Shelter You

by

ALICE MONTALVO-TRIBUE

*Lisa,
Thank you
for the support
· XOXO ·
A.M.
Tribue*

Other titles by Alice Montalvo-Tribue

Translation of Love (Of Love #1)

Desperation of Love (Of Love #2)

Copyright © 2014 by Alice Montalvo-Tribue

Published by Alice Montalvo-Tribue

All rights reserved. This book may not be reproduced, scanned, or distributed in any form without written permission from the author. Please do not participate in or encourage piracy of copyrighted materials in violation of the author's rights. All characters and storylines are the property of the author.

This book is a work of fiction and any resemblance to any person, living or dead, or any events or occurrences, is purely coincidental. The characters and story lines are created from the author's imagination and are used fictitiously.

Cover Image licensed from Big Stock Photo
http://www.bigstockphoto.com

Cover design by Distorted Edge Designs
https://www.facebook.com/DistortedEdge

Editing by Whitney Williams

Formatting by Integrity Formatting
https://www.facebook.com/IntegrityFormatting

Table of Contents

Prologue 1

Chapter 1 5

Chapter 2 13

Chapter 3 21

Chapter 4 33

Chapter 5 39

Chapter 6 49

Chapter 7 61

Chapter 8 69

Chapter 9 79

Chapter 10 89

Chapter 11 103

Chapter 12 117

Chapter 13 129

Chapter 14 137

Chapter 15 145

Chapter 16 153

Chapter 17 163

Chapter 18 173

Chapter 19 179

Chapter 20 191

Chapter 21 197

Epilogue 209

About the Author 221

Acknowledgements 222

Excerpt: Three of Diamonds by W. Ferraro 225

Excerpt: Translation of Love by Alice Montalvo-Tribue 245

Excerpt: Desperation of Love by Alice Montalvo-Tribue 263

Dedication

To Arbin for telling random people at bars and movie theaters that your wife is an author.

For Eva Rose because the love I feel for you is the love that inspired this book.

Prologue

"I can only give you thirty minutes to get out of here before I have to report it to my supervisors that you're gone. The clothes I brought for you are in the closet over there," she says, pointing to a long closet built into the wall.

It reminds me of a high school locker, long and narrow. At the age of 17, I've become very familiar with those lockers, having used them all throughout my years in school and they were great years, happy years, right up until the end. It's hard to believe that just a few months ago I was graduating high school, Miss Popular, top of my class, my pick of universities. To everyone on the outside looking in, it appeared that I had my whole future ahead of me. The perfect life, great grades, an amazing family, the world was my oyster. Little did they know that my future had already been decided, mapped out and planned for me. None of which I had any say in, none of which I was comfortable with.

I turn my attention back to the tall gangly woman in front of me. She's unnaturally thin, but I can almost see the attractiveness there, that she might have been beautiful once upon a time. Her blond hair is coarse, straw like and brittle, and her glasses are too big for her face, but I don't care about any of that. To me, right now she's an angel. A real live angel sent down to help me get out of an impossible situation.

"Besides clothes I was able to get you all of the basic supplies you'll need. It's not much, but it'll get you by until you can afford to buy more," she says, as I nod.

"When I leave this room, pick up the phone and call the operator. Ask for a volunteer to bring a wheelchair up to your room because you are being discharged. Once she comes up, tell her that your car is already waiting and that you need her to wheel you to the east entrance. Show her your hospital bracelet. It matches Lily's so you'll be fine; she won't know any better. She'll ask if you have a car seat, so just tell her that it's already in the car."

My heart starts to beat faster as I listen to her directions. Am I really doing this? Am I strong enough, brave enough to defy my parents, go against their wishes?

"The taxi driver will be waiting for you. His name is Seth, he's a friend of my husband's. He'll take you to the bank first. Take out every single penny that is in your savings account and then have him take you to the bus station. Take the first bus out of here, Mia. Leave your cell phone behind and get a pre paid one the first chance you get. You'll be eighteen in one month, and at that time you can call and request a copy of Lily's birth certificate. This way, even if they can track you, they can't legally force you to come back.

It takes me a minute, but I finally find my voice. "I don't know how I can ever repay you for this."

"No one should be forced to give up their child; it's wrong. Just promise me you'll be a good mom and that you'll call me if you need anything at all."

I look up at her with tears in my eyes. If not for this kind woman I'd be handing Lily over to her adoptive parents in a matter of hours. It may seem cruel of me to have promised to give my baby away to a couple who desperately wants one and then to just pick up and run away but none of this was my choice. Four months before my high school graduation I found out that I was pregnant. As you can probably imagine for a seventeen year old to hear that she's going to become a mother is shocking and scary. So I did what I thought would be the right thing, I went to my parents and asked for their help. Their

solution? Hide my pregnancy until after graduation and then keep me a virtual prisoner in my own home until I gave birth. When I expressed to them my desire to keep my child they gave me an ultimatum: Give the baby up for adoption, or keep the baby but leave their house with absolutely no financial help from them. What else could I have done? I had no choice but to agree to their demands and I thought I could do it. I thought I could go through with it until I held her, my Lily, and I knew that giving her away would literally kill me—would make it difficult to go on with the knowledge that she was out there in the world somewhere, living a life apart from mine. And because of this I made her a promise and I'll die before I break that promise. I'll die before I ever let her go.

Chapter 1

Nurse Kelly's plan went down exactly the way she said it would. The volunteer that came up to take Lily and I out to the car barely checked that our bracelets matched before she helped me into the wheelchair and took me down to the exit where the cab was waiting for me. Seth, the driver helped get Lily in the car seat and then got us the hell out of there as fast as he could. He took me to my house and after verifying that my parents weren't there, I ran inside. After packing some more clothes, all of my important documents and some cash that I had stored in my desk, I took one last look at my childhood bedroom and left.

Seth quickly took me to the bank where I was able to liquidate my entire savings account, a little over ten thousand dollars that I had been saving ever since I could remember. Every single dollar I'd ever been given from birthday and Christmas presents and from working at the local ice cream shop every summer was now in my backpack. Seth thought it would be a good idea to take me to a bus station a couple towns over. I wasn't about to let anyone find me now that I had come this far, so I hopped on the first available bus out of state heading to Savannah Georgia, and told myself that once I got there I could stop for the night and make a decision on where to go next.

I've been traveling for about five hours now. We stopped earlier in Jacksonville, Florida, for about an hour—giving me just enough time to hide in a large bathroom stall to feed Lily in private and grab a bite to eat for myself. I'm terrified that she might start crying and disturb the other passengers on the bus, but the continuous motion seems to help her sleep. I close my eyes and wonder how I'm going to make this work, how I'm going to be able to take care of Lily without any help. The truth behind my situation is daunting. How will I know what she needs, why she's crying, how to get her on a sleeping and feeding schedule? Will I know what to do and how to take care of her when she gets sick? What will I do for childcare when I find a job? The thoughts overwhelm me but I try not to panic. I have to keep it together for Lily, because I have to believe that a life with me is better for her than any life she could have had without me.

It's a little after ten at night when we finally arrive in Savannah. I gather Lily and my belongings and grab a taxi cab. I tell the driver to take us to the most affordable hotel in the area and a little while later he drops us off at an inn right on Bay Street. It's much too dark to explore outdoors but from what I can tell, it's gorgeous here, someplace I'd love to come back and visit one day. When I reach the front desk the clerk eyes me suspiciously as she checks me in but mercifully doesn't ask me any questions. I pay for my room in cash, grab my room key, and hop on the elevator. I get to my room as quickly as I can.

I can't help but to feel exposed when I'm out in the open, as if by some off chance someone might recognize me.

I change Lily's diaper and put her in a pink one piece pajama, turn down the bed and crawl in with her. I lie on my side with her snuggled close and offer her my breast. Kelly showed me what to do that first night after my parents had left for the evening. I remember being grossed out initially but I wanted to be able to feed her even if it was only one time. To be able to give her even just a small piece of me was important, it felt right. I'm thankful that I did it now because given my limited resources nursing her seems to be the most cost effective way to keep her fed. It doesn't take long for me to give into the exhaustion, my eyes start to get heavy and before I know it I'm asleep.

I was looking forward to at least taking in a few of the sites in Savannah but fear of being found or recognized kept me a virtual prisoner in my hotel room. We stayed for two days and then hopped the midnight bus to Richmond, Virginia. We stopped a few hours into the trip in North Carolina and then drove straight through the remainder of the night; thankfully Lily slept most of the way but I sat in the back of the bus and when she woke up for her feeding I was able to cover her up with a blanket and nurse her privately. It helped that almost everyone on the bus was asleep.

The hotel in Virginia is not quite as nice as the one in Georgia but it's safe, clean and affordable. I allow myself to wander around Richmond a bit more than I did in Savannah, but I keep to myself and keep my head down most of the time. I find a small pharmacy near the hotel where I pick up diapers, baby wipes, infant Tylenol just in case of an unexpected emergency, a pair of scissors and two boxes of brown hair dye. If anyone is looking for Lily and me we'll be a lot harder to recognize if I alter my appearance and making my hair darker seems like the easiest way.

"Well isn't this a beautiful baby." I look up and see an elderly woman standing behind me in the line to pay.

I instantly tense up, and go on alert. Maybe I'm paranoid. I mean, it's only a little old lady but I can't be too careful. I'm not sure if there's anyone out there looking for me. I don't know if the police were called, if the media was alerted, or if a reward was offered, but I certainly wouldn't put anything past my parents.

"Thank you," I respond quietly, never actually looking at her and hoping that she'll just leave me alone.

"Is she yours dear?" She questions, just as the person ahead of me is done paying for his items. I ignore her and quickly move up, putting my things on the counter and paying for my purchases as fast as possible. I get the hell out of there and back to the hotel in record time.

Lily begins to cry and I know that she must be hungry because she's just woken up so she can't be sleepy and her diaper is dry. I lie down in the king size bed with her and feed her until she falls asleep again. Strange as it may seem these moments with her calm me down, they give me the reassurance I need that running away was worth it. I'm beginning to feel more and more confident with her, like maybe I can do this, make this work with her and be a good mom. I think about the things I'll have to give up, the things that I have already given up — my friends, enjoying my youth. I know I should be out doing the things that normal kids my age do, partying, dating, living the college life but all of those things were taken away from me and replaced with this life instead and the thing of it is, I'm okay with that. Yes, I'm young, inexperienced and I know that making the decision to keep Lily will never be the easy choice. But when it came down to it, when I was given the option, it was the only choice.

I look different as a brunette, I barely recognize myself when I look in the mirror. I feel better to a certain degree now that I've changed my hair, coloring and cutting it shoulder length, my long blond locks were always my signature look so it will take some getting used to for me but it's what I need to do to keep my anonymity. After weighing out my options, I decided that I prefer traveling at night when there aren't many people out and about. Lily and I left the hotel in Virginia and hopped on our next bus at three o' clock in the morning driving through the night and stopping at eight the next morning in

Baltimore Maryland. I decide to stop here for the night and let myself get some rest before catching my final bus into Pennsylvania. I'm not sure why I'm drawn there of all places, it was just a random choice plus it's a big enough state that I can hopefully just blend into.

By the time Lily and I finally reach our final destination, a small Pennsylvania town about forty five minutes outside of New York City, I'm exhausted but grateful that we made it here without getting caught. It's early fall and the colors of the trees here are stunning. I've never seen anything quite like it; the brilliant orange and red leaves fill the streets and it makes me glad that I chose this as the place for Lily and I to start our new lives together. I get us settled into a hotel and snuggle up close to her after feeding and changing her surprised at how connected I feel to her. Yes, she's my daughter and instinctively there should be a bond there, but I was so prepared to let her go, give her up to make my life less complicated. Looking at her now, I know that she's the kind of complication I wouldn't trade for the world. No matter how unexpectedly she was created. I close my eyes and rest. I know that I'll be up at least two times tonight to feed her and I need to be up early, I'm planning on beginning my search for an apartment first thing in the morning. Before long both Lily and I are fast asleep.

I don't know why I thought that finding an apartment would be easy. We don't need much room for now, a studio or a one bedroom apartment will work. I've been searching for days but the places I've seen within my budget dangle on the disgusting and unsafe side.

I'm running out of hope by the time I go to see the last apartment on my list. It's on a busier street but the building is clean and well maintained. A tall and slender middle aged woman meets me out front. She looks at me as if though she's surprised someone as young as me is here alone with a baby and looking for an apartment. I can tell she's not judging me, I think she's probably more concerned than anything else. She stares at me for a second with her kind eyes.

"Are you Kelly?" She questions.

I didn't want to give anyone my real name in case my family really is looking for me. When I called to set up appointments I used the first name that popped into my head, Kelly, the name of the nurse who helped me get myself and Lily out of the hospital. "Yes, I'm Kelly. You must be Janet."

She extends her hand and I reach out and take it. "Yes, I'm Janet."

She shakes my hand and quickly releases it. "Thank you for meeting me today."

"Of course. Come on in and I'll show you the apartment." She opens the front door and allows me to walk in ahead of her. "It's just down the hall and to your left."

When we reach the door she puts the key in the door, turning the knob but stopping just before she opens. "I'm sorry Kelly, I don't mean to pry but what is a young girl like you doing looking for an apartment? Shouldn't you be at home with your family?"

I know she means well but I'm not prepared to answer this question. I answer the best way I can on the spot and what I come up with is not a complete lie, just an altered version of the truth. "My family kicked me out when I got pregnant. I was staying with a friends family but it's time for me to find a place of my own."

"Oh honey, I'm so sorry to hear that. Forgive me for asking." She pushes the door open and allows me to walk through.

"It's alright. I understand what it must look like, an eighteen year old and a baby." I give her a small smile and quickly walk away from her, moving to stand in the middle of a small living room. I look around at the bare white walls and though it's small, it's by far the nicest place I've seen. It's sparsely furnished with a worn old blue couch and chair.

"The bedroom is through that door over there," she says pointing to my left. "It's pretty spacious…big enough to fit a full size bed and a crib for the little one."

I try not to read into it but her words give me hope. "Does that mean you'll rent it to me?"

"We normally require a credit check but I'm assuming since you're so young you haven't built up much of a credit rating?"

"Yes ma'am."

"And you have no furniture?"

"Not yet, no ma'am."

"And can you afford the security deposit and first months rent?"

"Yes I can."

"Alright then, I have the lease with me, if you want the apartment it's yours. You can use the furniture that's here too if you'd like and I'm pretty sure I have some old baby things that you can use. I don't live too far away. I can have my husband drop it off and set it up this weekend."

I look up at her wide eyed, stunned and seriously trying not to cry. "I don't know how to thank you. I promise you I won't be any trouble."

She simply smiles and nods at me.

By the time I leave the building, I have a lease, a set of keys, and permission to move in right away. I grab my belongings, and check out of the hotel. By nightfall Lily and I are all moved into our new apartment.

Chapter 2

It's been almost a month since Lily and I ran away from the hospital in Florida. I remember how scared I was when I took my baby and hopped on that first bus. I remember thinking that I would never be able to take care of her on my own. I have to admit that being a mom and taking care of an infant is hard work. There are times when I feel lost and alone, there are days when I'm exhausted and wish I could take just a few hours away for myself but that isn't possible right now and being able to raise Lily makes it worth it. I'm merely a few days away from my eighteenth birthday and I'm certain that our life will be so much easier when that happens. For starters, I can stop lying about my name, about my story. I'll be able to get a job and find childcare and use my real name. No one will be able to come and take Lily away from me once that happens. In the meantime, I came across a free clinic where I was able to take Lily to get her first vaccinations. Sticking to a budget hasn't been too difficult. The apartment's utilities are included in the rent, I have basic cable which consists of about twenty channels, and that's enough for me for now. Since I'm still breastfeeding and I've never been a heavy eater, I've only had to go to the grocery store a couple of times.

The day after I moved in, Janet's husband dropped off an infant swing, highchair, play yard and a simple stroller for Lily. I honestly couldn't believe it but he explained that the items had been sitting unused and collecting dust in the basement. He actually thanked me for taking it off of their hands. I'm almost positive that he was just trying to make me feel better about having to take the handout but I'm grateful nonetheless. These are the things that I didn't think about when I left, taking Lily and virtually disappearing into thin air and even though I still have the majority of my money I know that it won't last forever. I need to find my way and take care of Lily at the same time.

At this time last year life was so different, the biggest decision I had to make was choosing which universities to apply to. My dream had always been to go to NYU and live in the city, finally free to live and experience everything that life had to offer. I never imagined that I'd end up pregnant and alone, without my family or any of my friends to lean on for support. I try not to get sad when I think about the dreams and the goals that I had set for myself, I try to look on the bright side but life has dealt me an unfair hand and I can't help but to feel sorry for myself at times.

Lily's screeching cry pulls me out of my head, I get up off of the couch that I've been lounging on for most of the afternoon and pad over to the play yard. I scoop her up into my arms and gently rock her back and forth. I fed her less than an hour ago and her diaper is dry. I continue rocking her for awhile with no luck. Her cries get progressively worse and before long I'm genuinely worried that there's something wrong with her. I try feeding her again but she's having none of it. I reach for my phone, thinking for a split second that I can call my mom and ask her what to do. If anyone would know what I should do it would be her, but then I realize that I can't do that. She didn't want anything to do with my child and because of it forced me to take matters into my own hands. The truth of my life is that there's no one that I can call for advice at a time like this, and normally that would make me sad, but right now all I can focus on is Lily. I quickly call a cab, pack up her diaper bag, and bundle her up. When the driver arrives, I instruct him to take us to the nearest hospital.

I check us in at the emergency room, telling the girl at the front desk that I was so nervous I'd forgotten my identification.

I know enough about the law to know that a hospital can't refuse emergency treatment so I feel confident with my excuse.

We're sitting in the waiting room for what seems like an eternity. Lily is still crying and my nerves are now frayed. I'm barely holding it together.

The emergency room doors open and a couple of paramedics are wheeling in a young man on a stretcher. He looks as if he's been beaten badly. They take him to the back immediately, which only serves to further frustrate me about my long wait. I walk over to the front desk again and question the receptionist.

"Can you please tell me how much longer it's going to be before we're seen? We've been here for over an hour."

"There's a few patients in front of you. You'll just have to wait," she answers me shortly.

I go to speak, but before I can she plasters a fake smile on her face and bats her eyelashes. "Oh, hi Officer Tate," she says. "How are you?"

I turn my head to where her comment is directed and I'm pretty sure my heart stops momentarily and I'm not sure if it's caused by fear or a totally different emotion. A police officer is walking in our direction and these days I try to avoid them at all costs but one look at this particular cop and my feet are rooted firmly to their spot. I can vaguely hear Lily crying as I take in the sight of him. I know that men of any kind are the last thing I should be thinking about, but his piercing blue eyes draw me in. He looks to be around six feet tall with a tan complexion and hair that's cut low in a military style buzz cut. His full lips are all kinds of sexy and when he looks me dead in the eye it takes every ounce of strength I have to look away.

"Hi, Jennifer. Assault victim brought in a few minutes ago?"

I didn't think it was possible for her smile to get any faker but it does. "Of course," she says, leaning over giving him the maximum view of her boobs and touching his arm in a blatantly obvious attempt to get near him. "They took him back already. He's in bed number ten."

"Thanks." He turns away from her and suddenly he's in my space. "Is she alright?" He questions, motioning to Lily.

His acknowledgement of me makes me both nervous and excited. Yes he's beautiful, sexy and he seems kind but he's still a cop and technically I'm still a runaway. As much as I'd love to have a conversation with Officer Tate, it's in mine and Lily's best interest if I extrapolate myself from this situation as quickly as possible. "She won't stop crying and I'm worried, but we've been here for a while and still haven't been seen."

He gives me a slow nod and turns back to fake Jennifer. "Isn't there anything you can do to get her seen? Poor thing looks miserable and I'm sure the rest of the people in the waiting room would appreciate a reprieve from a crying baby." He looks back at me. "No offense," he says with a slight grin.

"None taken." I return.

We both turn to face fake Jennifer again. She looks like she's just swallowed a sour pill but quickly plasters on her smile that she clearly reserves only for Officer Tate's benefit. "Well, since you asked so nicely I'm sure I can make an exception for this cute little one." She walks over to the bin of patient files, moves mine to the front and then gives him a wink.

He gives her an equally fake smile and in that moment I can tell that he sees right through her syrupy sweet routine. "I really appreciate it." He pats Lily on the back and then looks back up at me. "I'll check in on you a little later okay?" he asks, and quickly walks away. (Although it sounded more like a statement of fact than anything else.) He wants to check back in on me and Lily? But why? Why would he care whether Lily gets seen by a doctor or not? If she's alright or not? He doesn't know us, has no emotional ties to us, and he doesn't even know our names so why should he care about our well being?

The sound of the privacy curtain being opened startles me. I turn to see Officer Tate standing there. He stares at me for a moment and gives me a timid smile.

"Hey, how's she doing?" He questions quietly.

I look down at Lily, sleeping in the hospital bed and I smile. "She's okay. We're just waiting on the discharge paperwork. The doctor says it was probably just gas." I respond. I look up and our gazes meet.

"Well that's good," he says with a nod.

"Yeah," I say with a light chuckle, shrugging my shoulders. "I guess I should have known that huh?"

He shrugs his shoulders too. "I don't know. You're a new mom, so I think it's understandable."

"I guess," I say, turning away from him.

"Hey," he calls out. There's a strength to his voice, a resolve that I can't help but respond to.

I turn, giving him my full attention again. "You did the right thing. She wasn't acting like her normal self and you made sure you got her checked out. That doesn't make you stupid or naïve it makes you a good mom."

"You don't have to say that. You don't even know me."

"In my line of work I see a lot of things. I know the difference between good and bad, and I promise you, just from what I've seen tonight I know that you're doing a good job."

I sigh, taking his words in, letting them wash over me and sink in. He's right, I may be young and unsure but I'm doing my best and I am a good mom. "Thank you. I appreciate you saying that."

"You're welcome." He walks further into the room and stands at the foot of the bed, looking down at Lily. He opens his mouth to speak but then hesitates, maybe thinking better of saying or asking whatever it is that he wants to say and then just like that he blurts it out. "Where's her dad?" he asks, his eyes never leaving Lily.

I'm silent for some time because really I don't want to talk about this, not with him, not with anyone. Talking about it won't change the facts, won't rewrite history. "He's not around, it's just me."

"I see," he says with a nod.

"But we're fine. We're doing fine on our own," I reply quickly, making myself sound a little bit too defensive.

He crosses his arms across his chest, a move I'm sure he uses to intimidate people. It makes him look like a no nonsense badass cop and it honestly terrifies the shit out of me. "What's your name?"

"Kelly."

He tilts his head to side and his eyes pierce through me. "How old are you, Kelly?"

"I'm eighteen. I recently turned eighteen alright, but like I just told you a second ago, we're fine."

"Are you working?"

"No." I mentally kick myself for being honest. What the hell is wrong with me? I need to be more careful about what information I divulge, especially to him.

"What are you doing for money?"

"I'm using my savings right now. I'm looking for a job but without a babysitter, it's kind of hard." My heart is racing again and I hold onto the railing on the bed because I think I might just faint if I'm not careful. I knew it was a bad idea for me to tell this man anything. A man who's a cop nonetheless. "Look, please don't call child protective services." I'm practically begging him now. "I know I'm young, okay? I get it. And ideally I'd like to have an amazing family by my side, helping me take care of her, but that's not how it worked out for me. My family didn't want anything to do with us so I had to grow up and do the best I can. You said it yourself, I'm a good mom. I'll be fine, I'll make sure that she's fine, and I'll be damned if I'm going to let you or anybody else take Lily away from me."

He looks at me for a minute, probably processing my outburst but he says nothing. He looks unsure of himself which is very different from the confident demeanor he displayed earlier in the evening. He pulls out a notepad and begins to write something down. When he's done he rips the paper out of the pad and hands it to me. "I have a friend who owns a daycare. She may be able to help you, maybe give you a job. I can't make you any promises but this is her number. Tell her I told you to call."

"Oh. Thank you. I…I'm sorry, I just thought…"

"I understand but you have to relax, alright? No one can take Lily away from you if she's not abused or neglected and clearly she's none of those things." He reaches behind him and pulls a card out of his back pocket and hands it to me. Our fingers graze and my body grows warm at his touch. "This is my card. You call me day or night if you need anything Kelly, alright?"

I nod my response, unable to say another word to him. He gives me a slight smile, and as quickly as he appeared he leaves. Yet, he leaves behind just a little bit of hope that maybe I can make a life for myself and Lily here.

Chapter 3

I called the number that Officer Tate gave me the morning after our emergency room visit. Sarah, the owner of the day care center scheduled me to come in for a tour this morning. He must have let her know that I'd be calling because she didn't seem surprised to hear from me at all. It almost sounded like she was expecting my call. I didn't have a suit that I could wear for interviewing so I paired a gray button down top with black slacks and a light weight black jacket. It isn't perfect but it'll have to do and at least I look presentable. The center is located in a nearby strip mall and is close enough for me to walk to, when I get there I'm met by Sarah at the front desk. She's young, I can't imagine her being older than twenty five. She's about my height, but thinner with blond hair and deep blue eyes. She gushes over Lily and takes her from me immediately carrying her around like she's known her all along.

"I'm so glad you called. Logan said you were looking for work but were worried about childcare. He knew I was hiring and thought that this might be a great fit for you." She has a warmth about her, it radiates through her pores. I don't know why but I feel safe when I'm around her, I feel like I can trust her but there's also that part of me that wants answers. It's the part of me that has thought of nothing more than Officer Tate since I met him. There's something about him that draws me in and I haven't been able to stop thinking about him since. But now I have to wonder if he and Sarah are more than just friends, and I find it even harder to justify the feeling that comes over me when I think of them together. It's nothing more than jealousy in its purest form.

"How do you know Officer Tate?"

"His sister is my best friend. I've known him and his family most of my life."

"He's a good guy," she says as she takes me on a tour of the center, showing me classroom after classroom as she goes. The center has several levels, the babies and younger kids on the lower level and the preschool age children on the second floor. There's also a basement that houses a small library and another classroom.

She leads me into her small office and takes a seat behind her desk, still holding Lily in her arms.

"This little girl is a doll. You seem to be doing a really good job with her."

"Thank you."

"So Kelly, what did you think? Is this the kind of place where you'd be interested in working?"

"I think so. What would I be doing exactly?"

"Well, we're hiring several teaching aids so you'd be helping the teachers watch after the children, helping prepare arts and crafts, getting snacks and lunches ready and some basic clean up."

"What about Lily?"

"Generally you would be required to pay tuition for Lily, but Logan is a good friend and he asked me for a favor. He never asks for favors so I know this is important to him. Lily can stay in the infant room while you work in the toddler class."

"I don't know what to say, that would be amazing."

"Alright then. How soon can you start?"

"Right away, today."

"How about you start at seven on Monday morning?"

"That sounds perfect."

"Okay. I just need you to fill out the employment package and I'm going to need a copy of your license and social security card for the file."

"I'm sorry, Sarah, but that's going to be a problem."

"Oh?"

"I'm sure Officer Tate mentioned that Lily and I are on our own. I won't have access to most of my documents for another few weeks."

"Well, what happens in another few weeks?"

"I turn eighteen."

"I see. Did your family really kick you out, Kelly?"

"Well, in a not so roundabout way."

"You can trust me. I'm not out to hurt you, you can tell me what's going on."

Inside I'm conflicted, telling her my story is risky. I would be giving her the power to decide my fate. If she wanted, she could call Officer Tate immediately and at that point I won't even have a chance to run. Can I really trust her to keep my secret to help someone who she doesn't know live a lie? Even if it is for a good cause, even if it is to keep a mother and daughter together? Looking in her eyes I can tell that she genuinely cares, that she really does want to help us but how far is she willing to go? I still don't trust that she won't report me, but I let the story take shape before I can change my mind and I'll think about the consequences later. "My parents were forcing me to give Lily up for adoption, It was either that or be cut off from my family. I didn't think I had a choice so I agreed, but it was never what I really wanted and once I gave birth and I saw her for the first time, I couldn't go through with it."

"So you ran away?" She questions. I can hear the shock in her voice.

"Yes."

"And you're afraid to use your license or social security card because you think they may be able to trace you somehow."

"Yes." I say, confirming her theory. "I'll be eighteen in just a couple of weeks and by that time it won't matter. They can't legally make me come home or try and take Lily away from me."

"Is your name really Kelly?"

I hesitate briefly then shake my head.

"I'm not going to turn you in. You can tell me."

"It's... It's Mia. My name is Mia."

"Mia... Okay," she says with a twinge of hesitation in her voice, as if she's trying my name on for size, analyzing if it really fits or not. She looks down at Lily who has fallen asleep in her arms. "You can work under the table until you turn eighteen and then I have to put you on the books, I'm taking a huge risk in doing this for you."

I breathe a sigh of relief. "I know. Thank you so much."

"You've already been through so much. I would hate to see you lose Lily when it's clear that you love her so much, that you're doing everything you can to be a good mother. I think you deserve a chance."

"I know you're sticking your neck out for me, I do...But can I ask you one last favor? Please don't tell Officer Tate what you know about me, at least until I turn eighteen."

"Mia..."

"Please."

"Logan is my friend. I can't lie to him."

"I know, and I'm grateful to him, to both of you. I'm just asking you to delay telling him the truth, just until I know that Lily and I are in the clear. I can't risk my family finding me. I can't lose my baby, not now, not after all this."

"I will keep your secret for now."

"Thank you." I return smiling at her.

The past few weeks have flown by, and we've quickly settled into a routine. I've been working at the day care center four days a week and even though I come home exhausted every single day, I love it. I love the kids and Sarah, and the staff has been extremely welcoming. I didn't want to at first but Sarah made me use my real name at the center, assuring me that no one would hear about my situation from her. Part of me is sad that I had to put my dream of going to college on hold, but for the most part I feel proud and empowered by the fact that I'm able to live on my own and take care of Lily without the help of my family. Regardless of how she came into this world, the events that led to her birth and my running away with her, I wake up every single morning happy with my decision, thankful that she's a part of my life. Even though I had to go through a lot of heartache, I wouldn't change any of it.

I make it home in a daze. The walk home is quick, normally only ten minutes or so; it's Friday, and not only do I have my first paycheck but tomorrow is my birthday. All these weeks of secrecy, fear and constantly looking over my shoulder are about to be behind me. I can start to use my real name again other than at work, maybe get a Pennsylvania license and finally order a copy of Lily's birth certificate.

I open the front door of my building, carefully getting Lily's carriage in without bumping it. She's bundled up and it's hard to see her but I'm pretty sure she's asleep. I get a wave of nausea when I make it to my apartment. I'm suddenly struck with fear, the front door is cracked open and I distinctly remember having locked it when I left this morning. At first, I think that maybe my family has found me, sent someone after me to bring me and Lily back home but when I gingerly push the door open what I see leads me to believe that my family had nothing to do with this. The more I look around the clearer it becomes that I've been burglarized.

I'm terrified to step foot inside the apartment as it looks now; it's completely ravaged, destroyed, the furniture has been overturned, my television set and DVD player are gone. I'm not sure of what else they've taken, but in a moment of realization I run to my bedroom with Lily. I put her down on the bed, open the closet door and lift up the broken panel on the floorboard in which I've hidden the remainder of my money. I pull out the duffel bag and open the zipper breathing a sigh of relief when I see it all there. I quickly store it again and rifle through Lily's diaper bag until I find my pre paid cell phone. I dial 911 and report the break in to the operator who advises me that she's dispatched police to my apartment. She offers to stay on the phone with me until they arrive but I'm sure that whoever has broken in is gone now.

It takes around ten minutes but the sound of sirens nearby starts to calm my seriously frayed nerves a bit, when the police officers knock on my door, I finally start to feel better. I put Lily down in her basinet and answer the door only to come face to face with him, the man who's been on my mind for over two weeks now. "Officer Tate?"

"Kelly? It was your place that was just broken into?"

The sight of him makes me nervous all over again, this time for a completely different reason. My mouth goes dry and I'm not sure if I can make a sound. I nod in response to his question. The look of genuine concern in his eyes makes my heart melt a little and for the first time since I got home I start to feel safe again.

"This is my partner Officer Clark." I look at the older, shorter man, curiosity on his face, he's wondering how his partner and I know each other.

"Hello," I say timidly, hoping that he's not inclined to ask too many questions.

"Kelly." I turn my attention back to Officer Tate. "Where's Lily?"

"She's in her basinet sleeping." I point over to where she is.

He nods, seemingly relieved that Lily is okay. "Can you tell us what happened?"

"I got off work a little while ago and when I came home, my door was slightly open. I came in and found my apartment wrecked."

"Is there anything missing?"

"From what I can tell so far, just my television set and DVD player. I called for the police right away. I didn't want to touch anything else," I say, wrapping my arms around my torso protectively.

"You did the right thing," says Officer Clark, with more of a concerned fatherly tone. I think of my dad for a second and wonder how he'd feel if he knew his daughter's apartment just got broken into. The apparent adrenaline rush that had me operating on pure instinct begins to wear off and the reality of what has just happened starts to set in, taking control of my emotions. I fight back against the tears that threaten to spill over and quickly look away from both men.

Logan moves around me until we're face to face and he gently grasps my shoulders. "Shit Kelly, you're shaking."

"I am?" I question through now chattering teeth.

"It's okay, you're going to be fine. You're doing great." He leads me over to what's normally my living room, bends down to pick up an overturned chair, and helps me to sit down. He crouches in front of me and looks up at me with worried eyes. "Is there anyone I can call for you?"

I shake my head, still fighting back the tears. "Will you be alright here while we have a look around?"

I nod in response and he gives me a smile that doesn't quite reach his eyes. I can tell he's watching me closely, making sure I'm not in shock or about to lose it. But at the same time he has a job to do and I'm sure he doesn't want to set off any bells and whistles with his partner, or make him think that there's something more going on between us than just a casual acquaintanceship even though there's not.

Lily starts to stir, in the basinet situated beside me and I have an overwhelming urge to hold her close, make sure that she's safe. I pick her up and I hold her as tightly as I can, snuggling her closely to me and letting her little body give me strength. I gently rock her back and forth in my arms, letting the repetitive motion soothe and settle us both.

After looking around and taking my statement (and that of a few neighbors), both Officer Tate and his partner leave, leaving me feeling alone and slightly terrified. The thought of sleeping here alone makes me nervous and jittery, and I try my hardest not to panic. All the baby books I've read say that children can sense when their parents are stressed. I make sure that Lily is clean and fed before I put her down in her crib, and then I quickly change into a pair of sweats—not wanting to be caught in anything skimpy if my intruder returns. I want to be able to run if I need to. I grab the sharpest knife I can find from the kitchen and place it on my nightstand—along with my cell phone, and settle into bed with the lights still on. A glance at the clock tells me that it's after midnight.

"Happy eighteenth birthday, Mia," I say to myself, feeling just a little bit victorious that Lily and I are both now free.

I'm not sure how long I've been sitting in bed, but my head starts to bob as I try my hardest not to doze off. A knock on the front door causes me to nearly jump out of bed. I look at the clock and it's after one. I grab my phone and my knife, and sneak a peek at Lily who's still sleeping soundly, and slowly tip toe to the living room. I start to dial 911 when I hear a familiar voice call out from the other side of the door.

"Kelly? I just wanted to make sure you and Lily are okay. Open up."

I let out a sigh of relief, set the knife down and open the door. I'm pretty positive that I've never been so happy to see anybody in my entire life. "Jesus Christ, you scared the shit out of me."

"I know, I'm sorry. I just got off duty and thought that you might be scared here all alone. I just wanted to drop by and check in on you," he says, his hands buried in the pocket of the jeans that he wears oh so well.

"I wasn't scared until some lunatic decided to knock on my door in the middle of the night."

"It's morning actually," he corrects me with a grin. "And if you weren't scared, why is there a carving knife in your living room?"

I look back at the knife, silently cursing its presence and then back to Officer Tate. "Just because I have protection doesn't mean I was sitting around like a damsel in distress. There's nothing wrong with having something to protect myself with."

He puts his hands up in the air as if telling me he surrenders. "Alright warrior princess, relax. I just don't want you to hurt anyone with that thing," he says with a chuckle.

"You know Officer Tate, I'm glad you can find humor in this situation. It's not every day that a young woman and her child come home to a burglarized apartment. You'll be able to laugh and tell stories about this for years to come."

"I'm not laughing at you, I promise. I'm just trying to lighten you up a little. The tension is rolling off of you," he says. There's a look of concern in his eyes that I'm starting to become accustomed to, it's penetrating right through me.

"Why do you care so much, Officer Tate?"

"My name's Logan. I think we're past the 'Officer Tate' thing, don't you?"

"You're a cop."

"And you're not a suspect or a criminal. You can use my first name." He looks around the destruction that is my apartment and takes it all in, in his plain clothes: He's donning a pair of dark jeans, and a black hoodie. He looks different out of uniform, younger, hotter if that's even possible. His gaze lands back on me and he looks me over for a while. I can tell that he wants to say something but the words don't come. I can't really take the silence anymore, so I walk away from him and plop down in a chair. Feeling his eyes still on me, I let out a huff of air.

"What? Why are you staring at me just say what you want to say already?" I'm not sure why I'm being so short with him. I think maybe it's a mixture of exhaustion and stress. I don't know why I'm pushing him to speak or more importantly pushing him away when the last thing I really want to be right now is alone. I honestly hate feeling afraid and powerless, and maybe if I can convince him that I'm not those things, I'll start to believe it myself.

"I'm not looking at anything. Are you sure you're okay?"

"I'm fine Officer T...Logan, we'll be fine."

"Alright, then. I guess I'll get going."

I try to mask the disappointment I feel at his imminent departure. I nod my head signaling to him that I'm fine with him leaving. I take a deep breath, get up and walk to the door — opening it up for him. He walks through the open doorway and turns back to look at me. I can almost see the inner conflict playing out in his eyes and I know the only thing I can do to help him is close the door on whatever this is.

"Thanks for stopping by, Logan. It was really nice of you to go out of your way like that but..."

He places a hand on the open door before I have a chance to shut it in his face. "I don't think I can leave you here like this." He blurts out and his eyes go wide, almost like he can't believe the words that have come out of his mouth either.

I'm speechless, unsure of what to say or do next, but he never wavers. "Kelly, pack a bag, get Lily and let's go. You're coming with me."

Chapter 4

I stare at Logan as if he has two heads. He's just *ordered*, not asked me to pack up Lily and my things and go with him. What's even more shocking is that for a split second I actually want to go, I actually *consider* going.

"What do you mean I'm going with you? What are you talking about?"

"I'm telling you that I can't leave you here with your apartment in shambles and at risk for another break in. You have shotty locks on the doors, poor lighting, and you don't even have a peephole for God's sake. Your landlord has been notified of the break in and until she brings this place up to code, you and Lily are not staying here."

"Where do you propose I go, huh? I'm not about to waste all of my money on a hotel and I can't exactly afford a better apartment right now. I have no choice but to stick it out here."

He crosses his arms over his chest, the air of confidence dripping off of him. "You're coming home with me. It's done, decided. Get your stuff, get Lily, and let's go."

"Logan, I barely even know you. We've met twice and both times were under intense circumstances."

"You can trust me."

"No, I can't!" I shout, sounding more and more agitated. "I don't trust you. Why would you put yourself out there for someone you barely know?"

"I put myself out there for people I don't know all of the time. Tonight I'm doing it because I want to, because I can."

I shake my head. "That's not good enough."

"I'm not asking you, I'm *telling* you. Get your things now." The authority in his voice causes me to flinch, he's not Logan right now, he's Officer Tate and with every passing moment it's becoming clear as day that I'm not going to win this battle. Truth be told, I'm not so sure I really want to win this battle. I weigh out my options: Do I really want to stay here alone with Lily when the place has been trashed and I'm understandably scared of a repeat robbery attempt? I'm not exactly keen on the idea of being anyone's target. There's also the fact that I'm beginning to develop a full on crush on Logan. I don't know whether to add that on the pros or cons list and the last thing I really need is to make a fool of myself in front of him. But if I had to choose between dying and acting a fool there really is no contest.

"Okay, fine. Just give me a few minutes," I say, stalking in the direction of the bedroom.

"Bring enough for a few days." He calls after me.

A few days? A few days of Lily and I living with Logan. I tell myself not to get excited about this. He's just a nice guy helping me out in my time of need. It means nothing more to him than that and even if it did, how irresponsible would it be of me to get involved with the first guy I meet after all that I've been through? Relationships are a foreign affair to me and the only real interaction I've ever had with a man resulted in me getting knocked up at seventeen and excommunicated from my family. I wonder at times if I had told my parents the truth, given them the entire story, if they would have been more supportive of me. If they'd been more understanding of my predicament, would they have stood by me then or would they have had the very same reaction? The thing is, in spite of the fact that they loved me, I always knew that keeping up appearances was the most important thing to them; perhaps the fear of them treating me this way even after they heard the truth is what ultimately led me to say nothing.

I scurry around my bedroom, vaguely aware of the fact that it's probably creeping up to two in the morning by now and throwing things into bags. This is a crazy thing to do, not that I'm a stranger to crazy, but right now all I can think about is getting out of here and having temporary protection from someone who's on the right side of the law. By the time I make it out of my bedroom with two bags full of clothes, one full of money, and a diaper bag filled to the max and a sleeping baby, Logan looks like he's about ready to pass out from a mixture of boredom and exhaustion.

"Sorry I took so long. It's not easy packing for a baby."

"That's okay. I already put her bassinet and play yard in my truck."

"Thanks."

"Here. Let me help you with that," he says, taking my bags from me, leaving me with only Lily to carry.

The ride to Logan's house is quiet, The only sounds I hear are those that come from the car driving along the uneven streets. I try to think of something to say, but small talk has never been my strong suit and the more time that passes by, the more uncomfortable I become. At this point I start to wonder if maybe I haven't made a mistake in agreeing to come stay with him. Maybe he's having second thoughts himself; no one should be held responsible for decisions that they make in the wee hours of the morning.

"Logan, you don't have to do this you know. Lily and I can be a real handful and…"

"It's really not a big deal. I have plenty of room and I'd really feel a lot better knowing that you're not in that apartment alone when it's not safe."

I don't reply, just turn my head and look out the window at the night sky. The moon is full tonight and it illuminates the sky in such a way that makes the night feel like it's a permanent fixture, like the universe is so filled with darkness that the sun might never shine down again. There are times when I feel like my life is like that, eternally submerged in the dark, like all of the sunlight has left my world and I may never see it again. Normally I can take one look at Lily and realize that I'm wrong, that she is the sunlight breaking through my darkness, the one thing that guides me to the warmth of day.

Logan unlocks the front door to his house when we arrive and quickly ushers me inside. He drops my things in the small foyer and turns on the lights.

His house is nice, nicer than I'd expect from a young bachelor. I assumed he'd live in a small one bedroom apartment, with minimal furniture and a large flat screen television. Evidently, I was way off the mark.

"You have a great house," I say with just a hint of awe in my voice. I look around taking in the massive living room with warm taupe paint, leather furniture, a stunning fireplace, and bay windows.

"Thanks. I bought it cheap and fixed it up," he says, picking up Lily's bassinet and my bags again. "Come on, I'll show you your room." He leads me upstairs to the second level and leads me into a bedroom that reminds me a lot of my bedroom back home in Florida. It's got lots of windows which gives it a light and airy feel. The full size bed looks inviting and all of a sudden I start to feel the exhaustion of the day that I've had beating away at me.

"The bathroom is through that door." He puts the bassinet down and points to a closed doorway, then turns to face me again. "It's connected to a second bedroom. We can set that one up for Lily tomorrow if you want, you might appreciate having your own space for a while. We can pick up a baby monitor so that you can keep an eye on her."

"Logan that is too much. I can't let you do all of that, besides it's only for a few days."

"I want you both to be comfortable while you're here."

I open my mouth to argue but he cuts me off. "My bedroom is just across the hall, just yell if you need anything. We'll talk more in the morning."

He hurries out the door and into his bedroom, leaving me standing here—wondering how I ended up in the house of a relative stranger in the span of just a few hours. I conclude that avoidance will work best for tonight.

All of my questions and concerns will just have to wait till morning. I feed and change Lily, get her situated in her bassinet, turn down the lights and settle into my new but temporary comfy bed. I shut my eyes and force myself to clear my mind, to let the stress of the day and the last few weeks go if only just for a little while. Before long I fall asleep and have perhaps the best night's sleep I've had in a long time.

Chapter 5

A crash of thunder causes my eyes to snap open. I take in the unfamiliar surroundings as confusion hits. I roll onto my side—searching for Lily, and see her bassinet next to my bed. Peeking over, I take in the sight of her sleeping peacefully. I look out the window and remember the events of last night as I watch the rain fall. It all comes rushing back: Logan, coming to my rescue, sweeping me away to his castle like a white knight come to save the damsel in distress. There were no promises made between us, no vows of love or lust, but still there was something there. A sliver of attraction, an invisible pull drawing us together and for now it's enough. I'm not ready for more and he's likely not willing to give it but it's still more than I could have ever hoped for in my situation. So why does my mood not reflect the optimistic thoughts in my head? Why do I feel like the unsteady raindrops that fall against the window, dark and gloomy, unwelcome. It's because I'm living a lie, because to Logan I'm "Kelly" and Mia is just a girl who I left behind in Florida. She's someone I left behind the moment a tiny little fist wrapped itself around my fingers; that's when I ceased to exist. The only problem is, I miss who I used to be, miss my identity and I want to share that with Logan, want him to know the real me. I want to be able to tell him as much of my story as I can, fill in the gaps of my past and hope to god that he's still willing to stick around after. Even if only as a friend…I think I can live with that.

The decision is made. Being honest with Logan is my only real option. I can't feel good about accepting his generosity or hospitality any other way. If Lily cooperates with her normal schedule, I have about another hour before she wakes up for a feeding. I leave my bedroom, making my way downstairs in search of Logan. The butterflies in my stomach take flight, alerting me to just how nervous I really am about coming clean about my past and with a cop no less. I give myself a mental pep talk, reminding myself that I'm eighteen now and no one can force me to go back home. I tell myself that I don't need his approval or acceptance; I've made it this far on my own, I'm sure I can keep on going.

When I reach the kitchen I see Logan sitting at a small bistro style table, drinking a cup of coffee. He looks up at me, our eyes lock and my nervousness becomes worse. My senses are heightened. I can tell there's something wrong.

He looks cold almost devoid of emotion. Maybe he's changed his mind about me and Lily staying here now that he's had a chance to sleep on it, a chance to think about what it really means to have us here. Biting the bullet, I decide to make the first move. I walk further into the kitchen and give him a timid smile.

"Good morning," I say softly.

He closes his eyes and rubs the bridge of his nose between his thumb and his forefinger. He releases with a sigh and looks back up at me. "Good morning, Kelly... I'm sorry, I meant *Mia*."

The moment he says my real name, my stomach drops. I feel lightheaded, like I might just pass out from the shock of hearing that name coming from his lips. My heart starts to race in my chest, mimicking the sound of the rain drops pelting on the shingles that cover the roof.

"That is your name, isn't it? *Mia*?" He reaches into his back pocket and pulls something out, it looks like...a passport. "Mia Reynolds of Winter Park, Florida," he says, tossing it on the table. He shoots daggers in my direction. "I found your birth certificate and license too."

The shock and fear start to dissipate and my blood quickly begins to boil. Anger takes ahold of me; the fact that he went through my personal belongings makes me feel violated. "How *dare* you go through my things, Logan! You had no right!"

A muscle jumps in his neck and I know that the level of his anger matches mine, but I don't give a shit. I'm ready for battle, my temper getting the best of me. "You're a stranger staying in my house. I have every right."

"I'm here because you wanted me here!" I yell, my voice getting louder with every word. "You insisted, I didn't ask you to come to my rescue! That was all you."

He takes several deep breaths. He appears to be walking a fine line between control and complete insanity, but I refuse to back down. "I want you to sit down now and tell me what the fuck is going on."

"Or what?" I spit out, my voice dripping with defiance.

"Mia, so help me God. Do NOT test me," he says curtly, the well of his patience running dry.

"Last night you said I wasn't a criminal, but now you're treating me like one."

"No. I'm not treating you like a criminal, I'm treating you like a liar. There's a big difference."

"You son of a bitch!" I shout and lunge for my passport on the table simultaneously. He gets to it before I do, and with his free hand he grabs my wrist. "Let go of me and give me my things back. I'm leaving."

"You're not going anywhere until I know what's going on here. Is that little girl upstairs even yours?"

"What! Are you crazy?" I shriek, pulling my arm away. "I can't believe you're asking me that. Of course she's mine."

41

"Then why, why are you lying about who you are and where the hell did all of that money come from? I get that you don't know me that well but I've never given you a reason not to trust me."

His eyes sear through me, the ice that crackled in them before is gone and now reflect his concern.

My anger from moments ago starts to disintegrate and it's replaced with my earlier remorse for having lied to him. "I didn't want to lie to you. I didn't have a choice at first, but after last night…I felt guilty. I knew I couldn't stay here without being honest with you. I was coming down here to tell you, I swear."

He says nothing, just looks at me, possibly weighing my words. The silence is deep, consuming, I shouldn't care but his forgiveness matters to me. "Tell me now." He finally says.

"I got pregnant in my senior year of high school. I was seventeen years old." I look at him searching for something only I'm not sure exactly what it is I'm seeking. Comfort, understanding maybe.

"Go on." His voice is soft, calm yet imploring, urging me to go on with my story.

"When I found out, I was terrified," I say taking the seat across from him. "I didn't know what I was going to do, but I knew that I needed to tell my parents. I knew I couldn't go through with terminating a pregnancy and there was no way I could have hid it from them."

He nods, the simple gesture telling me that he understands where I'm coming from. His eyes never leave mine, coaxing me to continue.

"They were angry, when I told them, humiliated. They couldn't believe that I had done this to them, that I had been so reckless. They were concerned about what their friends would think, what the community would say."

"That must have been hard for you."

"It was. I was devastated. To think that how they would appear to their friends was more important than their daughter and what she was going through was a hard pill to swallow. I mean, I know I got myself into the situation but I'm still their daughter, right? They told me to keep quiet, made me promise that I wouldn't tell anyone at school, not even my best friend."

"What about the father?"

This is the question I don't want to answer, the one that sends me spiraling into depression every time I think about it, every time I remember him. I answer the question as calmly as I can. "He knew, he... He didn't want anything to do with it, Logan. He had his whole life ahead of him and didn't want to get tied down with a baby and I just figured *I* got myself into this mess. Why drag him down too? Why take away his brilliant future because of my fuck up?"

His eyes go wide. He looks angry again and I guess right now anger is better than indifference. "It doesn't work like that, Mia."

"Why not?" I challenge. "I'm fine with it. My parents tried to get me to tell them who he was. They grounded me, threatened me, did everything they could think of but I never told. And you can't force me either, Logan. I won't do it. It's my choice — *mine*, and I chose to give him his freedom."

"Mia..."

"No!"

He places his face in the palms of his hands and scrubs, obviously frustrated with my stubbornness. "Fine. What happened next?" He probes after finally looking up at me.

"They made me keep quiet and hide my pregnancy until I graduated. After that, they kept me a prisoner in the house. They rarely let me leave unless it was to go to the doctor's appointments and they were with me the entire time."

"What about your friends? Didn't they wonder why you just disappeared?"

"My best friend Kelsey left right after graduation. Her family sent her to Europe for the summer as a graduation present. The rest of my friends would call and they'd ask me to go out sure, but it was easy enough to blow them off. After a while they just stopped calling." I pick up the sugar spoon which lies on the table and start twirling it between my fingers, using it as a conduit to channel all of the nervous energy in my body. "When I was seven months along, my parents sat me down and told me that they'd decided adoption was the best choice for us. That I was too young and irresponsible to care for a child and they were not willing to take on the responsibility of a child after having raised me or explain to people how their only daughter wound up pregnant with a bastard child."

"Mia," he says softly, reaching over the table to wipe a stray tear I didn't even realize I'd shed off of my cheek.

I didn't think that telling Logan my story would be this difficult, this painful, but I can almost feel the same emotions I felt as I was going through it all. I guess in reality I'm still going through it. Every day with Lily is a new struggle, a hardship that I was not prepared for.

"It's okay," I say, lowering my head to look down at my hands—still twiddling with the spoon. "I told them I wanted to keep my baby, that I had spent seven months bonding with the life growing inside of me and I was not willing to hand her over to strangers."

"How'd they take that?"

"They were furious. I'd never seen them so angry and it scared me. They told me that I didn't have a choice. This was their decision and it was final, and if I even thought of defying them or embarrassing them I could not live there anymore. They wouldn't pay for me to go to college, they'd take away my phone and car, and they'd let me fend for myself. I didn't know what else to do, Logan. I didn't know my options or my rights. I was a minor and they were my parents so I agreed."

"That's understandable."

I nod my head and wipe away more tears. "I spent the next couple of months mentally preparing myself to give away my baby. I didn't let myself think about her, talk to her. I barely even looked at my stomach. I knew that detaching myself emotionally and mentally from her was the only way I'd be able to go through with it without going crazy. My parents had taken care of everything, found the adoptive parents and arranged for them to take Lily from the hospital after she was born. They never even let me meet them."

"What did you do?"

"When I went into labor and was taken to the hospital, I didn't allow my parents to be in the room with me. It was the only place that I had any say. I did it all alone, and they waited outside with the adoptive parents. After Lily was born I asked to hold her. Legally they couldn't deny me that, I still had rights you know. So the nurse reluctantly handed her over to me. I looked at her and I knew Logan, I knew that I would die before I let anyone take her away from me. That I would die if someone *did* take her away from me."

"How did you manage to get away, Mia?"

"The nurse," I say, looking up at him again. "The one who let me hold Lily. After everyone had left for the night she brought her in to me. She was kind, and I found myself trusting her, telling her my story, telling her how I didn't want to give

Lily away. She didn't say anything, just sat and listened," I say through tears. I think of Kelly the nurse and smile. "The morning I was supposed to check out and Lily was to go with her adoptive parents, she came into my room. She had worked it all out: how I would escape, how I would get the money that I had saved away. *My money.* It was my only shot at getting away so I went along with it. I felt bad for the adoptive parents...I really did but legally I didn't do anything wrong. I'm her mother. I hadn't signed the papers yet and even if I did, I still had time to change my mind. My biggest problem was that I was only seventeen and if my parents found me they could force me to come home and if that happened there was no telling what would happen to Lily. I couldn't trust that they'd just let me keep her. You have to understand I did the only thing I could think of to keep my daughter." I cry. "I wanted to tell you that night, when I met you at the hospital but I couldn't risk it. Not when I was so close to turning eighteen, being legal. I knew that it was the only way that no one could force me into anything."

"And you made it. According to this," he says, holding up my passport, "your eighteenth birthday was yesterday."

I let out a chuckle. "Yes, I made it. I'm free to be me. I'm free to be Lily's mom and no one can change that now. No one can take me away from her, not you, not them not anyone."

"I would have never done anything to take her away from you. I'm not your enemy," he says defensively.

"No, but you are a cop. It's your duty to do what's right."

"Sometimes legal doesn't equal right. I'm not a robot, Mia. I would've helped you."

"But I had no way of knowing that, so I had to be careful."

"Does Sarah know?"

I exhale slowly. The last thing I want to do is throw Sarah under the bus, but I'm learning very quickly not to underestimate Logan. He'll get to the truth eventually and I'm done living a lie. "She wanted to tell you. I made her promise."

He shakes his head and rolls his eyes. "Fuck…"

"I had to tell her. There was no way I could work on the books by giving her a fake name. She would have found out about me. I took my chances and told her the truth. It was a crapshoot, but she decided to help me. I promised her that if there was ever a need I would tell you myself after I turned eighteen."

"God Mia, I don't know what to do with all of this."

"Just put yourself in my shoes. Think about what you would have done. I'm not a liar by nature, but I did what I had to do. Giving Lily up was not an option for me."

The sound of Lily crying from upstairs puts an indefinite end to our conversation. I'm glad for it, relieved for the ability to take even a small break from this soul crushing confession. I'm exhausted from having to relive any of it.

"Go take care of her. I'm going to go to the grocery store. I'll bring you back some breakfast."

"You're not kicking me out?" I question, not hiding the surprise in my voice.

"No. I'm not kicking you out. Are eggs okay with you?"

I nod. "Yes. Eggs are fine."

He gets up, grabs his keys off of the kitchen counter, and heads for the front door."

"Logan." I call after him. He turns but says nothing, just stands there motionless, waiting for me to speak. "Thank you," I say quickly and head upstairs to take care of Lily.

47

Chapter 6

❧

It's over an hour later by the time Logan makes it back. I don't go downstairs right away—just lay on the spacious bed with Lily, relaxing and trying to wrap my mind around the events of the morning. Part of me is afraid to face him, to see the disappointment in his face because I still feel awful for having lied but when push comes to shove I still wouldn't change it and that thought causes me to feel guilty.

"Mia?" Logan calls out from the other side of my door. "Can I come in?"

I sit up in bed and let out a sigh, not sure I'm ready to face him just yet but not wanting to be rude either. "Uh yeah."

He opens the door and leans on the frame. I can't help but to look at his arms. The curves and lines that form his muscles protrude in just the right way. I tear my gaze away and look him in the eyes, which in this instant is worse than looking at his body. I feel like I get a tiny piece of him every single time I look at them. I'm drawn to them like a moth to a flame. I tear my eyes away and look back down at a cooing Lily.

"I bought you an egg sandwich," he says. "It's getting cold."

"Thanks," I murmur, tucking a stray piece of hair behind my ear. "I'll be right down."

"How's she doing?" he asks, motioning toward Lily.

"She's great," I say with a smile because I know it's the truth. She is thriving and beautiful and strong and that has everything to do with me. Every single doubt, every single negative word that my parents spewed at me about not being ready to take care of a child was false and it gives me a surge of pride in knowing that I've proved them wrong, even if they'll never know it.

"Good. That's really good."

The insecurity I've felt since we had our conversation this morning returns. I don't want my staying here to be full of anger or animosity. I know that I lied to him but I keep hoping that he'll see that lying was my only choice at the time. "Logan?"

"Yeah."

"Are we okay?"

He lets out a breath. "Yeah Mia, we're okay. I get it, alright?" He states, crossing his arms over his chest. He looks guarded, defensive and I can't help but to feel a little sad about it. "I understand why you did what you did. You're a legal adult now so it doesn't even matter. Nothing bad happened to you, you've done a great job with Lily, and you're making it work. It's over."

"But you don't trust me, right?" I ask, biting my lower lip, clearly showing my nerves about his answer.

"Do you need me to trust you? I'm not your boyfriend and I'm not your father."

"No, but you're my friend."

"Friends, huh?" he asks, raising an eyebrow. "Do you trust me?"

I avert my gaze, looking past him and out to the hallway rather than at him. He knows, gets enough about me to know that I don't trust him. I don't trust anyone, and I know that I'm a hypocrite for wanting him to trust me when I can't give him the same thing. That I'm incapable of it because life has taught me that trusting people gets you nothing but heartbroken and

hurt. I hate that I'm this jaded at eighteen, that I've felt enough pain to get me through a lifetime, but if I could choose to let myself trust somebody, I would choose to trust him.

"Alright," he says, putting me out of my misery. "I can live with friendship." He pushes himself off the door frame and shoots me a smile before walking away.

Logan watches Lily while I eat breakfast and take a shower; it's strange not having to rush through these seemingly normal tasks, to have someone around to give me a break, even if it's only for fifteen minutes. I don't want to take advantage of him but God it feels good to have a little time to myself. After my shower I head out of my room in search of Logan and Lily. I pass an open door on my way downstairs and come across the two of them in the bedroom adjacent to mine. Lily is in her play yard while Logan is sitting on the floor with a toolbox setting up a crib. I'm confused by the scene being played out before me. It seems natural yet wrong, a contradiction.

"Ah what are you doing?" I ask.

"Hey, I'm putting this crib together for Lily. I thought it would be good for her to have a place to sleep while she's here."

"You bought her a crib?" I ask, the disbelief evident in my voice. Why would he buy something as permanent as a piece of furniture for Lily when we're only going to be here a few days. I'm not sure what to make of the gesture, but Logan seems to make an art form of confusing me. From the day I've met him, every interaction with him leaves me more and more mixed up about his intentions.

"Umm."

"Logan, I can't accept this. You have to take it back." I try to sound firm, but he just glares at me looking annoyed by the fact that I'm protesting his generosity.

"Relax, Mia. I got it at a thrift store for practically nothing. You can take it with you when you go. She's getting bigger, she's not going to fit in a bassinet forever."

He has a point but I hate the idea of accepting charity from him, especially from him. I desperately need for him to see me as capable, as someone who can take care of herself. "Alright fine, but I'll pay you for it."

He stops what he's doing and looks up at me. "It's a gift."

"I don't need your gift." I challenge.

"Ahh but it's not a gift for you. It's a gift for Lily." He declares with a smug look on his face.

"Are you always this controlling?"

"Yes." He confirms and continues working on the crib again. "Are you always this irritating?"

"Yes… Can I at least help you?"

"That would be great. Why don't you hold that piece over there up for me? It connects to this railing."

I move quickly, getting the piece he needs and kneel on the ground next to him. "So now that you know my story, how about you?"

"What about me?"

"What's your story?" I probe, trying to get him to open to me some. Maybe then the fact that I've spilled my past won't seem like such a huge deal.

"No story, I'm just your average guy."

"I don't know about that. I think everyone has a story, Logan."

I can swear I hear him groan. "Not me."

"Okay. Do you have a girlfriend?" I ask nonchalantly, not wanting to let on that his answer matters to me one way or another. It shouldn't matter, nothing good can come of me developing stronger feelings for Logan; the crush I've admitted to myself is bad enough.

He looks me in the eye and smirks. "No, I don't have a girlfriend."

I can feel the flush reaching up to my cheeks. Why his reaction embarrasses me I have no idea. I change the topic as quickly as I can. "What about your family?"

"What about them?"

"This is like pulling teeth. Where are they, do they live nearby?"

"Yes," he says with a chuckle. "They're nearby. My mom and dad live a couple towns over in the same house I grew up in. My sister lives about fifteen minutes away and my brother lives in New York City."

"Are you all close?"

"Yeah. We're pretty close."

"What did they think about you becoming a cop?"

"Wasn't what they wanted for me, but…they're proud of me anyway."

"It must be scary for them, huh?"

"I imagine it is scary at times, but they know that I'm very careful, that I don't take any unnecessary risks."

"Right."

"Any more questions, detective?"

"Haha. You're a regular comedian."

For the first time today, I feel a little bit of that chemistry, that attraction that lingers between Logan and me.

Logan spends the rest of the day doing odds and ends around the house and I do my best to stay out of his way. I'm still not sure how to act around him or how to wander freely around his house without feeling uncomfortable. For the most part I lounge in my room—reading a book with Lily at my side, until he comes upstairs to let me know that dinner is ready.

I meet him downstairs, and he's in the kitchen serving up a plate of pasta.

I look to the dining room and see he's already set the table. "I hope you don't mind pasta," he says, handing me a plate.

"It looks great. I can't remember the last time I've had a home cooked meal." I regret saying that as soon as it leaves my mouth. I hate seeing that look in his eyes; it's pity and the last thing I want is for Logan to pity me.

"Have you not been eating well?" The tone in his voice gets to me. It resonates through me, cloaking me with a feeling of sadness. It's like his emotions have been transferred to me but I don't comprehend them. The sadness confuses me, why would he be sad for me? A girl he barely knows.

"No, I have. It's just that I don't really like to cook just for myself," I say, taking a seat at the table. He sits down across from me. "It's just me and Lily and she obviously can't eat what I make. It's really pointless to make big meals so I just make a lot of soup, sandwiches, and TV dinners."

He gives a slow nod and sighs. "I want you to feel free to take whatever you want, make whatever you want while you're here."

While you're here...

For some reason those words are like a weight on my chest. When I ran away, I wanted my freedom, to be independent, to raise Lily on my own. Yet the thought of leaving this house causes that kind of involuntary reaction from me. I've only been here a day and already it feels more like a home than I've ever known, but I know that this is temporary and the longer I stay here the harder it will be to move on and that's not good for any of us.

"That reminds me," I say, "Janet, my landlord called. She says my apartment should be ready to move back into on the fifteenth."

"Okay."

"You realize that's almost two weeks right?" I query. Staying here for a few days is one thing but two weeks is a long time. I don't want him to think that I'm taking advantage of him.

He picks up his phone and opens up the calendar. "I have a late shift on that Friday," he says, picking up his fork and stabbing a piece of pasta. "I'll take you by your apartment and we can make sure that it's acceptable together."

I let out a chuckle and roll my eyes. "Acceptable? Really, Logan?"

"Yes. Really, Mia. I want to make sure that everything I spoke to her about is done. You're not going back there until I know you'll be safe."

"You just can't help acting like a cop all of the time can you?" I tease, after chewing my bite of food.

"I take my job seriously Mia, but we're *friends* remember? And as your friend I'm not letting you move back into a place that's not up to code. You have Lily to think about and you shouldn't take things so lightly where her security is concerned."

His statement sobers me up and I know that he's right. Our safety and security are what's most important, but if I don't get back to my life as soon as possible, I might never want to leave this house.

We spend the rest of dinner talking like real friends. I ask him about being cop, and tell him about my job at the day care center. He tells me about his love of cars and about his favorite sports teams and I find myself soaking it all up. Relishing in the normalcy of it, of sitting and having a meal with someone who isn't totally self-centered and absorbed in their own universe, someone who actually cares about what you have to say. I make a silent promise to myself to give this kind of normalcy to Lily, to let her know that she matters, her likes and dislikes, fears and dreams, I want her to know she can tell me all of it and I'll always listen. I'll give her what I never had, the things that money and status can't buy.

"This was really great, Logan." I praise, after I've eaten all of my meal. "Thank you."

"You're welcome."

"I'll do the dishes."

"No, it's okay. I'll just toss it in the dishwasher later." He looks at me with a hint of gleam in his eyes. "Stay here, okay? Don't move."

"O…Okay."

He smirks at me. It makes him look boyish and I love it because he has a tendency to be too serious. I hope I can get to see more of this side of him. He stalks off and comes back a minute later with a small chocolate cake; a single lit candle sits in the center of it.

My heart rate picks up and my eyes start to tingle and burn.

"Happy Birthday, Mia." He grins at me. "I know it was yesterday but I think everyone deserves to celebrate their birthday, even if it's a little late."

I put my head down and try to shield my smile and water rimmed eyes from him. "Thank you," I say on a whisper as he sets the cake down on the table. "This is really sweet of you." I swipe away at a falling tear, embarrassed by my reaction to his thoughtfulness.

"Hey." He calls out gently, tipping my chin up so that our eyes meet. "What's the matter?"

"Nothing." I brush out of his hold with a shake of my head. "It's just... I can't remember the last time I got a birthday cake." He looks up at me resting on his haunches and gives me that look that's becoming all too familiar, the one that tells me he feels sorry for me.

I hate it, hate that he looks at me that way and hate that I care. I shouldn't care what he thinks or feels about me but unfortunately I do. "Don't pity me, Logan. Please."

"I don't."

"I see how you look at me."

"That's not pity, Mia. Do I feel bad for some of the things you've gone through? Yes. Of course but mostly I'm just in awe of your resilience. You're a really tough girl."

"I'd like to think so."

"You are. I know strength when I see it. Now make a wish and blow out the candle so we can eat this thing."

*Make a wish...a wish...*What would I wish for if I could have anything I wanted? The answer to that question scares me for as much as I'd like to deny it, the only thing I want right now is more of Logan Tate. I blow out the candle, letting the thought linger in my mind.

"What'd you wish for?"

"I can't tell you."

"Right...I've got one more thing for you," he says, walking over to a nearby hutch and pulling something out of a drawer. "I picked this up earlier today. Don't freak out, okay? It wasn't that expensive." He sits down and hands me a box wrapped up in blue paper with a white ribbon on top.

I stare at him in disbelief. I want say something but I can't, and after a moment I gently undo the ribbon and open up the wrapping paper, careful not to tear it. Inside the box is a small black digital camera. I look up at him, stunned at the fact that he got me anything at all for my birthday, let alone a camera. It's without a doubt the most thoughtful gift anyone has ever given me and because it came from him I know I'll treasure it always.

"Lily's getting bigger and I thought you might like to capture it on camera."

I can hear the excitement in his voice, the joy that he feels in giving me something that he knows I need. He's right, I've thought about it several times in the last few weeks. How I've wanted to document her growth in photos. How I've wanted to capture moments with her but haven't been able to. "Shit, Logan... I don't know what to say."

"You don't have to say anything. Just use it."

I will… I will use it. Thank you. This was so nice of you."

"I can be a nice guy." He shrugs his shoulders and chuckles.

"I know. I feel like I'm racking up debts with you and I'm afraid that I may never be able to repay them."

"I don't want you to pay me back. I just want you and Lily to be happy, that's all."

I'm not sure how to accept his words of kindness, his wishes for me and Lily, but I'm quickly learning that Logan Tate is nothing like what I'm used to. In fact, he's the complete opposite.

Chapter 7

❧

Logan worked most of the day yesterday, leaving me and Lily in his house alone. I snuck on his laptop and ordered a copy of Lily's birth certificate, then passed the rest of the time by watching cable television, setting up my camera and doing most of our laundry. By the time he got home I was already asleep. True to his word he set up a video monitor in the spare bedroom so that I could check on Lily while she's sleeping in her crib. A crib that after careful inspection appears to be brand new and not thrift store material. A fact that was proven when I found the empty box for said crib in the basement while I was searching for the laundry room. I also found the receipt for the crib mattress, bedding, and baby monitor. Every time I think that I've seen the extent of Logan's thoughtfulness he surprises me with something else. I find my guard slipping a little bit more every day and it scares the hell out of me. It's hard to understand the fear of others but for me, "trust" is the biggest one of them all. To trust someone means being weak and vulnerable, and I promised myself that I would never be either of those things again.

After a long hot shower, I dry off and cover myself up in a plush white towel. I decide to check on Lily to see if she's awake yet. I use the door that connects to her bedroom and open it up slowly so that I don't wake her if she's still asleep. I tread lightly into her room and stop dead in my tracks as I take in the sight before me. The early morning sunlight is beaming through the window, shining like a spotlight on Logan who's sitting in an old rocking chair and rocking Lily back and forth. He has a sleepy look on his face, his short hair is a bit disheveled, and he's holding her as if it's second nature.

Something inside of me churns at the sight of them, witnessing them together like this makes me melt a little. He looks down at her lovingly and she holds onto his finger innocently and just for a second I allow myself to believe that they fit. That it's not totally out of the realm of possibilities for a guy like Logan to take on a girl like me, to love a child like Lily. I'll never understand Logan's penchant for taking care of others, maybe because I never had anyone to take care of me, not in any real way. He's yet to notice my presence so I run back to my room and grab the camera that he gave me. I quickly set up the shot and snap a few pictures of them together. The sound of the shutters click alerts him to my being there.

The corner of his mouth twitches up into an almost smile.

"Hey," he whispers. His face flushes a little and I think that I might have embarrassed him by taking his picture, but then I catch his gaze roaming the length of my entire body and I realize my nearly naked state is likely the cause. Suddenly I'm only all too aware that my attire consists of nothing but a towel.

"Shit, sorry." I grimace, backing up slowly. "I didn't know you'd be in here and then I saw you guys and thought I'd take a picture. I forgot that I had just taken a shower."

He tugs at his lower lip, tilts his head and stares at me.

"I don't normally walk around in just a towel." I ramble, shaking my head. I sound like an idiot but I'm mortified and I don't know what else to say.

"That's a shame," he replies with a mischievous grin

His words cause a reaction that I'm not at all used to. My traitorous nipples strain and peak under my towel, my skin starts to tingle and I feel flushed everywhere. I'm sure that I must look like a deer caught in headlights but I have very little control over my body at the moment. I hear him let out a chuckle as I make haste to my own room, shut the door, and quickly change into a pair of stretchy black yoga pants and a dark gray t-shirt.

After beating myself up mentally for being so stupid, I go back into Lily's room just as Logan is putting her back in the crib. I'm still shocked at how natural he seems around her, it's like he's been caring for her from the beginning. He turns around and glances at me from across the room. "I see you've changed into something more comfortable."

"Yeah, sorry about that," I reply, shrugging my shoulders. "I didn't think you'd be in here."

He runs a hand through his short hair. "I couldn't really sleep. She was crying," he says, motioning to the crib, "so I came to check on her. I heard the shower running so I thought that picking her up might help calm her down until you were done."

"Thanks." I look around the room and stop at the newest piece of furniture, the pretty white rocking chair with matching cushions. My lips tug up into a bright smile. "So..." I tease. "Where'd the rocking chair come from?"

He returns my smile and shakes his head. "My parent's garage."

"You do know we're only here for a short time right?"

He chuckles. "I do. I do know that. You can take all of this stuff with you when you go. It would make me happy to know that Lily has what she needs."

I can't meet his eyes. His generosity is hard to accept and I hate the fact that I'm at his mercy right now. I'm at war with myself, craving my independence, wanting to be able to do what I need to do as an adult without having to depend on anyone. I was finally beginning to feel like I was achieving that when the break in occurred and threw everything out of whack. Now I feel like I'm back to square one. On the other hand, I find that I still love the feeling of being here in Logan's home, under his care. I'm reminded that I have to work at the center tomorrow and that transportation might be an issue.

"Logan, I have to work tomorrow and…"

"What?" He presses.

"Well, the daycare center is within walking distance of my apartment. This is a lot further and I don't have a car." I feel like a loser saying this to him. I had a car back home, a really nice brand new car that I gave up when I left. I don't regret the decision, but God that car would surely come in handy right now.

"Ahh. Right," he says, realization dawning on him.

"I mean, if there's a bus nearby I should be fine."

He places his hand on his hips and stares out the window for a moment. "Get Lily ready and meet me downstairs."

I squint my eyes, giving him my most confused look. "Where are we going?"

"I'm taking you to get a Pennsylvania license."

"How does that help me with no car?" I question, confused by the rapid turn of events.

"Trust me." He remarks as he walks past me, leaving me standing in Lily's room.

Trust…There's that word again. Am I capable of trusting anyone, of trusting Logan? He seems worthy but if there's one thing that I'm sure of is that people are not always what they seem to be.

A few hours later, Logan and I are walking out of the department of motor vehicles with my new license in hand. He straps Lily into her car seat in the back of his truck while I look on. He shuts the door and tosses his keys at me. I barely catch them and look up at him with what's now becoming my familiar perplexed glare and shake my head.

"You're up. Drive us home chief."

"You want me to drive us home in *your* truck?"

"Yes," he says giving me a slow nod. "That's what I said. I have another car in my garage. If you can drive my truck without incident, I'll let you use my car to get to work."

"Are you serious?"

"Yes, you need to get to work, I have an extra car… Get us home in one piece and it's at your disposal. It's really that simple." He sounds more like a drill sergeant than his normal self right now, but I don't care. I'm just excited to be able to drive.

"Sometimes I think you're completely insane," I say, walking around the car and getting in the driver seat. I turn the ignition and put my seat belt on, Logan does the same.

"I'm not insane, Mia. I'm just trying to help you, and I think you need someone you can turn to for help whether you want to admit it or not."

I pull out of the parking lot and onto the road, not responding to his last statement. The last time I willingly turned to someone for help I was almost forced to give my daughter up for adoption. That's not to say I haven't met good people since then: Kelly the nurse that helped me get out of the hospital with Lily. Sarah for giving me a job and yes Logan. Logan has been more than incredible, which is why I find it so hard to understand the reasons why. I wasn't always this cynical but sometimes life has a way of beating the optimism out of you.

"People don't normally do nice things for others without expecting anything in return."

"What could I possibly want in return?" He reaches over and turns the radio off. I glance down at his hand and images of him touching me with that very hand fill my brain, which is strange because normally the idea of anyone touching me like that is repulsive.

Oh my God, what am I thinking? Having a crush on Logan is one thing but actually entertaining the idea of more, of taking my feelings for him beyond the point of something innocent, is too much of a stretch.

"I'm ah… I'm still trying to figure it out." I shut down my inappropriate thoughts about Logan and focus my attention on driving.

I can see him jerk his head to the side from my peripheral vision. "Is that how you really feel about me?"

I let out an exasperated sigh "I don't know." What does he want me to say? I can't figure out what it is that he gets out of helping me, why making sure Lily and I are safe is so important to him, or why I want to believe in him so badly. Have I really been that starved for affection?

"You're full of it." He tosses out, jutting his chin in my direction. "You know I'm a good guy and you just can't bring yourself to admit it."

"Maybe." I concede with a smirk. "Still, I'm sure you can't wait to get rid of us. You can get us out of your hair in just a few weeks and then you can go back to a life of bachelorhood."

"Bachelorhood?" He tosses his head back and laughs. "Wow, you've got me all figured out huh? A different woman every night of the week."

I clutch the steering wheel until my knuckles turn white and attempt to mask the frown that is fighting to form on my face. The thought of different women with Logan every night stirs something in me. I feel like a child on the verge of throwing a temper tantrum. In fact, I'm gripped with jealousy, an emotion I've never really experienced when I think of Logan with other women.

"What did my truck ever do to you, Mia? You can relax the death grip you have on the steering wheel."

"Ugh, I'm just concentrating," I reply, brushing off his comment.

"I have a really demanding job." The humor is now gone from his voice. "I don't have a lot of time for dating, and I hardly lead a life of bachelorhood. I want what every one else wants."

"And what's that?"

"To find *one* woman to love, to settle down with, build a family with."

"That's a nice dream," I say softly, never taking my eyes off the road in front of me. Of course he wants a family of his own one day. Why would he want to be tied down with a mess of a girl and her child when he could have his picture perfect life?

"Do you have a similar dream?"

A year ago I had so many dreams: I dreamt of going away to college, starting a career and making a life for myself apart from my family. I dreamt of finding an amazing man and falling in love. All the dreams of a girl that were viciously ripped away from her.

"My dreams don't really matter anymore. All I can do is make sure that Lily has the chance to make her dreams come true."

"That's not true. You're young, you can do whatever you want."

"How old are you, Logan?"

"I'm twenty four. Why?"

"At age twenty four you have two cars, a home, and a career. What you don't have is a lack of a college degree, an apartment in shambles, and a baby. You can do whatever you want. I can't," I say, knowing all too well that my options were taken away from me, my hands tied. I took back what I could the day I snatched up my daughter and ran. I took back some control but I also signed up for what promises to be a very difficult life.

"What is it that you want?" The tone of sadness returning to his voice.

"Did you know that I had my choice of colleges?"

"You can still go to college, Mia. It might just take you a little longer, but you can make it happen. There are programs for people with children and families." He says the words but I'm not sure he believes them himself. Not really. He's saying what he's supposed to say, words to motivate and inspire me, but in what reality does a single eighteen year old mother get to achieve all of her wildest dreams?

"My focus has shifted. There's nothing wrong with that."

"No, there is nothing wrong with that as long as that's what you want," he says, just as I turn into his driveway.

"So? Did I pass? Do I get to use your car for work?"

"Yeah. You did great, passed with flying colors," he says, making me grateful that he allows me to drop the previous topic of conversation.

Chapter 8

I get to work bright and early the next day. True to his word, Logan gave me full use of his spare car. He made sure to fill up the gas tank, and got Lily's car seat secured in the back seat last night. I spent most of the night hiding in my room—pretending to read a book, because it's becoming increasingly more difficult to be around him without letting my imagination get the best of me. He sparks something in me, brings something to life that's been lying dormant. I could have sworn that I caught him casting glances at me from across the table at dinner last night but I can't be sure and I'm not confident enough to act on my own urges.

I'm working the front desk this morning since the normal receptionist is out sick. I prefer being in class with the children, but I do whatever they ask of me because I need the job.

"Good morning Mia," Sarah says as she enters the front door. She sets her oversized sunglasses down on the desk and tilts her head looking somewhat confused. "Is Officer Tate here for something? His car is in the parking lot."

The fact that she can specifically pick his car out of a parking lot full of vehicles intrigues me. "No, Logan's not here, I drove his car here."

Something resembling jealousy flashes over her features. She purses her lips and gives me a tight smile.

I know I could have explained the circumstances better, let her know the reason why I'm driving Logan's car instead of walking to work, but a part of me wanted to witness what Sarah's natural reaction would be. The frozen look on her face and stiff posture speaks volumes, and as grateful as I am to her for the giving me a job and keeping my secret, I can tell I need to be on alert now. The nature of our friendly relationship may have just shifted.

"You're on a first name basis with him? I hadn't realized you two had gotten that close. Does he know the truth about you, *Mia*?"

I don't respond to her question right away, I understand the hidden meaning behind it. She's threatening to tell him, but I give her a bright smile. "Lily and I are staying with Logan, so he's letting me use his car…and yes. He knows the truth," I say, just as the phone rings.

I love this phone right now, I pick up the receiver never taking my eyes off of Sarah and keeping my smile intact. Her shock is evident as she leaves me to my work and heads back to her office. I'm stunned by the fact that she has feelings for Logan and even more stunned at how angry that makes me.

After work, I stop at the grocery store with Lily and pick up a few ingredients so that I can cook dinner. Logan has done so much for me that the least I can do is make him a meal. The rest of the day at work was awkward to say the least. Sarah and I went out of our way to avoid each other, and it seemed as though neither of us wanted to discuss my relationship with Logan. I thought of nothing else for most of the day—my relationship with Logan, if you can even call it that, and his relationship with Sarah. I keep wondering if she's really just his sister's friend or if there's something more between them.

When I get home I place Lily in her baby swing and get started on making dinner right away. I opt to make pork chops with rice pilaf and baked potatoes. It's a simple meal I taught myself how to cook but I'm excited to be able to make it for Logan. I turn on some music and focus on cooking dinner, allowing the stress of the day to fade away. I let the music soothe me, loosen me up and carry my thoughts away. By the time Logan gets home I'm completely zoned out. My head is rocking back and forth to the beat of the music, I'm lost in the rhythm, and I don't hear him approach. He taps me on the shoulder and startles me, snapping me back to reality. I jump, pull out of his reach and let out a shriek. I turn to see Logan standing there with a remorseful look on his face.

"Shit, are you alright?" He questions, then shrugs his shoulders. "I'm sorry I didn't mean to scare you."

I clutch my chest and close my eyes. My heart is pounding in my ears and my hands have a slight tremble to them. I try to breathe through the feeling of panic that has washed over me and I hope he doesn't notice just how scared I actually was a minute ago.

I take a deep breath open my eyes and force the words out of my mouth. "No, it's okay. I'm fine. You just surprised me that's all."

"I shouldn't have snuck up on you like that. It was stupid of me." He looks at me intently. He can see that my fear wasn't just a normal reaction, that it's very real, but he says nothing. I don't want him to say anything, to ask me questions that I can never answer—questions that are too difficult, too painful to answer. I move away from him and turn the music off.

"It's okay, Logan." I smile, trying to reassure him. "I was in my own little world and didn't realize you'd gotten home already. I think maybe the break in at my apartment affected me more that I realized, made me a little jittery. That's all."

He lets out a sigh and nods. "That makes sense."

I think he accepts my explanation but I can't be sure. "Dinner will be ready in a few minutes," I say, attempting to change the subject as quickly as possible.

He turns in the direction of the stove and smiles. "You didn't have to do that but I appreciate it. Thanks."

"I wanted to."

He's wearing his police uniform; it looks different on him today. It's the first time I've seen him in it when it doesn't intimidate me or even frighten me. I can see the man behind it, I can see that Logan wears the uniform it doesn't wear him and it looks amazing on him.

"Do I have time for a quick shower?"

"Sure, I'll keep it warm for you," I reply, using the time away from him to gather my thoughts and calm myself down.

Logan and I sit at the dining room table eating. I'd fed Lily while he showered and she is now sleeping up in her room. We eat most of the meal in companionable silence with little strings of conversation here and there. We're just about done when he finally asks about my day.

"How was work?"

"It was okay," I say, taking a final sip of my drink. I stand up, taking my plate and his to the sink. "I think Sarah was kind of shocked that I was driving your car. She was even more stunned by the fact that I'm staying here." There's a question hidden in that statement and I know he gets it. I turn on the water and begin to rinse off the plates.

He comes up behind me, reaching over me to put the glasses in the sink but doesn't move away. I clutch the sponge in my hand for dear life, the proximity of our bodies causes my breath to hitch, and a rush of warmth floods my belly causing butterflies to take flight. Logan's left hand rests on the edge of the sink and his right grazes my hips, initiating a whole slew of sensations that I've never felt before.

"Mia," he says softly. If he were to move anoth— lips would be touching my ear. "Sarah is my sister's best friend, she's *my* friend, there's nothing between us."

I shrug at his response, feigning disinterest but secretly elated by his answer to my hidden question. "It's really none of my business."

He turns the water off and takes the sponge out of my hand, tossing it back into the sink. His hand on my hip pulls at me, guiding my body to turn around until we're standing face to face and inappropriately close. "So you wouldn't care if I told you that I *did* have a relationship with Sarah?"

"Why would I care, Logan?" I ask, averting my gaze.

"Look at me, Mia." I do as he asks, our gazes lock but neither of us makes a move, our bodies are frozen trying to comprehend the electric charge between us.

"Did you?" I whisper.

"Did I what?"

I let out a huff. I know he's doing this on purpose; he wants me to say it. "Did you have a relationship with Sarah? Did you sleep with her?"

A hint of a wicked smile tugs at his lips. He pulls a strand of my hair between his thumb and his forefinger as if he were examining it for a moment then he gently pushes it behind my ear, his touch makes my body go on hyper alert, my most sensitive areas coming to life. His gaze drops to my lips then quickly rises back up until our eyes are locked on each other. He shakes his head. "No. I never had a relationship with Sarah. I've never slept with her."

I force my features to remain neutral but I think he can sense my relief, and I'm almost positive that he enjoys my reaction. His fingers gently stroke my cheek and I can't help but to lean into his touch, I'm lost in it, no longer in control of my actions or reactions. I tilt my head up, push off of the counter and onto my tiptoes and before I can think it through mesh my lips to his. His hands grab onto my hips, pushing me back down again until I'm leaning against the sink. He follows me down, using his strength to take control of the kiss, using his tongue to coax my mouth open and slowly guiding it into my mouth. And just like that my crush on Logan is gone, replaced with lust and few other emotions that I have no desire to think about. My arms slide around his neck as his slip around my waist pulling me closer to him uniting us like two puzzle pieces locking together. It's a brilliant rainbow in an otherwise dark and cloudy day. I never knew a kiss could be like this it feels like more. It's as if though I'm opening up a part of me to Logan that no one else has ever been privy to and he's doing the same for me. It excites me and scares me at the same time; no one has ever ignited the fire inside of me the way that he does.

The sound of Lily crying comes through the baby monitor that I brought downstairs with me earlier. I pull away from Logan and instantly the spell is broken, it's as if someone has thrown a bucket of cold water over my head. I can't tell by looking at him what he's thinking but I can only assume that it's not good. I can't believe that I actually kissed him. I can feel the heat rushing up to my cheeks and I'm completely mortified. He reaches out for my hand but I dodge him.

"I'm so sorry. I shouldn't have done that," I say.

He cocks his brow, looking as confused as I feel. He shakes his head at me. "No, Mia."

"I know." I groan covering my eyes with my hands. I don't want him to see my mortification. "It was completely inappropriate, you've been nothing short of amazing to me and Lily and…"

He reaches for me again but I take a step back. "It's okay, I..."

"No, it's not okay." I sigh, looking away. "I have to go check on her." I move out of the kitchen and quickly bound up the stairs, going into Lily's room and locking the door behind me. I pick her up out of her crib and sit in the rocking chair. I hold her to my chest, and place a kiss on her little forehead. I close my eyes, biting back tears, mentally kicking myself for what I did and hoping that I haven't just outworn my welcome with Logan.

After I get Lily back to sleep I use the connecting bathroom to get back to my room. I just don't think I can handle a run in with Logan right now. I change into a pair of pajama pants and a tank top then crawl into bed. I can't shake the embarrassment that I'm feeling. I mean, yes Logan has flirted with me a time or two, but there's a huge difference between innocent flirting and sucking someone's face off. As stupid as it was of me to do it, I can't help but relish in how good it felt to be in his arms, how good it felt to feel his arms around me; my lips are still tingling.

A gentle rapping on my door pulls me from my thoughts. I lift my head just in time to see Logan slowly opening my door and peeking his head in.

"Hey."

"Hey," I reply, inwardly praying that he'll just take pity on me and go away. Let me wallow in my misery and self-hate all alone.

"Can I come in?"

What am I supposed to say? No Logan, you can't come into a bedroom in the house that you own? A bedroom that you're letting me use for free?

I let out a sigh and push up onto my elbows so that I can get a better look at him. "Of course you can come in. It's your house."

He crosses the room in a few quick steps and before I can question or protest he's hopping up on the bed and lying down next to me on top of the covers.

My eyes go wide with surprise. "What are you doing?"

He brings his arms up and places his hands behind his head, using them as a pillow. "Relaxing for a minute it's been a long day."

"You have your own room to relax in, don't you?"

"Yeah," he replies, turning his head to the side so that he can look at me, "but I wanted to talk to you. This kills two birds with one stone."

I know Logan enough to know that he's not going anywhere until he gets his way so I do the only thing I can do. I let out a huff and roll my eyes. "Fine, talk."

"Do you want to tell me what happened downstairs?" There's no anger in his voice, no reproach in his tone. He's cool, calm and collected; right now I envy his ability to remain level headed.

"I… I don't know, I just thought that maybe… I…"

"What?"

I bury my head in the pillow and muffle out an answer. "I thought that maybe you wanted me to kiss you."

"You're wrong."

Oh my God, if ever there was a time I'd like for the floor to open up and swallow me whole this is it. This is by far the most humiliating moment of my life. "Yeah, I got that." I croak out.

76

He slips his hand between the pillow and my face and tugs at my chin, forcing me to look up at him. "I didn't want you to kiss me because I wanted to be the one who kissed you, and I would've but you beat me to it, and I liked it. I wanted it."

I inhale a sharp breath, this was not what I was expecting him to say. "I thought…"

"I know what you thought and I'm telling you that you're wrong." He strokes my cheek like he did earlier in the kitchen. "You flipped out and ran away before I could say a word, Mia. I care about you, I like you, and maybe I always have. From the first day I met you, I knew there was something about you."

"Logan, I'm glad that you feel that way about me, I am pretty sure you must know that by what happened earlier, and as happy as I am that I wasn't out on that ledge alone this is probably not the best idea. I come with too much baggage and I have too many issues to get involved with anyone right now."

"Lily isn't baggage."

"I know, I didn't mean it that way, I just… I can't."

He nods slowly. "Alright, I respect you, Mia. If that's how you feel about this then we'll do it your way. We'll just be friends."

"And you'll really be okay with that?" A part of me is hoping that he'll say no but I know that it's for the best. He wouldn't want me if he knew everything there was to know about me and he deserves better. Someone who can love him and give him a family of his own, not a ready-made family.

"Sure," he says, closing his eyes.

"What are you doing now?"

"What does it look like I'm doing? I'm going to sleep."

"This isn't your room."

"Go to sleep, Mia. I've had a long day and I'm too tired to move now." I should fight him, tell him to get out and that I have no intention of sharing my bed or my heart with him, but he would be able to see right through the façade. He knows every single word I've just said was done so with very little conviction, I'm starting to realize that I've never wanted anyone to love me more that I want Logan Tate to. Instead of fighting a losing battle, I turn on my side and close my eyes—taking comfort in the fact that even if it's for a little while longer Logan is here with me.

Chapter 9

It's been two weeks since the break in at my apartment and it feels like an eternity since I kissed Logan in the kitchen. Since the night he came into my room and slept in my bed. Things have been otherwise normal but every night since then, after I've put Lily down for the night and after I've gone to bed, Logan comes into my room and sleeps in my bed.

He always stays on top of the covers and we talk and laugh. He tells me about his family life and what it was like growing up here, and though the sexual tension is there, neither of us has acted on it again. What we've built in the last few days is so much more than the desire to act out on our feelings. It's more than a stolen kiss in the kitchen. It's two people spending time together, getting to know each other, and day by day coming to trust one another.

Work has been a little awkward to say the least but Sarah finally made good on her word and put me on the books last week. That means I'll be eligible for health benefits for Lily and myself, and I can stop going to the clinic and get her a real pediatrician in a few months.

Logan picked me up on my lunch hour and he and I are on our way to do a walk through of my apartment with my landlord, Janet. I left Lily at the daycare center and when I walked out to the front desk to meet Logan I found he and Sarah in what appeared to be a heated conversation. I didn't want to assume but I could pretty much assume that I was the topic of discussion. Not to mention the fact that all conversation ceased when I approached them.

"What were you and Sarah talking about before?" I ask from the passenger side of the truck. I try my best not to sound bothered or catty even though that's exactly how I feel.

He looks uncomfortable as he glances at me out of the corner of his eye. "Um…"

"Sorry, it's none of my business. You don't have to answer that."

"No, it's fine. She just wants to make sure that I'm not…" He hesitates.

"You're not what?"

"Taking advantage of you. She thinks you're too young for me."

"I bet she does." I mumble under my breath and roll my eyes. "I think she's more worried about you getting tied down with just another teen mom than she is about anything else."

"Mia, you're not a stereotype to me. The fact that you're young and have a baby doesn't bother me. I am completely in awe of you, of what you did for Lily."

"Thanks." I look away from him quickly in a poor attempt to hide the blush creeping up my cheeks.

We pull up in front of my building and a sense of sadness washes over me. This is it. As long as all of the repairs have been done, I can move back into my apartment with Lily tonight. I should be happy about getting my own place back, but the empty feeling in my chest is gnawing away at me and it has everything to do with Logan. Everything to do with how much I'm going to miss him.

Janet is already there when we arrive. "Kelly, Officer Tate," she says with a cheery smile. Logan looks down at me at the mention of the name that I was using up until a few days ago.

"Hi Janet," I respond as Logan shakes her hand.

She leads us into my apartment.

Janet unlocks the front door. "We've changed the locks on the door for you and added a security chain," she says, more for Logan's benefit than for mine. He barely acknowledges the change.

We walk around the apartment while Janet points out more of the changes that she's made in order to make it a safer place to live.

"So what do you think, Officer Tate? I think that we've addressed everything on your list."

"I didn't notice these bars on the window," Logan says, pointing toward the living room windows.

My mouth opens in shock. "Logan!" I sputter out, trying to get him to stop.

"Well, they're child proof windows." Janet announces, looking back and forth between the both of us. I think she's as confused about our relationship as I am.

"No, ma'am. What they are is a fire hazard and they have to be taken off."

"Logan..."

"*Kelly*...If there is a fire, you and Lily would be stuck. There would be no way to get out of this apartment." He turns back to Janet. "I also noticed a large crack in the bathroom ceiling and some evidence of leakage."

Janet looks as if though she's been slapped in the face. "Well, I..."

"Look Janet, you seem like a really nice person but given the circumstances, I'm just not so sure that this is the best place for a young mother and her child."

"Logan!" I demand in a warning tone. It doesn't phase him, he practically ignores me.

"I just think that maybe *Kelly* is a little in over her head here, Janet. She needs more of a move in ready kind of place, a place with more room for Lily. You can understand that, right?"

"Well, she's only been here a few weeks. She signed a lease for a year."

"And I'm sure that given what transpired here last week you'd be more than willing to let a young mother out of that lease. I mean, would you have been comfortable coming back to live in an apartment that was just burglarized?"

"Janet," I say, pushing myself in front of Logan and into the conversation, "Logan is just being really overprotective..."

"No *Kelly*, I'm just being honest." He comes around from behind me and moves to stand next to me. "What do you say, Janet?"

She looks about ready to throw something; she avoids Logan's cop stare and turns to face me. "It's clear that Officer Tate is not comfortable with you staying here sweetie. Perhaps it's for the best for me to let you out of your lease. If you leave me a forwarding address I'll cut you a check for your security deposit."

"That's very kind of you, Janet. We'll make sure to have everything moved out by Sunday."

And just like that I go from independence to homelessness.

I'm seething by the time we make it back to the car.

"Well, that went well."

"Are you fricking *crazy*? Are you serious right now?"

"What? You're getting your security deposit back, *Kelly*. You should be happy."

"Stop calling me that." I growl.

"Why? That's the name you wanted to be known by, Kelly."

"You're a real jerk you know that? I'm homeless now, Logan. Are you happy? You must be so proud of yourself making me lose the only decent apartment that I could afford."

"Oh, Mia."

I can hear the remorse in his voice now and some of the anger begins to dissipate but it's quickly replaced with fear. What the hell just happened? I can't stop the onslaught of tears that start to fall. "What am I supposed to do, Logan?"

"Hey. Don't cry, Mia. Do you really think I would do that to you and not have a plan?"

"A plan? What plan?"

"I want you and Lily to stay with me."

"That's your plan? You want me and Lily to stay with you? For how long Logan, huh? Until you get sick of us, until you meet some girl you want to bring back to your house but wait… you can't, because you have house guests."

He smiles brightly at me, genuinely and I have to fight the urge to melt into him. "I want you there, I like having you there."

"Okay, but there's going to come a time when you want your life back, so what's going to happen to me and Lily when that time comes?"

"It's not going to happen, Mia. You need to relax. Just trust me."

And there it is again, the word that I've come to despise with everything that I am: Trust. I want to trust him, and up until a few minutes ago I think I was starting to trust him but now this has thrown me for a loop. Why would I trust him when he's just made me lose my apartment, when at any moment he can decide that having a young mother and baby in his home isn't conducive to the type of lifestyle he wants to have? The only thing that I'm sure of is that he really hasn't left me much of a choice. I have no other alternative but to take him up on his offer to stay with him.

"Fine. You win, but this is only temporary. It's only until I can find a new place that I can afford."

"Deal." He agrees with a mischievous grin.

I huff and put my seatbelt on. "Are you taking me back to work?"

"Sure." He turns the ignition and pulls out onto the road. "So, about once a month my family gets together for dinner."

"Oh?"

"Yeah and...well it's this Sunday at my parents' house."

"Oh okay, well Lily and I can fend for ourselves."

"I know, but actually I was hoping that you'd come with me."

"You want us to come with you? I'm not sure that's such a great idea."

"Why not?"

"Well for starters what would they think of me? The girl and her infant who are living with their son."

"They're not going to judge you, Mia. They're not like that. I know they're going to love you. Just think about it," he says, pulling into the parking lot of the daycare center. He turns to face me and gives me a shy smile. "I work late tonight so don't wait up for me, alright?"

"Okay. Be careful," I reply, extricating myself from the car quickly, not looking back as I enter the building. I can't help but to notice the frothy glare I get from Sarah as I walk past her and head back toward my classroom. Maybe he sees them as only friends but Sarah sees Logan as way more than that and now she sees me as competition. I just hope she doesn't fire me because of it.

It's almost one in the morning by the time Logan crawls into my bed. I have a hard time coming to terms with the sense of peace that comes from knowing that he's back home, safe and with me because I know that I shouldn't care. That his comings and goings shouldn't affect me, that his safety shouldn't worry me, but it does. We lie silent for a moment, facing each other, taking one another in.

"Did I wake you?"

I shake my head. "No I was awake."

"Were you waiting for me, Mia?"

"What? No," I reply so weakly that even I don't believe it.

"Really? Because I couldn't wait to see you."

"I don't know why you say things like that."

"Like what?"

"Like…" He looks into my eyes, silently encouraging me to speak to him. "I don't know, nice things."

"You should have someone to say nice things to you. You deserve it."

"And you want to be the one to say those things?"

"Why else do you think I just got you evicted from your apartment?"

"Logan…" I wail, smacking him on the arm.

"What? I like having you here and I'm serious that that place still needed work. I would have never been comfortable leaving you there."

"But why? What is it that you want?"

"I guess I just want to shelter you. And not just in the literal sense but I have this crazy need to protect you, to make sure that you and Lily are okay. I know I haven't gone about it the best way, but I want you here."

"I want to be here too." I admit quietly.

He strokes my cheek gently, a gesture from him that I'm starting to love. Instinctively, I lean into him, wanting to get as close to him as I can. He places his free arm over my waist, his hand lands just above my butt—pushing me even closer to him.

"Does you wanting to be here mean that you want to be with me too?" His hands move upwards slowly, starting to rub my back, forcing my muscles to relax.

"Is that what you want?" I query, slipping further into a fog,

"I don't know how to do this, Mia. I usually just go for what I want, say what I mean, I don't hold my tongue at all, but with you I sense that I need to tread carefully, like you need to time to process what's really happening here."

"What if you decide it's all too much? I'm scared."

"I know baby, but you're here, you're with me and you and Lily are safe. And when it comes down to it, I want you, I want you both, I want you to be mine. Do you want that too?"

"I… Yes. Yes, I think so."

"Then we can start off slow. We can take our time, keep on getting to know each other and see how it goes."

"I don't want to bring you down or hold you back. Why would you want a ready made family when you can start from scratch and have your own?"

"Because that's not what I want. You want an explanation that I can't really give you. I can't tell you why people want what they want, they just do. It just is and I need you to believe in it, trust it."

"Trust doesn't come easily to me."

"I know that, but do you think you can try? Do you want to try with me?"

I know what I want my answer to be. I want Logan and even though the thought of being with him, of trusting him is terrifying, I know I owe it to myself to try. "Yes, I want to try," I whisper.

His grip tightens on me and I tilt my head back as his descends and our lips meet. Warmth spreads throughout my body making me feel alive, the way only Logan can make me feel. We break apart a few minutes later, both smiling, both happy for what's just transpired.

"Can I sleep under the cover now?"

I try but fail to stop the giggle erupts in me. "Yes, you can sleep under the covers."

"I'm glad you get a kick out of this." He murmurs, situating himself under the blankets and pulling me into his arms.

"Goodnight Logan."

"Goodnight Chief."

Chapter 10

I've had the urge to throw up since I woke up this morning. My nerves are shot and I'm trying not to panic. Logan, Lily, and I are on our way to his parents' house for dinner. I'm unaware as to what I should expect tonight and I'm pretty confident that his family is going to hate me. Who in their right mind would want a girl like me for their son, and more importantly who in their right mind would bring a girl like me home to meet the parents?

I tried to convince him to go without me, tried to explain to him that it was just too much too soon but he insisted that his family would be happy to meet me. I on the other hand am terrified to meet them. I'm terrified to walk into their home on Logan's arm with a baby in tow. Nevertheless, I found one of two conservative dresses that I have in my possession and I put it on. It's a simple black dress that sits just above my knees and I've paired it with a jean jacket and a pair of flats. I feel ridiculous but it's the best I could do given my situation. Logan looks mouthwateringly sexy in a pair of black slacks and dark blue button down shirt. He holds my hand the entire way there, silently giving me encouragement.

We pull into the driveway of a massive brick house. Floodlights shine like a beacon on Logan's truck as we approach; it's like a spotlight on us making it impossible for me to hide. The house reminds me a lot of my parents' home back in Florida, which tells me that his family has money. In my world, when people have money they have a skewed sense of reality and priorities, but I'll do my best to withhold judgment.

Logan turns his head toward me. "You ready?"

"Do I have a choice? We're here already," I reply with a hint of sarcasm in my tone.

"I promise you that it's going to be fine. I know my family. They're going to welcome you with open arms." He reassures.

"Even though I have a baby?"

"Yes." He reaches over and strokes my cheek. "Even though you have a baby."

"Fine, lets just get this over with."

He exits the car, strides around the front and opens my door. He practically has to drag me out of my seat, but once I'm securely out of the car and standing by his side he grabs Lily's car seat from the back seat and with his free hand grabs hold of mine. I look down at our entwined fingers and my heart skips a beat.

Normally, I'd be over the moon by this publicly open display of affection but right now it just puts me more on edge. He leads me across the long gravel driveway, up a short flight of brick steps and inside the front door with lightning speed.

I can barely catch my breath or mentally prepare myself for the upcoming introductions. *God, please don't let me pass out in the middle of this house.*

"Mom!" He bellows. "Dad! Where are you guys?"

"In the kitchen sweetie!" I hear a sing-songy voice call out. By process of elimination, I deduce that the voice must belong to his mother and I already like her more than my own mom. She sounds happy, gleeful, and kind, not miserable and cold like the voice that I was used to coming home to.

Logan puts Lily's carrier down and takes his jacket off before helping me remove mine. I pick Lily up and hold her close to me, needing to have her near, my protective mother gene kicking in. Logan grabs my hand again and instinctively I try to pull away but he just grips me tighter. One way or another, whether I like it or not, he's making some kind of statement about me to his family.

"Trust me," he says with a smile that does little to reassure me right now.

"Oh, I hate when you say that." I huff as he pulls me through the house heading for what I can only assume is the kitchen.

"Hi guys," he says as we cut through the dining room in order to reach our destination. His parents have their backs to us and turn around in unison. They take in the sight of us together, me holding Lily, Logan holding me and I expect for them to have a reaction to say something, lose the smiles that are plastered on their faces, have a mild coronary but unbelievably they don't even flinch. They never miss a beat, there's no question in their eyes, no obvious disappointment or concern.

"Logan." His father greets him with a nod.

"Hi honey." His mom gleams, walking over to us and placing a kiss on his cheek. "Aren't you going to introduce us to your friend?"

"Mom, Dad, this is my girlfriend Mia and her daughter Lily."

I'm floored by his use of the word "girlfriend." I'm Logan's girlfriend and though I'm still a little surprised by it, I'm mostly elated. I look back and forth between his parents and again I wait for a negative reaction, a secret look from mother to son that says *What the hell are you thinking*? And again I'm astonished when there is none.

"Mia, it's so nice to meet you. I'm Logan's mom, Carol and this is his dad, Steven."

"It's nice to meet you both," I reply timidly.

"Look at this gorgeous baby. How old is she?"

"Um, she's almost two months old," I say. God, I feel like a slut. They probably think I moved from one man to the next without so much as a second thought. I knew that this would be a bad idea.

"Oh, she's big for two months, but that's great. She looks really healthy. May I?" she asks, opening her hands up to indicate she'd like to hold Lily.

I hesitate, but only for a split second. I don't want them to think that I'm anti social or one of those moms that doesn't let anyone hold her kids. I gingerly pass Lily into her arms and watch as she smiles at her, kisses her little forehead and rocks her back and forth. "She's a doll, Mia. You should be very proud."

"Thank you."

Steven smiles at me and shakes his head. "Good luck getting her back now." He jokes and Logan lets out a chuckle.

"Where are Mandy and Chris?" he asks, looking between his parents.

I'm struck by the similarities, I can see pieces of both of them in Logan, His father's eyes and hair, His mother's nose and lips. It's like he got the best features from both of them. What strikes me the most is how they look at Logan, the love in their eyes for him is plain as day. There's no neglect or resentment just pride in their child, acceptance and joy. It makes me sad for the childhood that I lacked, the cold upbringing I had.

"They should be here any minute." Carol chimes in. "You know Mandy is always late and Chris is driving in from the city."

"Right."

"So Mia," She says, turning her attention back to me. "How did you and Logan meet?"

"Um, well I was at the hospital," I reply timidly.

"Oh no, is everything okay?" she interrupts, showing real concern.

"Mom, relax." Logan intrudes. "I was there on a call and Mia was there because Lily was a little under the weather. I ran into her, we talked, we became friends. You get the picture."

"You suck at telling stories," she says, turning to me and winking. "I'm sure it was a lot more romantic than that. We'll talk later." She walks over to Logan and gives up her hold on Lily, passing her over to him so that she can check on the oven.

"Don't let her get you started talking, Mia," says Steven. "She'll never stop asking questions. She'll have your whole life history by the time you leave here tonight."

"*Steven*." She scolds him and I can't help but smile at their lighthearted bickering.

"What? It's true." He teases, placing a kiss on her cheek. "Call me when dinner's ready. Football is on." He plucks Lily right out of Logan's hands. "Come on son." He commands, walking out of the room and taking my daughter with him.

Logan pulls me into his side and kisses the top of my head. "Don't worry she'll be fine. He's a pro. Do you want to come watch some football with us?"

"She's fine here." His mother smiles. "You go ahead so Mia and I can get to know each other."

"Will you be okay?" Logan looks at me.

I look at him and nod like a deer caught in headlights. Maybe she was saving her negative reaction for when she had me alone. Logan gives me a gentle squeeze before leaving me on my own.

"Can I help you with anything?" I ask her.

"No thanks sweetie. Take a seat and relax. I'm sure you don't get a lot of down time with an infant."

"No, I definitely don't," I reply, taking a seat on a stool by the breakfast bar. This is awkward and I'm not much for small talk, but at this point I'll say just about anything to fill the silence. "You have a lovely house."

"Oh, thank you dear. I'll give you the full tour when I finish up here."

"That would be wonderful. How long have you lived here?"

"Oh ages. The kids grew up in this house."

"Right. I think Logan might have mentioned that."

"Lily is *beautiful*. How are you getting on with a baby? Are you doing alright?"

"Yes. Thank you. I'm doing okay. I mean, some days are harder than others but for the most part I think…No, I *know* that I'm doing a good job."

"I can see that. She's thriving, Mia. You should be proud of yourself."

"That's nice of you to say."

"Can I ask about Lily's dad? I don't mean to pry and you can tell me to mind my business if you want. I won't take offense."

"No, that's okay. He's not in the picture. He didn't want to be."

"I'm sorry."

"Thanks."

"Are your parents helping you?"

"No ma'am."

"Call me Carol."

"Carol, right. My parents wanted me to give Lily up for adoption and told me that if I didn't go through with it I could no longer live with them. So I took Lily and I left."

"You left? Where are you from?"

"Florida."

"You came all this way from Florida with a baby?"

"Yes."

"Wow. You're a brave girl," she says softly. There's a familiar look in her eyes and I can tell she's holding something back. There's a story in her eyes and a pain that I'm all too familiar with. "I'm sorry about your parents, Mia. They made the wrong choice and they should have been there for you. If you ever need anything just let me know." I don't know what to say so I just give her a small smile and she continues. "Logan is a good man. If he's cares about you there's nothing that he wouldn't do for you. I can tell that he cares about you a great deal and I think that you need someone like that right now, Mia. Hold onto that."

"I'm sorry, but shouldn't you be telling me to leave your son alone right now? That I'm the wrong kind of girl for him?"

She shakes her head and tilts it to the side. "Why would I do that?"

"Because I'm an eighteen year old mother. How could you really be okay with that?"

"How can I be okay with my son dating a beautiful girl who just happens to have a child? Maybe because I was an eighteen year old mother once."

"What?"

"Shocking I know," she says with a chuckle. "I had Chris when I was eighteen years old."

"I had no idea."

"I was a single mom too. Chris's dad wanted nothing to do with us. I met Steven when Chris was a year old. He was twenty two and being groomed to take over his father's business. Let's just say his parents were none too thrilled with me when they found out about us. To this day, I swear they never got over the fact that he settled for me and they never really warmed up to me. So... what I'm saying is that I know better than anyone how hard it is, Mia. I know what you're going through and I thank God every day that I met a man who was willing to take me along with all of my extra baggage. I hope that you find that too and if it just so happens to be with Logan then I would welcome you and Lily with open arms."

"I don't know what to say. I just assumed you'd all hate me."

"Nope. We're a happy bunch."

"Thank you. It means a lot to me that you're so understanding."

She gives me another one of her warm smiles. "Come on, let's go watch some football. This chicken is going to take a while.

Carol gives me a tour of the house before we make it to the living room. Logan is on the loveseat with a sleeping Lily.

He holds out his free hand to me, and when I take it he pulls me down on the couch with him and settles me into his side.

"How'd it go?" he whispers in my ear.

"Your mom is amazing," I reply.

He gives me a squeeze and I melt into him even more. I still can't believe how far I've come in such a short while. How my life has changed, how a few unwelcome moments have altered the course of my future, but now I have Logan by my side and I never would have imagined that someone as amazing as him would be within my reach, in my realm of possibilities. But when I'm with him, when I see him bonding with Lily, I can't help but to hope that he'll be a permanent fixture in our lives. I can't help but want to trust him.

The front door opens, pulling me from my inner ramblings and in walks a man. He is clearly Logan's brother Chris. He's a few inches taller than Logan with more chiseled features but they have a few similarities that make the connection prevalent. By his side is a beautiful woman who I assume is his sister Mandy. Her long dark hair is pulled to one side and hanging over her shoulder, and her eyes match Logan's perfectly, along with her radiant smile. Interestingly enough, behind her is Sarah who stops dead in her tracks as she takes in the sight of Logan, Lily and I snuggled up together like a cozy little family. She doesn't even attempt to hide the disgust in her eyes. Her nostrils flare and all of a sudden this evening just got a lot more interesting. Sarah stands there for a moment, looking as if though she's just swallowed a bitter pill but she quickly recovers; she paints a fake smile on her face and puts forth her best attempt at pretending that she's unaffected by the sight of us.

"Mia? What are you doing here?" She drawls in a syrupy sweet voice. "I had no idea you were coming."

His sister walks further into the room taking us in. "Hi, I'm Mandy, Logan's sister and this is our brother Chris."

"Hello," I say, rising to my feet and holding out my hand to them both. "I'm Mia."

I can feel Logan stand right behind me as they take turns shaking my hand. Mandy looks between me and Sarah, confusion evident on her face and questions, "How do you two know each other?"

"Mia works for me," Sarah responds, chiming in. "Logan called me a few weeks back and asked me to help Mia out of a tight situation."

"Mandy," Logan says, interrupting, "Mia is my girlfriend and this is her daughter Lily."

I hear Sarah gasp and flick my gaze to her, catching her stunned and angry expression when Logan declares me his girlfriend. There's no hiding the disdain on her face and for just a brief second I hate myself because I find myself loving her reaction. I love the fact that Logan is making this statement in front of everyone that matters to him and simultaneously squashing any hope that Sarah may have had for a romantic relationship with him.

Mandy gives me a reassuring smile. "Well, welcome Mia. It's nice to meet you." She turns to Logan and just like all of the other members of this family, she snatches my baby right out of his hands. "Hello, Lily. Aren't you just the most gorgeous thing I've ever seen?" She coos, rocking her back and forth as she walks up to her parents, greeting each one of them with a kiss.

Dinner is served shortly after everyone exchanges their hellos. Carol was nice enough to set up her bed into a makeshift crib for Lily to sleep comfortably in while we eat. Logan makes sure to secure me a spot at the table next to him and places his hand reassuringly on my knee. I look around at everyone, taking in their comfort with each other and I wonder what it must have been like to grow up in a house like this, with a family that loves each other this much.

Chris gives Logan a nudge on his arm. "How's work little brother? Still keeping the streets safe and all that?"

"It's good," he replies but doesn't elaborate. He doesn't like talking about work, I've gathered as much from our short time living together.

"Well if you're ever ready to get off the force, you know I'll be more than happy to set you up with a job and your own office in the city. The family business is waiting for you."

"Thanks man, but I'm good," he replies almost uncomfortably.

"So Mia," calls Sarah, "when do you move back into your apartment?"

"What happened to your apartment?" asks Mandy. If I didn't know any better I'd say she almost seems worried.

I push a strand of hair behind my ear and give the crowd a timid smile. "Um, it was burglarized a few weeks ago."

His mom's mouth gapes open in horror. "What? Logan!"

"It's fine mom. Mia and Lily weren't there when it happened."

Sarah chimes in as if on cue, clearly trying to make an already uncomfortable situation worse. "And you know Logan, always the hero. He took Mia and the baby in."

"You guys are living together?" asks Chris with a grin on his face. I'm glad someone is getting a kick out of this conversation.

"Just until your apartment is ready." All eyes go back to Sarah who has evidently claimed the role of ring leader. "That's what you told me right, Mia?"

"Um, yeah well actually."

"Actually…" Logan chimes in, gripping my hand underneath the table. "The apartment wasn't up to code so Mia and Lily are living with me now, permanently."

"Permanently?" Sarah gapes at us. "You two have only known each other for a few weeks? Isn't that a tad bit impulsive? What if it doesn't work out? What happens to Mia and Lily then? Where would they go?"

Carol glares at Sarah as if giving her a silent warning. "Logan would never do anything to hurt Mia or Lily. If he wants them to live with him it's because he's sure it's the right decision. You can't always control what feels right, can you Sarah?"

Mandy shoots me a wink from across the table. "I think it's romantic. I'm happy for you two."

"Thank you," I reply with a smile, "but it's not exactly permanent. Logan and I agreed that it was just until I can find another apartment."

"Well I think it's wonderful," Carol says, giving me a knowing smile. "You know too much upheaval isn't good for the baby, Mia. If Logan says you can stay long term you should consider it. His house is big enough and he has plenty of room."

God his mom is good. She knows exactly what she's doing, she can see Sarah's frustration and she's twisting the knife and letting me know she has my back all at once.

"I'll consider it," I say timidly.

Logan pulls me into his side and places a kiss on my forehead. "I'll convince you," he whispers in my ear in a teasing tone.

A smile breaks out on my face, and it hits me that I've been smiling a lot more lately and Logan is the reason. Not even Sarah's repeated attempts to make me look bad in front of his family can bring me down now. The rest of dinner is uneventful but by the time I leave the Tate's home I feel a little lighter, happier, like I actually belong.

Chapter 11

The next few weeks fly by, and I do my best to stay away from Sarah at work and luckily she's professional enough to do the same for me. I love working with the kids and having Lily nearby all day is ideal. Carol has met me for lunch a couple of times and I can't help but to feel thankful for the bond that is forming between us. Having her around makes me a more confident mom. It's great to have someone that can give me a little parenting advice from time to time.

Logan and I have fallen into an easy routine. We spend as much time together as we can with our differing schedules and no matter what, every night he sleeps in my bed. Although we're getting closer and closer with every passing day, we still haven't crossed any lines. We kiss a lot, hug, and cuddle, but we have yet to go past that. I think that he can sense my hesitation at taking our relationship to the next level. He likely believes that it's due to the fact that I don't want to become a teen mother again. Little does he know that the thought of having sex with him terrifies me. It's not that I don't want to, or that I don't want to experience that kind of connection with him. The truth is, I really do want to, but the fear of being hurt and used is still in the back of my mind.

I snuck out of the house early this morning while Logan was still asleep after having plotted with Carol and dropped Lily off at her house for the day. At her suggestion, I'm taking the reins and planning a fun day with just me and Logan. It's my first time away from Lily other than when I'm working and even then she's in the same building. I'm not quite sure how I feel about it, but I know that Carol will take good care of her and Logan and I can use some alone time.

The smell of freshly brewed coffee permeates my senses as I walk through the front door; Logan is obviously awake. I make my way to the kitchen and walk straight into Logan's arms. He rests his chin on the top of my head and circles his hands around my waist.

"Good morning." I sigh, enjoying the feel of being enveloped by him.

"Morning chief. I woke up all alone. Where'd you run off to?"

"I just dropped Lily off at your mom's house."

He pushes me back to arm's length and gives me a questioning look. "You did? Why?"

"Because she wanted to spend time with Lily. She actually insisted and I decided to take advantage. You and I are going to spend the whole day together…alone. I have it all planned out."

"Shouldn't I be the one taking you out?"

"Nope," I respond with a shake of my head. "Today you're giving up all of your control to me. I'm taking over and you just have to go with it."

"Just go with it, huh?

"Yup," I reply with a lopsided grin.

He brings his head down and touches his forehead to mine, giving me a heated stare that causes me to tingle everywhere. He weaves his thumbs through the belt loops on my jeans, effectively keeping me connected to him. "I'll go anywhere with you," he says, just before he brings his lips down to mine for what might go down in history as the sweetest kiss ever.

I order Logan to put on warm comfortable clothes while I deal with my body issues. I know that breastfeeding was the best choice at the time but having to pump on schedule is not my favorite part of motherhood. I try to finish up as quickly and as discreetly as possible; the idea of Logan knowing that I have to do this is embarrassing to me. I don't want him to look at me as a milk pumping factory. I like that he sees me as more than just a mom. Thirty minutes later, we're packing into his truck with me in the driver's seat.

"You sure you're okay with me driving your truck? We can take my... I mean your other car."

"I'm sure. This is more comfortable than *your* car."

"Okay," I say, getting that familiar warm and fuzzy feeling I get whenever he says something sweet to me. Something thoughtful that throws me off balance and causes my resistance against his charm to slip further.

"So..." He prods, clapping his hands together loudly and rubbing them together. "Where are we going?"

I bat my eyelashes at him in a teasing fashion just before turning onto the main road. "You'll see."

"Why the sudden need for secrecy, huh chief?"

"Your manipulation won't work with me, Logan," I say, giving him a playful punch on the arm. "It's not a secret. It's a surprise. There's a big difference you know."

"Watch that punch there, you hit like a man. You can hurt someone with that thing." He teases.

"Ohhhh yeah right. Big bad Mia."

He reaches over and slips his hand on my neck, giving it a gentle squeeze. "There's nothing big and bad about you, Mia. It's all soft and sweet."

We spend the next hour or so listening to music and talking about any and everything. I can tell by the directions that his built in GPS is spewing that we're getting close.

"So we're obviously going to somewhere in Philly. Can you tell me where yet?"

"Guess?"

"Museum of art?"

"No."

"Franklin Square?"

"Nooo."

"Ugh, Liberty Bell?"

"Something you'd actually enjoy." I tease.

"Baby, it's a Sunday. The only thing I'd enjoy on a Sunday in the fall is football."

I smile brightly at him.

"Nooo. Are we going to an Eagles game?"

"According to this thing," I say, pointing to the GPS, "we are."

"What? How?" he asks, looking completely adorable, a mixture of surprised and excited.

"I know people," I say. When Steven found out I wanted to do something nice for Logan, he was able to get me a pair of seats from a friend of his who has season tickets. I knew it would be the perfect surprise for him.

Moments later we're parked and making our way into the stadium.

We're ushered to our seats and Logan looks at me and grins. "How'd you get seats right on the forty yard line?"

"Is that good?"

"Is that *good*? Mia, these seats couldn't possibly get any better." We settle into our seats and for the next few hours, Logan and I are a couple. A real couple. He explains what's happening down on the field to me. We hold hands and snuggle into each other to keep warm. It's beautiful, simple, and normal and it feeds a part of my soul that's been empty for so long, a darkness in me that's starved for sunlight. I feel as though I've been fighting against the current for so long and with Logan I can finally just let go. I can finally be free to be me, I can finally allow myself to trust a little.

Logan can tell that I'm exhausted by the time the game ends and opts to drive home.

"Are we picking Lily up?" he asks as we pull onto the highway.

I hesitate for a moment, all of a sudden very aware of my answer. "No. Your mom and dad are keeping her for the night."

He looks away and clears his throat. "Oh, okay. That was nice of them."

"Yeah, I mean we can always call them and pick her up if you think it's too much."

"No, no. I think it's great that they're giving you the night off, plus they don't have grandkids yet so I can guarantee you they're eating this up."

"Us. They're giving *us* the night off. I know her crying wakes you up too."

"It's no bother. I love that kid."

I inhale a sharp breath, hearing him say he loves Lily is like a dream. It causes a pang in my chest and my eyes start to burn with unshed tears. The thought of Lily having Logan in her life, a good man, an honest man who could teach her and show her the difference between right and wrong is almost too much for me to hope for. I had already resigned myself to the idea of raising her on my own as a single mother. I never would have believed that someone as amazing as Logan would want to be with me, an unwed teen mom on the run.

"She um... She loves you back," I say quietly.

He pulls my hand into his lap and entwines our fingers together, a connection that feels different somehow. Stronger, if that's even possible, and all of a sudden I can't wait to get home. I can't wait to be alone with him, and see what the night has in store for us.

The car coming to a stop jostles me awake; Logan pushes a few strands of hair off of my face and kisses my nose.

"We're home." He announces quietly, while he strokes my cheek with the back of his hand. "You okay to walk?"

I look into his soulful blue eyes and smile. I could get lost in him, I want to get lost in him. "Yeah, I can walk."

He shuts off the ignition and removes the key. He exits the car and rounds the hood coming to the passenger side and opening the door for me. I give him my hand and he helps me out. We make our way inside the house, and he switches the lights on and closes the door behind me as I take off my jacket and hang it up. He comes behind me and circles his arms around my waist; instinctively I lean back into him.

"Are you ready to go upstairs?" He questions, his lips inches away from my ear.

My heart rate picks up and I try to speak, but find that I've lost my voice. I nod my head in response to his question and with a slight push of his hand on the small of my back he leads me up the stairs. I turn to face him and place my hands on his chest. "I think I need a shower, it's been a long day."

"Yeah me too. How 'bout you meet me back in my room when you're ready."

"Your room?"

"Yeah, I thought that maybe we can stay in my room tonight. I have a bigger bed it's more comfortable."

"Okay."

I take my time in the shower washing my hair, shaving and getting myself mentally prepared for what may or may not happen tonight. We've never actually spoken about furthering our relationship, never discussed the impact of throwing sex into the mix. I've been happily living in a bubble here with Logan all the while in denial about the fact that at some point he would expect more, he would need more. It's not that I don't want to give it to him, I want to. With everything I have I want to be that for him, I want to be everything that he needs and expects me to be and I think that I want those things too. I'm just scared, scared to give myself to him willingly because what if it's not what I keep hoping it will be. What if it's exactly what I experienced in the past? The idea is not exactly appealing to me and not that I regret having Lily, but the process of creating her was not by any means romantic or enjoyable. I make a promise to myself not to use my past experience as a point of reference for whatever happens with Logan. He's different. He cares about me and whatever we do we do it because we both want to.

Once I'm done in the shower and my hair is all dry I linger in my bedroom trying to figure out exactly what to wear. I don't think that my normal attire of flannel pajamas is appropriate for tonight but I don't own anything that is outright sexy. Lingerie has never been a top priority on my list of things to do. I pick the best pair of undies that I can find—a cute pair of pink boy shorts with black lace trim, and toss on a white t-shirt that I snatched from Logan. I open my door and walk across the hall, taking deep soothing breaths.

I pause for a moment at his door, placing my forehead on the cool wood. *I can do this.* I say to myself trying to calm my nerves. I lift my hand and gently rap on his door. Moments later it opens up and Logan is standing there looking nothing short of beautiful, freshly showered and in a pair of dark gray boxer briefs.

He takes my hand and gently tugs me into the room. "You never have to knock baby," he says, closing the door after me.

I simply nod my response and hope that he can't sense just how nervous I am.

"Hey," he says, pulling my chin up until our eyes are locked. "Nothing has to happen here tonight. We only have to go as far as you want okay?"

"Okay."

"I like you in my clothes, you look beautiful."

"Thank you."

"Come on, come lay down with me." He pulls back the covers and climbs onto the middle of the bed. I take his outstretched hand and join him. He pulls me close until we're snuggled together face to face. He strokes my cheek the way I love so much and pulls his hand through my hair. His hand starts to move, he runs it up and down my arm, never breaking eye contact as he moves on to my back rubbing lazy circles around my spine. Slowly his hand travels down until it reaches the hem of my shirt and slides underneath it, I jump a little at the direct contact to my skin but I quickly recover and begin to enjoy the impromptu massage.

"Logan."

"Hmmm?"

"Kiss me, please."

There's no need to ask twice. He would never make me beg for what I want, that's just his way, giving, needing to please and take care of me and God help me I love him for it. I do. I love him and I think I may have loved him after he rescued me from my apartment but I was too scared to think it let alone believe it.

His lips are soft, accommodating. He takes his cues from me only taking more when he's sure that I'm comfortable. He moves us so that I'm on my back and he's on top of me, his hand slipping under the front of my shirt. I'm surprised by how much I like his hands on me, how good what he's doing to me feels. Heat pools between my legs when he finally finds the swell of my breast cupping it firmly and then gently thumbing the nipple. The sensations that he elicits from me are intense and leave me wanting more, needing more of what he can give me because he's so good at it.

Before I can protest, the kiss is broken and my shirt is gone. My cheeks turn pink with embarrassment at the thought of Logan seeing me with nothing but a pair of panties on. I gave birth to a baby just a few months ago and my body is nowhere near being back to what it used to be and it makes me self-conscious. I try to cover up with my arms but he shakes his head. "Don't. You're fucking beautiful baby."

"I'm not."

He circles my breasts with his fingertip and takes in every inch of me with nothing but lust in his eyes. "You are the most beautiful thing I've ever seen." He tugs at my earlobe with his teeth causing a sharp intake of breath from me. "I want to taste every inch of you, Mia."

"You do?"

"Yes. Do you want me to? Would you like that?"

"I...I don't know." I stammer.

"You don't know? Haven't you ever had anyone do that to you?"

"No."

"No? Oh baby," he says with a chuckle. "I'm about to show you what you've been missing." He gently tugs on my underwear until I'm completely bared to him. I look into his eyes and all of a sudden I don't feel so embarrassed. I feel beautiful, Logan makes me feel beautiful. His hands begin to roam again, gently massaging their way down to my legs where he runs his hands up and down my calves, making me relax my muscles with every single touch. His hands slip into my inner thighs and gently pulls them apart, giving him an all access view to everything that is me. "Oh baby, you're gorgeous."

His words make me shy. I'm not used to being on the receiving ends of compliments of any kind. I cover my eyes with my hands.

"Uh uh," he says, tugging at my arms until my hands are free of my face. "Don't hide from me, I love everything that I see and I want you to feel confident, okay?"

I open my mouth to reply just as his fingers rub against my wet core. My hips buck off the bed as I let out a cry. "Yes."

"Yes?" he asks with a grin. "*Yes* you feel confident or *yes* you like me touching you like that?"

He rubs me again and I let out a moan.

"Which one baby? Hmm? Should I stop?"

"No. Don't stop."

"That's my girl," he says, spreading my legs further apart and lowering his head giving him better access to me. I'm pleasantly shocked when his tongue meets my wet folds and he licks his way up to my clit where he begins his gentle assault. With every second that passes I lose more of my control, bucking my hips until I find a circular rhythm that meets the motion of his tongue. A persistent pressure starts to build in me. It peaks then resides, again and again, and every time it reaches that peak it gets stronger, causing my legs to quiver. Logan's hands clutch my hips, keeping me firmly rooted to the mattress. I grab onto his head and hold on for dear life as he works his tongue into every crevice until I'm gone, lost to an explosion that courses through my entire body, igniting me from within. In a haze I hear myself calling out for Logan as he extracts every ounce of pleasure from me. I close my eyes and toss my head to the side as I come down from the high I've just experienced.

"Oh my God," I say breathily.

He chuckles and buries his face in my neck. "Was it good for you baby?"

I can't help but to giggle at his comment. I never imagined after everything that I've been through that I could feel this happy. That I could feel this free and that I could actually experience what being intimate with someone feels like. Logan hovers over me again, his eyes go liquid with desire and that's all that it takes for me to want more, to need more of him. He grabs my hands and pulls them up and over my head, wrapping his hands around my wrists and pinning me down to the bed as he buries his head in my neck and starts kissing me there.

A sense of panic starts to hit me and a memory resurfaces—crashing into the forefront of my mind, transporting me back in time, and all of a sudden I'm stuck under strong hands unable to move. A large frame hovers over me whispering horrible things in my ear. Making me afraid to move, afraid to fight, making me an unwilling participant in a series of cruel acts, forcing me to grow up long before my time, to snatch away all of the innocence and naivety of a young girl. I fight against the memory, fight to keep my wits about me, to remember that this is Logan I'm with and not…not someone who would ever intentionally hurt me. A solitary tear escapes from my eyes and I shake my head, trying to dislodge the memory from my mind, alerting Logan to my discomfort. He looks up at me his eyes wide at the sight of my tears. I can feel myself trembling and I hate that I've had this reaction to him.

"Babe?"

"Let go of me." I plead through a now steady stream of tears.

He looks startled, obviously confused. "What? Mia?"

"Let go of my wrists, Logan." I cry. "Now."

"Okay, okay… Babe, it's just me alright, I'm sorry," he says, letting go of me.

I pull myself up to a sitting position and wrap my arms around my trembling body. I try to force it to be still but it's no longer following commands from me. "I don't like to be held down." I admit softly.

He moves from my side until he's in front of me. Hesitantly he pulls my chin up so that I can look in his eyes. He shakes his head slowly. "I'll never do it again… Shh it's okay baby. Please don't cry."

I grab onto his shoulders and pull him into a hug, digging my nails into his back as I try to calm my sobs. "I'm sorry, I'm so sorry, I'm just being stupid."

"You could never be stupid, Mia. Look at me," he says, pulling away slightly so that I can see his face. "You could never be stupid to me, alright?"

"Alright." I nod slowly.

He strokes my hair slowly, lulling me back into a calmer place. "Do you want to talk about it?"

"No, I... I just have a thing about not being able to use my hands."

He nods then rearranges us until we're lying down in his massive bed with me tucked away safely in the crook of his arm. "How many people have you been with, Mia?"

"What?" I question, wishing that he could just let this go.

"Sexually, how many have there been?"

"One, just... Just one." It's the truth, even if I can't tell him all of it, if I can't give him the sordid details of the past I can give him one truth.

"Lily's father... Did he? Mia, did he do something to you? Make you..."

I shut my eyes not wanting to look at him. Trying to shut his words out of my mind. "No, just please...please Logan don't go there, just leave it alone please."

"I can help you...If something happened to you."

"Nothing happened, alright?" I snap at him. I try to pull away but he just holds me a little tighter. It's not menacing, just forceful. I take a deep breath and check my attitude. "I'm sorry. I just started having sex way before I was ready and it wasn't all that great, just let it go."

115

The look of concern in his eyes and his heated stare tells me that he understands that sex for me has never been an option but I will never confirm that for him. I'll never speak of it with him or anyone else.

"Mia…"

"Will you just hold me? Please," I say, pulling his shoulders in an attempt to get him closer to me.

"Of course," he replies, wrapping me in his arms.

"I'll do better next time I promise," I say softly.

"Baby you did fine. You did great," he says, stroking my cheek again. God I love that so much. "I told you only what you're comfortable with, okay?"

"Okay." We lie together in silence, my mind running a mile a minute as I'm sure Logan's is too, but I snuggle deep in his arms, letting their warmth envelope me, hoping that their strength will help keep me strong, help me to let go and wash away the dark memories of the past.

Chapter 12

Logan and I haven't spoken of my meltdown again. When I come home from work with Lily on Tuesday, he has moved all of my belongings into his bedroom, making space for my things in his closet and drawers and moving Lily's baby monitor to his bedside table. He said that if I was going to live with him and we were going to be together, then we should use the master bedroom and make it our own.

I love when he does things like that, when he takes charge of making certain decisions, in turn making it easier for me to focus on other things like my job, Lily, and most importantly healing the wounds of my past because there's nothing that I want more than to move forward with Logan.

"I had a dream last night," I say quietly to Logan while we snuggle in bed with Lily, who was fussy tonight sleeping on his chest.

"What was it about?"

I stare at Lily, looking so sweet and peaceful and she's just so easy to love. "I dreamt that I was visiting my mom. That I was at her house and she was holding Lily, cradling her in her arms and singing her a song. She looked at her with such love in her eyes, the way any grandmother would look at their grandbaby, the way that your mom looks at Lily, and she was so happy to see her. When I woke up and realized it was just a dream it made me so sad. Why couldn't she just love her? Let me love her? Give me the choice instead of trying to force me to do something I would have never been able to live with?"

He rubs my arm. I've come to find that Logan uses touch as a way to calm me down, to make me feel better and I wouldn't have thought it but it actually works. "Maybe she thought she was making the right choice?"

"Do you think it would have been the right choice for me to give Lily up?"

"No," he says, giving me a reassuring smile. "I think that you were put in a difficult spot, an impossible situation, and you made the absolute best choice you could."

My eyes drop to Lily resting on his broad chest. "Look at her. How could anyone not love her?" I wonder out loud.

"I don't know babe." He strokes Lily's back and gives her a kiss on the top of her head.

He's quiet for a moment, just staring at her little face. "Mia, have you tried to call her?"

"Who?" I question, already knowing the answer but not wanting to hear it.

"You know who, your mom."

I purse my lips at the thought of picking up the phone to call a woman who was so ready to cast my child—her grandchild, away. Who made it evident that if I chose this life I would no longer be welcome in her home. "No. She made her position very clear. I don't want her to feel like she can have any more input in my life or my decisions."

"It's up to you, but she can't hurt you. No matter what she says, she can't force you to do anything you don't want to do and I'm here to make sure of it. Will you at least think about it?"

I let out a sigh of frustration and answer, "Yes. I'll think about it." We both know I'm lying, we both know that I have no intentions of calling her. Maybe not ever.

"I forgot to tell you, I'm going out of town for a training on Thursday but I'll only be gone one night. I'll be home by the time you get home from work on Friday night."

"Oh, okay," I say, acting as if his absence won't affect me. I haven't been alone for an entire night since the break-in at my apartment and even with Logan's crazy hours I'm still able to sleep securely knowing that he'll be home eventually. "Where are you going?"

"I'm going to New York. Will you be alright here alone? I don't like leaving you."

I don't want to let on that being alone makes me a little bit nervous. It's not healthy for me to be so dependent on him or anyone else. I need to be able to deal with things on my own and being home alone is just one of those things that I need to conquer. I smile up at him and give him a wink. "Well, I'll miss you, but I'll be okay."

"I know you will be. You're the strongest girl I know." His faith in me is humbling. Being with Logan has taught me what a real relationship should be like. What it means to have someone who you share your dreams with, your fears and everything in between.

Logan left early this morning and then called me in the early afternoon after he had already settled into his hotel. He promised to call me before I went to bed tonight. I snuck outside when he called, not wanting to take personal calls at work. Sarah was heading out for lunch and overheard us on the phone. She had a sour puss look on her face for the rest of the day. As grateful as I am to her for having helped me out and given me a job when I desperately needed one, her attitude toward me has changed dramatically. She makes it very uncomfortable to be around her and I find myself hiding in my classroom for the majority of the day. I don't want to be her enemy, but she's made it very difficult for me to be her friend.

When I leave work I get a phone call from Mandy inviting me out to dinner. I'm tired and really just want to go home and sleep, but she's Logan sister and I really want her to like me so I agree. I meet her at a small little Italian restaurant not far from Logan's house and in true Tate fashion, she snatches Lily away from me immediately. God this family loves babies. We're seated at a two person table with Lily positioned in her car seat between the two of us.

"It's only been about a week since I've seen her and she's already gotten so big." She says playing with Lily who's kicking her little feet.

"Yeah, she's growing so fast," I agree. "She's starting to hold her head up more now and she's smiling, it's really cool."

"Logan told me he'd be out of town tonight. I hope you don't mind that I invited you out. I just thought you might like some company."

I take a sip of my soda and give her a smile. "That was really nice of you, Mandy."

"So how is it working at the daycare center?" She probes and I wonder if she's really asking about my job or if she's wondering how things are with Sarah. What if she really invited me out tonight to warn me off from her brother, to clear the way for Sarah. She is her best friend after all. Why wouldn't she want her to be with Logan?

"It's great, I love working with the kids and the teachers are amazing. I've really learned a lot," I reply giving her a muted version of the truth.

"What about Sarah, how do you like her?" She presses.

I give her a tight smile. "She's fine," I reply, not wanting to give her any more information, any ammunition to use against me.

She sighs and rolls her eyes at me. "She's in love with Logan, Mia. She always has been and I know that you can see it. You don't have to lie to me about it. I've told her countless times that he'll never see her that way. They're just too different and she's not his type."

I'm sure she can see the surprise on my face as I give her a questioning look. "How do you feel about that?"

"Who my brother chooses to love is none of my business. My loyalty is to him not to Sarah, so if he wants to be with you then I want that for him too. You make him happy and that's all that matters to me."

I can't believe how the dynamic within this family works. It just reinforces the fact that my family is in fact the perfect picture of dysfunction. "Are you all this nice? I'm really not used to it. My family can be brutal, so being surrounded by kind loving people is kind of throwing me off here."

"We just love each other and realize how important family is. We know that you should never take anything or anyone for granted. Don't worry about Sarah. I love her but she's misguided where Logan is concerned. She can't do anything to hurt you."

"Well, it helps to have all of your support. It really means a lot to me. I never knew having a family could be like this." I say, shrugging my shoulders.

"I just wanted you to know where we stand. We're all happy to have you and Lily around. Logan is really happy with you and that's so good to see."

"He makes me really happy too. I never knew I could be this happy, I keep waiting for something to go wrong."

"Don't think like that, Mia. Everything will be fine," she says.

I want to believe her, but in my life happiness has always been a fleeting emotion.

Even after Logan called me last night I couldn't sleep. He sounded distant, tired maybe, and I couldn't help but to wonder what was wrong. Had the training not gone the way he anticipated? Was he just tired from the driving or maneuvering his way around the city all day? I think I'm starting to worry about him and his safety as much as he worries about mine. Over time I've been letting it sink into my brain exactly what it is that he does for a living. How he puts himself out on the streets all the time and puts his life in danger. I'd be lying if I said it didn't scare the hell out of me. To make matters worse, the regular receptionist at the day care center is out again and of course I'm stuck manning the front desk. Sarah's been in her office for most of the day and has thankfully stayed away from me but she makes an appearance just as I'm packing up for the day.

"Oh, hey Sarah. Have a good night," I say, trying to maintain a cordial atmosphere.

"Mia, I didn't see you there," she replies, turning to face me. "Are you heading out?"

"Yeah, I'm just going back to get Lily."

"Right." She drawls out, and gives me the fake smile I'm becoming more and more accustomed to. "So how is the apartment hunt going?"

I hesitate, not really wanting to let on to how serious things are really getting with Logan but then I think that it might be better for her to know. Maybe it will encourage her to move on. "I think I'm staying put for right now. Logan's made it pretty clear that he wants us to stay."

She purses her lips into a tight line and drops her handbag on the front desk, just as she lets her true feelings go. "God Mia, your plan to find Lily a dad has worked."

"Excuse me?" I ask incredulously. I'm thrown off by her completely untrue and inappropriate statement. I'm starting to see that Sarah is borderline delusional.

"I mean, how long were you even in town before you set your sights on Logan? And let me tell you he was the perfect mark. He took one look at poor pathetic Mia with her sad little life and just had to jump in and rescue you. You really should pat yourself on the back."

My eyes go wide and I swear I can almost feel my blood start to boil over. "Are you actually suggesting that I planned to have my apartment burglarized, made it so that Logan would be the officer on duty that night, and then brainwashed him in to taking me and Lily in, all so that I could get him to play daddy?"

"Oh come on, Mia. You play the damsel in distress perfectly down to a tee."

I place my hands on the desk and shake my head at her. "You don't know me. You know nothing about me. You have no idea what I've been through, how dare you judge me."

"I know your type and you know what? You can have your fun. Logan will see you for exactly who you are one way or another."

Clearly she's not holding back maybe it's time that she understands that I know the truth about her feelings. "You're just jealous that he wants me and not you. It kills you, doesn't it? It burns you to see him with me, to see how he loves Lily."

"You're wrong." She growls and points her bony little finger at me. "He is my friend."

The finger in my face throws me over the edge. I'm done with her and her accusations. "A friend who you've been dying to notice you. The friend who you want to make your boyfriend so desperately that you would accuse me of the most absurd things. Everyone knows it, Sarah. Even Logan knows it, but guess what? He doesn't want you. He wants me! And I want you to stay away from him and leave me the hell alone."

"Well… Mia. I've never done anything but support your cause. I gave you a job when it could have cost me my business and as the owner here. I can't tolerate anyone speaking to me the way that you just have," she says with a smug look on her face.

"*What*? You started it."

"I'm sorry, Mia but I have to let you go. Please collect your things and do not come back."

"Oh my God," I say, straightening my spine. "This is exactly what you wanted all along. Go to hell, Sarah." I spit out, storming back to the infant room to get Lily. I pick her up and get the hell out there as quickly as I can. I pull over as soon as I get out of the daycare parking lot so that I can calm down before driving home. After a few deep breaths I get on the road and make it home safely. As I pull into the driveway the tension of the day starts to ease off of me when I see Logan's truck in the driveway. I park and have Lily out of the car in the blink of an eye.

I unlock the front door and look around, no sign of him anywhere.

"Logan?" I call, looking around the lower level. When I don't find him I make my way upstairs. I can hear the shower running from the hallway so I take Lily into her room and get her ready for bed. Once she's fed and settled down in her crib I walk across the hall to mine and Logan's bedroom. He's tossing clothes into the laundry bin when I walk in. "Logan."

He turns at the sound of my voice and when his smile hits me I know that I'm home. I don't stop, don't speak, words aren't necessary, I walk straight into his arms and when they wrap around me my whole world clicks back into place.

"Hi baby." He greets me as he kisses the top of my head.

"I missed you," I whisper as I fight the urge to cry.

"I missed you too," he says, pulling away slightly.

I grab on tighter holding on for dear life. "Don't let go."

"Are you okay?"

Instead of replying, I start to walk forward pushing him until we hit the bed, I crawl into the middle and pull him down with me. I place a gentle kiss on his lips and that's all the motivation that he needs to take over. He slips his tongue in my mouth and I tighten my hold on him, letting myself get caught up in the moment.

"How was your trip?" I giggle after we break apart.

"Enlightening. I'm glad to be home though. How about you? How was it here without me?"

I let out a sigh. "It was okay up until tonight. I got fired."

"What?" He questions, propping his head up on his hand "Why?"

"Sarah started with me and then she used the confrontation as a way to get rid of me," I say plainly. I don't know if I have it in me to get into detail.

"What did she say to you?"

I rub my face with the palms of my hands. "That I'm using you so that Lily can have a dad. She accused me of planning the whole thing, the robbery, everything."

"What the hell is wrong with her?"

"It's simple. She wants you."

"God, I'm so sorry babe." He strokes my cheek, soothing me with his touch. "I never thought she'd do something like this."

"It's not your fault. I just don't know what I'm going to do now," I say, snuggling into his side.

"Don't worry about it, Mia. I know that you want to do everything on your own and you want to be independent but I'm here. I want to take care of you."

"Logan..." I warn.

"No, just hold on. If I lost my job and you could help me, if you could take care of me would you?"

"That's not fair. It's not the same thing." I argue.

"Yes it is." He chuckles. "Answer the question."

"Of course."

"Then let me do the same for you. If you want to get another job fine but I don't want you to rush into something that you don't want, okay?"

"Okay," I say with a huff.

He pulls me into a tight hug and nips at my shoulder. "My parents are taking Lily for the weekend."

"What? Why?"

"Because I'm taking you to New York."

"Really?" I squeal, unable to hide my excitement.

"Yeah. My parents have a small apartment in the city, they're letting us use it for the weekend."

We stay up for hours, making plans for the weekend — hugging, kissing and just enjoying each other's company. I think about Sarah and her reaction to our relationship, I know that I should care, that I should be sorry that I lost my job. But I would do it all over again if it meant keeping Logan.

Chapter 13

❖

The Tate's place in New York is beautiful. It's a three-bedroom penthouse in the heart of Tribeca, one of the best neighborhoods in Manhattan. Everything is white, crisp, state of the art and modern with amazing views of the city. It's everything I ever dreamed of when I imagined myself as a student at NYU.

I'd once pictured myself living in an apartment exactly like this — enjoying my youth, living up my college years in the city. I'd thought that once I'd gotten to experience it all I'd be ready to go home and focus on building a career and starting a family. Of course, it didn't work out that way since life has a way of throwing a wrench in carefully laid plans, but the fact that I only live a short drive away from this beautiful city is a nice consolation.

Hand in hand, Logan and I spend the day walking around the streets. He even lets me drag him into a museum, where the hours slip away as we look at the many exhibits. I'm sure it isn't his idea of fun, but he seems content to just let me admire the art while standing by my side and listening to my interpretations of the different uses of color and light.

Later, we walk around Central Park, where he takes me to a hot dog cart for lunch. Then we find a bench to sit on side by side as we eat our food and watch the world go by.

"Does it ever bother you to know how much younger I am than you?" I ask in between bites.

He throws his head back and laughs. "Thanks babe, you just succeeded in making me feel ancient."

I giggle at his reaction. "What? It's true that you're older than me."

"Yes, I am. It's only a six year age difference. What's the big deal?"

"The big deal is that we're at completely different stages in our lives. You've got your whole life figured out, a home, a career, and you're pretty much settled. I on the other hand am just starting out. I'm eighteen with a baby and have no idea what's in store for me."

"It doesn't have to be that difficult. If I was thirty six and you were thirty we wouldn't be having this conversation."

"I just don't want to hold you back or tie you down when you could have so much more."

"Are we really doing this? Having this conversation in the middle of the city? Mia, you are *not* tying me down, and there's nothing that you are holding me back from."

I'm looking down at my feet now. I don't want to look in his eyes for fear that he might see the fear that lives in mine.

"Mia, look at me." He demands.

I lift my head and lock my gaze with his. I know he reads it; he can see through me.

"This is probably the worst possible moment... No, no it IS the worst possible moment," he says, "but I feel like if I don't tell you now, if I don't make you see what I see when I look at you we will never be able to move forward."

I inhale a sharp breath. The thought alone of not moving forward, of not being with Logan hurts like hell. "What do you see?"

"I see someone who is beautiful, a stunningly beautiful person. A person who doesn't see her own strength and beauty.

Someone who would go against anyone and anything to protect someone that she loves." He strokes my cheek, causing the butterflies in my stomach to take flight. "What I don't see is a number, because at the end of it all it doesn't matter. The only thing that matters is that I love you and you could be eighteen years old or thirty years old and it would make no difference, I would still love you."

His words cast a spell that makes the world fade into the background. The whole city is moving in slow motion until all of the movement and noise around me virtually disappears. I try to break down the words, try to process them one sentence at a time as I attempt to commit them to memory.

He loves me. He *loves me?* He loves *me!*

The words are full of magic, they're beyond powerful. They have the ability to erase fear, to make the thing that kept me at arm's length completely irrelevant, to make me feel larger than life when moments ago I felt so small. Most importantly they make me brave.

"I love you too, Logan," I whisper.

He grins as our lips gravitate together, as they touch and engage in a kiss that feels unlike any other, because this one kiss holds so much hope, so many wishes, a hint of desperation and an unexpected declaration of love.

"Sky's the limit." Logan promises as he pulls away.

Sky's the limit.

We're both tired by the time night shrouds the city. There's an electric charge in the apartment, an excitement drawing us closer and closer together.

I come out of the bathroom showered and wearing one of Logan's t-shirts, my new preferred bedtime attire. I bound over to the bed and get under the covers just as Logan turns the lights off, just as the lights from the city shine through the windows and illuminate the room.

He looks at me with a hint of humor on his face. I love when he looks like this. Light and free, no stress, no work to worry about or lives hanging in the balance. He's just allowed to be carefree. "Did you have fun today?"

"It was one of the best days ever," I reply.

"Yeah?"

"Yeah," I say, settling into his arms, my head in the crook of his neck. "Logan?"

"Hmm?"

I touch his ear lightly with my mouth. "Say it again."

"I love you, Mia."

"Logan?"

"Hmm?"

"Make love to me."

He snaps his head up and looks down at me, shaking his head slowly. "Mia, I didn't tell you that I loved you so that you'd let me…"

"I know that," I say, placing my hands on his bare chest, loving the warmth that radiates from him. "But I want to, I want to know how it feels when it's between two people who really love each other. I want it to be you and I want it to be tonight."

He stares at me for a moment, looking for some kind of doubt or hesitation on my face, a hint of fear maybe but there's none.

Making the decision to be with Logan is an empowering one because it's my choice to make. It stems from my own desire and love for him and maybe even the trust that he's managed to slowly earn from me.

He bends down, appearing to have made his decision and covers my lips with his, bringing my body to full alert.

I let out a soft moan at the feel of him, giving him the perfect opportunity to slip his tongue into my mouth. I let my hands roam the expanse of his back, using them as a tool to bring him down closer to me.

He breaks the kiss and I whimper at the loss of him.

"Take off your shirt." He commands. His eyes are liquid with desire and the way he looks at me makes me feel beautiful, makes me want to do any and everything to please him.

I push up slightly and pull the shirt over my head, tossing it on the floor and then lying back down.

He takes in the sight of me, and gives me a barely there grin.

"So fucking beautiful," he says, lowering his head to place a kiss on my forehead, my nose and finally my mouth again. His hands begin roaming, circling around my sensitive breasts, down my stomach, tracing the outline of my belly button and then finally... "You're not wearing panties."

I bite my lip and shake my head at him.

"Miss Reynolds, I'm shocked. If I didn't know any better, I'd think that you were trying to seduce me."

"You'd think right," I say with a proud nod.

"Oh yeah?" He questions, clearly amused by my reply. "Well then, I promise that I'm going to make it worth your while." He slips his finger in between my legs.

I inhale and close my eyes at the contact.

He continues to kiss me and explore with his hand, and when he finally reaches my clit, it's like he flips a light switch and I'm immersed in light. He massages gently at first, eliciting uninhibited whimpers from me.

I gasp as he slips a finger inside of me and begins pumping it in and out of me slowly. As the sensations increase, his pressure and rhythm increases. His lips are everywhere now, making every square inch of me his, taking possession of me in a way that makes the cracks in my heart whole again. The orgasm hits me fast and hard sending me over the edge as I cry out for Logan.

"That's it…I've got you," he whispers, drawing out every ounce of pleasure he can from me.

I close my eyes as I float back down to earth trying to recover from the fall. I vaguely notice Logan moving away from me. Then I hear the crinkling sound of a wrapper and moments later he's back, naked and hovering over me, using his lower body to draw my legs apart. I can feel his hardness as he positions himself at my entrance, his hand now on either side of my head. He's careful not to touch me or hold me down.

"Are you okay?" he asks, kissing the corner of my mouth.

"Yes," I reply, searching his eyes for reassurance.

"Are you sure you want me to keep going?"

I know he'd stop if I asked. He'd make it okay for me to back out and put an end to this, but backing out means giving up; it means quitting and letting my fear rule me and I truly want to let all of that go.

"I'm sure. I'm ready."

"Is there anything else that might scare you?"

"No, just don't hold me down...and go slow." I add quickly, burying my face in the crook of his neck.

"Baby look at me," he says. I pull back slowly and look up at his beautiful face. "I will not hurt you. I promise."

I nod my head.

"I'm going to link my hands with yours okay? But I'm not holding you down, I'm just holding your hands." He joins our hands together as he said he'd do and looks for my reaction. "Is this alright?"

"Yes. It's good."

"Just look at me, concentrate on me. It's just us." He brings his forehead down to mine and slowly slides inside of me. "It's just you and me..."

He continues to whisper, understanding my need for reassurance. Understanding that bad memories have a nasty habit of resurfacing at the most inopportune times but not tonight, because tonight is about us and Logan's love makes me stronger. It's just us and the past can't touch me. The past can't hurt me when I'm with Logan, because the past is all about darkness, but Logan is the light and as long as I'm in the light I'm safe, I'm protected.

Once I adjust to the feel of him inside of me, I nod my understanding of his words just barely rocking my hips to indicate my desire for him to move.

He kisses me again, tangling his tongue with mine as he starts to move inside of me, slowly thrusting in and out in a circular motion. Our hands joined, lips mashed together, bodies connected, my legs instinctively wrap around him as we meld together every single part of me is tied to him, bound together and nothing else matters. There are no ghosts here, no fear. It's just me and Logan, in love, expressing that emotion in the most natural way. I begin to pant as his rhythm increases, quietly moaning, as the pressure starts to build again.

"Oh God, Mia." He calls in my ear as he increases his pace yet again, squeezing my hands tighter and effectively pushing me to the edge again.

"Logan…" I cry out as I try to breathe through the stirring of sensations fighting to take over my body.

"I'm right here, just let go." He lets go of my hands and lifts my bottom to give him better leverage.

His eyes are on me, lustful and frantic, and as his mouth descends on mine the dam breaks open and I'm flooded with my climax—overpowered by sensations, all of which make me want him even more. I want him for loving me, for making love to me and for freeing me from the chains that have held onto me for too long. His release rips through him, his face buried into the crook of my neck, all the while I'm wishing that I could bottle up this moment and keep it close, carry it with me always so that I'll always be able to recall what perfection feels like.

Chapter 14

I'm a little sore this morning when I wake up, but I like it. For a long time now I've been going through the motions, taking life one day at a time, finding pieces of happiness here and there. Today I feel alive, I feel whole and it's funny that it took making love to get there but doing it on my own terms was like taking my power back.

Logan and I take a warm shower together; he makes breakfast while I get myself put together.

I'm standing by the glass windows with a cup of coffee in my hands, I'm staring out at the city wondering what my life would be like if this was an alternate universe, if this was my reality. Logan comes up behind me and rests his head on my shoulder as his arms circle my waist. "This was my dream." I tell him.

"What was?" he asks, bringing his lips to my neck.

"New York," I say, taking a sip of my coffee "You asked me a while back if I had a dream. This was it. I got accepted to NYU, I was going to move here and study psychology. I did what my parents wanted and applied to colleges in Florida but I knew that this was the only place I wanted to go."

"I'm sorry that you had to give that up."

"I am too."

"Maybe it can still happen for you."

"How?"

"We can figure it out somehow. Maybe not tomorrow but in a year or two."

"Maybe," I say with little conviction in my voice. I know it will never happen now and I wouldn't change that. I sacrificed this for the chance to raise Lily and I wouldn't trade that for the world. Maybe I can go to a community college once Lily gets older. "Should we be heading back home soon?" I ask, effectively shutting down the topic.

"Yeah, we should go get Lily. I miss her."

"You do?"

"Of course."

"How did I ever get so lucky? How did this even happen? I ran away thinking it would just be Lily and me forever and I was okay with that as long as I got to be with her but you... this... not even in my wildest dreams would I have ever imagined finding someone like you."

"I know you think it's all going to go away but it's not. I promise you that I'm not going anywhere. I love you, both of you."

I hold onto his words like a life preserver, keeping me afloat when just the thought of losing him causes waves of sadness and fear to crash over me.

The ride home is quick and Logan's parents were running errands most of the morning and since they were already out they're waiting for us at the house when we arrive. When I finally have Lily back in my arms I'm ecstatic. It's amazing to have Logan's family around to watch her. Every once and a while I need a break and I know I wouldn't get that without them, but I really miss her when she's gone. Logan lets me have my bonding moment with her and then snatches her away from me. Her face lights up at the sight of him could he be a father figure to Lily, could he really play that role in her life and would he even want to. What if we break up? How will that affect her? I try not to let these questions dampen my good mood, but fear is a hard emotion to let go of and as much as I love Logan, there's still a small part of me that wonders if he knows what he's getting into, if he's really in it for the long haul.

His parents stay for lunch and by the time they leave I'm feeling a little run down. My head is achy, my eyes feel heavy and my body is tired. I sit bundled into a ball on the couch, while Lily lies on the floor kicking at the play gym that Logan bought her last week.

"Babe, you want coffee?" Logan calls from inside the kitchen.

"No thanks!" I call back, lacking the energy to say much more than that. I hear his footsteps but don't bother looking up.

"Since when don't you want coffee?" He stops in front of the couch and crouches down in front of me. "What's wrong?" He inquires, the worry evident in his tone.

I attempt a smile and shake my head. "Nothing, I'm just a little tired is all."

He places the palm of his hand on my forehead and then circles it to the nape of my neck. "You have a fever."

"What? No."

"Yes," he says, scrunching his nose at me. "Why don't you go upstairs and lie down for a bit. I'll bring you some aspirin."

"Maybe when Lily takes her nap. I just fed her so she should be tiring out soon."

"I've got Lily. You go." He orders.

"Are you sure?"

"I'm positive. Go."

"Okay." I make my way upstairs to our bedroom, change into a pair of sweats and ungracefully throw myself onto the bed. Logan comes up a few minutes later with aspirin and a bottled water. I'm shivering cold so he tucks me under the comforter to warm me up. It doesn't take me long to fall asleep.

The room is completely dark when I wake up. I look over at the clock on the nightstand and I'm shocked by how late it is. Immediately my thoughts go to Lily, she hasn't been fed in hours. I throw the covers off of me and stand up. My limbs are sore, it hurts to walk, and I can tell that the fever is back.

I open the door and step into the hallway. I'm about to head downstairs when the sound of running water registers in my head. I turn towards the direction of the bathroom that connects to Lily's room. I can hear Logan's voice, but it's too low for me to hear what he's saying.

I tiptoe to the doorway, lean forward, and when I peek into the bathroom, I see Lily perched in her baby bath and pumping her feet.

When the water splashes, Logan wipes his face and chuckles. "Alright little stinker, this is your bath not mine," he says to her with a smile on his face. He shuts the water off and grabs her towel, laying it out on his lap until it's completely open. He plucks Lily out of her little tub, rests her on his lap, and gently swaddles her in the towel.

He takes Lily into her room and lays her down on the changing table. Then he puts her diaper on with no hesitation, making sure that it's secure and in place. He squirts baby lotion on his hands and gently works it into her skin. Finally, he pulls a warm pajama from her drawer and gets her dressed. All the while having playful one-sided conversations with her.

"I know you're standing there, Mia. You can stop snooping."

I let out a giggle. "I'm not snooping, you're just so good with her. It's adorable."

"Are you feeling any better?" He looks up at me, eyes dancing over my body as if he's looking for signs of life.

"I still have a fever I think."

He picks Lily up one last time before placing a kiss on her head and putting her down in her crib. "Go back to bed. I'll bring you more aspirin and some tea."

"I need to feed her."

"I already did."

I tilt my head in question. "You already fed her?"

"Yeah."

"What did you feed her?" I look at him like he's lost his mind. I'm almost scared to hear his answer.

He strides across the room and stops when he's just inches away from me. His face shows a hint of humor as he grins down at me. "One of the many packets of breast milk you have stored in the back of my freezer."

I gasp and cover my eyes, pretty sure I've turned several shades of red at this point. "You knew that was there?"

"Kinda hard to miss babe."

"Do you think it's gross?" I ask, peeking through my fingers.

He pulls my hands off of my face and shakes his head. "No. I think it's life. I think that you're an incredible mom and you don't have to hide it in the back of the freezer. I already know it's there."

I say nothing, just rest my head on his chest and circle my arms around his waist.

He holds me for a moment, swaying me back and forth gently. "Let's get you to bed." He tucks me into his side and walks me back across the hall. Then he helps me into bed and promises to come back with some aspirin.

I lie here, my mind running a mile a minute. I've seen glimpses of Logan bonding with Lily in the past, but seeing him with her now just melted me. I feel my eyes pooling with unshed tears. It's not that I'm unhappy, just sad that Lily was born into this situation. That she couldn't have a mother and father who loved and wanted her from the start. Instead she got someone like me who knew nothing about being a parent, except for that I wanted to be nothing like mine. She got me, taking her on the run as soon as we got out of the hospital, going from town to town hiding out in hotel rooms until we finally made it here.

What kind of start is that to her life? I push those thoughts out of my mind reminding myself that this was the only choice, the only way for Lily and me to stay together. I did the best thing that I could for our little family and finding Logan was just an amazing bonus. Whether he sticks around or not will be entirely up to him.

"You alright?" Logan asks, sitting down on the edge of the bed.

"Yes. I was just thinking about how far Lily and I have come. I worry, you know? I worry that I'm doing damage to her, that I'm not giving her what she needs."

"That's crazy. Could she have had a good life with adoptive parents? Yes, Mia she could have and she might have been happy but you're her mom. You wanted the chance to raise her, you deserved that chance and babe you're doing an *amazing* job. She's happy, she's loved and she's well taken care of. What more could she want?"

Two parents who love her...

I want to say it but I don't. I don't because it's really not his problem and I really don't want him to think that Sarah was right. That I'm with him just so that he can take the place of Lily's dad because that's not true.

"You're right," I say with a small smile. "I just doubt myself sometimes."

"Well don't. Don't ever doubt yourself." He kisses my forehead and hands me more aspirin. He takes the bottled water from me when I've finished drinking and hands me a bowl of soup. "Eat up. You need to have something in your stomach."

I do as he asks, not realizing how hungry I was until I've eaten some of the warm soup. It feels strange having someone to look out for me this way.

When I was younger and sick, I'd had to fend for myself. I could barely get my mom to take me to the doctor, let alone take care of me. I'd see the relationship that my friends had with their parents and wish that I had the same thing, but my parents were more concerned with money and financial status. I honestly think that they had me so that they would look like they had the perfect family.

It was all about appearances to them, which is why I'll do whatever it takes to ensure that Lily's upbringing is different. I want her childhood to be better than mine and I'll make sure that it happens with or without Logan.

Chapter 15

Logan has the late shift again tonight. I find that these are the times when his job is the hardest for me to accept. When he's gone long into the early hours of the morning, my mind runs wild wondering what he's out there doing. I try my hardest to get sleep in between Lily's feedings but it's difficult and I imagine that it never gets any easier.

I let out a sigh of relief when I hear the front door open and close; he's home and I know that he's safe. I see the light from the master bathroom flicker and figure that he must have accessed it from the hallway. He normally comes in to say hello to me before he showers but tonight he doesn't. I toy with the idea of going in there to make sure he's okay but I think better of it. I push the worry out of my head and wait, wait for him to come to me. To tell me if something is wrong, even though deep down I feel that something is definitely off.

A few minutes later, Logan enters our bedroom wearing just a towel. He bypasses the dresser where he keeps his boxer briefs and heads straight for the bed, straight for me. He pulls the sheets back, tosses the towel to the ground and climbs into bed. His head lands on my chest and my hands instinctively reach out for him.

I gently massage the top of his head. I don't know why his behavior scares me, but it's not a fear of him hurting *me*, it's more a fear of him being hurt.

"Logan?" I whisper softly. I don't need to say anything else, he can hear the question in my voice.

He angles his head so that he can look at me. When our eyes meet I can see the sadness dancing in his.

"Tim was shot tonight," he says.

"Tim?"

"My partner."

I let out a gasp. "Officer Clark?"

He says nothing, just nods.

I wrap my arms around him and hug him tightly. My heart breaks for him because it's clear to see that he's struggling with this. "Oh my God, Logan. Is he alright?"

He shrugs his shoulders. "I don't know...He was hurt pretty badly and he's in stable condition now, but we just have to wait and see." I can hear the defeat in his voice, the sadness and the fear. It's overwhelming and I want to protect him, shelter him from the pain but I know it's not possible.

"What happened?"

"A robbery at a convenience store. The owner tripped the alarm behind the cash register, and we were the first unit at the scene. We got there just as the robber was trying to get away. Tim approached first and the guy took a shot, didn't even think twice about it. Hit him right in the chest. He didn't get away though. I fired my weapon, shot him in the arm."

"Babe, I'm so sorry. I don't know what else to say."

"What you're doing is great. It's perfect. This is exactly what I need."

He lies there for a while, resting in my arms, his breath starts to even out and I think he's finally fallen asleep but his soft voice breaks through the silence.

"I just don't know if I can lose somebody else."

I go on alert, unsure of what he's saying exactly. "What do you mean? Who have you lost?"

He pushes off of me and falls back onto his pillow then covers his face with his arm. "No one, I just…"

I pull his arm away from his face. "Do you trust me?" He looks at me with sad eyes and strokes my cheek. "Trust me, you can tell me."

He takes another moment but finally answers. "Amy."

"Who is Amy?"

He takes a deep breath and gives me a sad smile. "Amy was my older sister. She died when I was eighteen."

I'm stunned by this revelation, Other than Mandy and Chris, I had no idea that he had any other siblings.

"I'm sorry, I…"

"It's okay. It happened a long time ago."

I nod my head slowly, knowing that he's experienced something traumatizing tonight and that I need to proceed carefully. I don't want him to shut down on me now. "Will you tell me about her?"

"She was twenty one when she got pregnant by some loser that she met at a party one night. They dated on and off for a while and the family never approved of him, but when she turned up pregnant they decided to move in together. No one was happy about it, but we supported her for the sake of the baby. To this day I'm not exactly sure what was going on between them but I remember that she would come back home and cry to my mom a lot. She was really stressed out. So stressed that she went into labor two months early.

I stroke his cheek much like the way he does to me. "What happened?"

"The baby was stillborn."

"Oh my God."

"Amy was devastated. She never recovered from that loss—she spiraled into depression, stopped talking to everyone, stopped going out and taking our phone calls. Occasionally though, I'd stop by her apartment and she'd let me in. I'd try to get her to talk to me, tell me how she was dealing, what was going on with her. Tried to get her to go see someone, a counselor, anyone, but she'd tell me that she was doing okay. This one time she told me that she had been battling insomnia, but her boyfriend had been giving her sleeping pills and that helped."

"Go on." I urge softly.

"It didn't take long for her to become dependent, Mia. It happened so fast, right under everyone's nose, and before long she had a full blown addiction. By the time we realized it, it was way beyond prescription meds."

"Wow." I'm sure I must sound like an idiot, but I honestly don't know what to say. I just feel so sad and I'm holding my tears back.

"It went on for the next few years. Every time I'd see her, she looked worse and worse but I kept trying. Once a week I'd drop by after school and just spend time with her. I'd try to get her to come home. I'd talk to her about rehab, but she'd just get angry and kick me out."

"I'm so sorry baby."

He nods in acknowledgment and continues the story. "I don't have to tell you what her fate was. One Friday afternoon, a few weeks before my high school graduation, I went to her apartment like I always did. Only this time she didn't open the door."

"Logan." I wince, dreading this part, not sure if I want to hear the rest.

"After standing there for God knows how long, calling out for her and knocking on the door, I tried the doorknob. Sure enough, it was unlocked. You know, I think about it all the time, Mia: Why didn't I try the doorknob earlier? Why did I wait so long to do that? What if I had gotten in the apartment early enough? What if I could have saved her?"

"No... Baby no. You couldn't save her. You did the best you could for her, you were there for her and that's all that matters."

"I wanted so desperately to help her, to save her. To bring her back to us but she was just too far gone. I didn't know how, no one did. Nothing worked."

"It was no one's fault. She had an addiction, she was sick," I say, hoping that my words are sinking in.

"It was after that that I decided to become a cop. To get people like her scumbag boyfriend off the streets and to help people like Amy. I figured if I could save just one person, *just one*, then maybe her death wouldn't be in vain."

Is that why he was so drawn to me, so invested in my well being and safety? It hurts to think about and he's been through enough tonight but still I have to know. I need to hear it.

"Logan? Is that why you helped me? Are you trying to save me because you couldn't save her?"

"No," he says, shaking his head.

"I'm not her... I'm not Amy," I say with a little bit more force than I intend.

"Hey... I know that. You're so much braver than she was, you're everything that she couldn't be. You're much stronger than she was. I know you're not her. I do. I know you're different, but maybe subconsciously she is the reason that I felt so compelled to help you. I'm sorry, Mia. This sounds so fucked up," he says, pulling himself up to a sitting position.

"It's okay," I say, sitting up next to him. "I'm not mad, I get it. I understand why you would see similarities."

"I couldn't get my mind off of you after that first time I met you. It wasn't just that I was concerned for you though, I…I thought you were beautiful."

I'm grateful for the cloak that the darkness that the room provides right now. I don't want him to see the flush in my cheeks.

"But there was that part of me that thought what if…"

"What?"

"What if something goes wrong? What if one bad thing happens to her? Will that be the thing that sends her down the same road my sister went down? Then when I got the report of a break in and I realized it was your apartment… I knew as soon as you opened the door that I couldn't leave you there, Mia. I couldn't do it."

"I'm glad. I'm glad that you didn't leave me there. I love you so much, Logan."

He leans over and places a kiss on my lips. "I love you too." He pushes me back down onto the bed, hovering just above me, looking down at me and seeking my approval. I wrap my arms around his neck and pull him down further. It's all the acknowledgement he needs from me.

He quickly removes my underwear, tossing them on the floor and reaching over to the nightstand for a condom. He rips the wrapper with his teeth and rolls it on lighting fast.

There's no foreplay tonight. He slides into me, pushing until he's all the way in. Logan is good at making sex about me, making it about my experience and my satisfaction, but tonight it's about him. He needs it to be and I want to give it to him.

I slide my hands down his back and hold on as he moves in and out of me slowly. He kisses my neck and I tug on his ear lightly with my teeth. I move my hips, slowly matching his rhythm, enhancing the delicious friction that comes with each move he makes. It doesn't take long before I feel the familiar buildup of sensation rising.

"Logan!" I call.

"Let go for me baby," he whispers.

I wrap my legs around his waist and my hands clutch his shoulders as my climax sweeps over me. Logan follows soon after with his own release, calling out my name as he comes. I hold onto him tightly, rubbing his back as he collapses on top of me — careful not to give me all of his weight.

He kisses me again, a final show of affection before he pulls away. He lies back down and pulls me into his side before closing his eyes and drifting off to sleep.

Chapter 16

Tim thankfully recovered from his gunshot wound and was released from the hospital a few days ago. Logan and I even visited him in the hospital a few times.

I think he needed to see for himself that his partner was going to be okay. Even though Tim is doing better, Logan is still a little bit off. He seems to be more pensive than usual, but I'm hoping that as the weeks go by he'll return to his normal self.

I've been looking for a job for the past week and a half and have yet to find anything. Logan tells me not to stress myself out about it and that he doesn't mind taking care of us, but I can't help but want to contribute. I don't want to become too dependent on him, because if we don't work out I'll be back at square one.

We ran into Sarah at the grocery store on Saturday. She took one look at us and turned her shopping cart around in an attempt to avoid us.

Logan however had other plans. He went after her and they had words. I'm pretty sure it was a heated discussion, but I wanted to avoid the whole dramatic scene so I stayed far away. Afterwards, I argued with Logan for confronting her but he told me it had been worth it and he would do it again. We made up pretty quickly because Logan is an expert at kicking up the charm when he needs to in order to get his way.

The rest of our week has been uneventful, I'm trying not to stress out about not working and really it is nice to be able to be at home and spend more time with Lily. She's so much more alert now. She's more active and smiles at everyone, but I can tell she prefers me and Logan.

I've started running as a way to clear my head because it really helps me to distress. Logan's been all about watching Lily while I take this time to myself, his only demand being that I don't run alone at night—a request which I'm only too happy to accept.

I turn out of the driveway and jog for the first few minutes. I turn right, heading towards the park, but right before I can break into a full run, a hand wraps around my arm and forces me to come to an abrupt stop.

I gasp as I'm pulled around to the back of a building, as my body hits the wall. My heart rate picks up, my mind is telling me to yell—to kick, punch, fight, but I'm too shocked to do a thing. I focus on the face of my assailant and my body instantly goes stiff.

I can barely breathe, but I manage to choke out his name. "Nick."

"Hi baby," he says, placing a hand on each side of my head, effectively caging me in. "I was beginning to think you fell off the face of the earth."

My skin is crawling at the feel of his chest touching mine. I'm panting now, barely able to stand up on my own, or make any moves to get away; the intense fear of seeing him is paralyzing me.

How did he know where to find me?

"What are you doing here?" I whisper, hating myself for sounding so weak when I'm around him.

"I came to see you darlin." He moves one of his hands from the wall and cups me through my yoga pants. I can feel the bile rising and fight to keep it down. "What do you say we get out of here? We can go back to my hotel and get reacquainted. One more time for old times sake huh?"

"Let go of me!" I yell, pushing his hand away from me.

"God baby, you've gotten feisty on me since you left. I like this new side of you, Mia. It would be great if you put up a little bit of a fight every once and a while."

"Fuck you!" I shout, the anger starting to make me bolder now. "How did you find me?"

"How did I find you? Your parents told me where you are. They're on their way up here to see you."

"What?" I breathe out. I always knew they'd be able to find me eventually; I'd just hoped that they wouldn't care anymore, that they would just let me live my life and let me be.

"I'm here to warn you, Mia. You keep that fucking little mouth of yours shut. Don't you go getting all honest on me now."

I jut my chin out in defiance. "Why would I lie for you? I have nothing left to lose."

"Oh you think not? Nothing has changed. The rules are still the same, only now instead of hurting your parents, I'll focus on that little boyfriend of yours. But first I'll make sure to tell him all about you and how you opened up those legs for me."

I can't stop the tears from falling. Logan can never know what happened to me, what I allowed to happen. "Leave him out of this."

He wipes a tear away and gently strokes my hair, which only causes me to cry more. "I've seen you two together, you and him with your little brat."

"Don't you dare speak about her!"

"Shut up!" He yells, grabbing hold of my neck. "Your parents will be here tomorrow. They're bringing their lawyer with them and they're going to try and make you sign those adoption papers."

"They can't make me do anything. I'm an adult."

"You will sign those papers and hand that kid over if you know what is good for you. That little brat is a connection between you and I that can not exist. Do. You. Understand. Me? You do what you have to do or I will." He spits out, throwing me down to the ground.

I cry out as my shoulder hits the concrete, but I do my best to recover quickly. By the time I look up, Nick is gone and he's left my life in the path of destruction.

I pick myself up from the ground and lean against the cold building, trying to get my emotions under control. I have to think. I have to figure out my next move and there's no way that I can let Logan see me like this.

My instincts are telling me to get Lily and run, to just go find another place to live—another state, but the thought of leaving Logan behind kills me; it causes an ache that I'm not sure I can live through. I may not have a choice though.

I can't ask him to help me, not because he wouldn't, but because I can't tell him the truth. I can never tell him about my past because he would never be able to look at me the same way. And if I do say something, if I do tell him what happened, Nick could do something to hurt him. I could never live with myself if that happened.

I start to walk back home, my feet feeling heavier with each step I take. This is my home, I love it here, and I love this town, the house I've come to share with Logan. The little life that we're building together is more than I could have ever hoped for but I always knew that keeping Lily meant sacrificing my own dreams. Maybe this life with Logan is just another dream that I need to sacrifice, something else I need to let go of, because as much as I love Logan it would absolutely kill me to lose Lily.

My mind is made up by the time I walk through the front door.

"You're back soon," Logan says, looking up at me from the couch.

"I got a cramp."

He starts to get up but I shake my head at him. "Are you alright?"

"Yes, I'm just going to take a hot shower." I head upstairs and look around my room, *our* room. My heart hurts, thinking that this will be my final night here.

I'll give myself one last night with Logan and when he leaves for work in the morning I'll take my things and go. I just hope it gives me enough time to avoid my parents, but even if it doesn't I don't care. They aren't the ones who I'm worried about; it's Nick that scares me, it's always been Nick.

I get in the shower and let the scalding hot water run over me. It should hurt, but it doesn't. In fact, I feel nothing. My whole body is numb.

I search my mind for solutions, other alternatives that don't conclude with me walking away from Logan. Would he come with me if I told him I had to go? Would he pick up and leave everything behind for me, to be with me and Lily? I can't ask him to do that, he has a life here, a family that I'm going to miss. A family that I've learned to love and even though I've never admitted it, a family I've come to think of as my own.

There is no happy ending for us, no happily ever after, no other way out of my situation. The only option is take Lily and run, and I'll keep running if I have to. I'll never give up, never stop fighting for the right to have my daughter and Nick will eventually have to leave me alone. Maybe then I'll finally be able to find peace.

I spend the rest of the day with Logan and Lily, pushing my sadness aside to try to make this night memorable for us. I pull him down on the ground and we lie there playing with Lily, trying to get her to smile and laugh. I know that in all my life I'll never forget this night. I'll look back on it and remember a time when we were both loved.

Logan is already in bed and reading a book by the time I get Lily to sleep in her crib.

"She asleep?" he asks, looking up at me.

I nod my answer and shut the door behind me. I stand there for a minute staring at him, taking in the sight of him because right now just for one more night he belongs to me and I belong to him. The knowledge that this is coming to an end makes my chest ache but I push it aside and walk further into the room. I lock my gaze on him as I push my pants and underwear down and step out of them. I can see the switch, the exact moment when his eyes get heated. They fill with lust quickly, and in response I pull the shirt over my head—tossing it into the now growing pile of clothes on the ground while he puts his book down.

It's funny. I've been thinking all along that it would be Logan to break my heart when in reality it will be me doing the breaking, but tonight I need him to know how much I love him. I need him to feel that he's it for me, that given the chance I'd spend my entire life trying to make him happy. I need him to understand it tonight so that when he realizes that I've gone away he'll have this memory and know that it wasn't all a lie.

I stand there a few seconds more, letting him take in the sight of me completely naked and aroused by him, for him.

Desperately wanting him to understand that he is the only one that I could be this way with.

I walk over to the bed and pull the sheets off of him. His hardness strains against his boxer briefs, causing me to grin. I climb on the bed and hook my fingers into the waist of his boxers and tug them off easily. I grab hold of him in my hand and gently squeeze, his head falls back onto the pillow and immediately I'm loving the surge of power I have over him. The power to make him feel what I want him to feel and right now I want him to feel loved.

I look up at him. "I've never done this before."

"You don't have to."

"I want to."

"Then just do what feels right," he says.

I lick the tip of his head then let my tongue run down the underside of his shaft and then up again before I close my mouth around him and take him in. Slowly, I move my head up and down, using my mouth to create a gentle suction.

Logan buries his hands in my hair as I find my rhythm. I take as much of him into my mouth as I can and use my hand at the base of him, stroking him up and down along with my mouth.

"Oh fuck, Mia." He cries, releasing my hair and hauling me up his body. "I don't want to come like that."

I smile at him then lean over to the nightstand and grab a condom. He takes it from me and rips the foil wrapper, then he hands the condom back to me.

I've watched him enough times to know how to do it. I pinch the tip then quickly roll it on. I stroke him a few more times before finally positioning myself on top of him, straddling him with my legs. I slowly lower myself onto him until there's nothing left of him to take. I throw my head back at the feel of him stretching me out. God he feels so good.

I look back at him, memorizing his face, burning it into my brain and fighting back the tears that threaten. "I love you so much. You know that right? I love you more than I ever thought was even possible."

He reaches up and cups my face in the palm of his hands. "I love you too, Mia. More than anything."

I pull his hands off my face and link my fingers with his, pushing our conjoined hands onto the mattress and slowly begin to move. I rock my hips slowly at first, savoring every single minute of this, knowing that this will be the last time I have him. He lets me have my control for a little longer before flipping us so that I'm on my back and he's on top of me.

"I like this side of you baby," he whispers in my ear, sending goose bumps throughout my body as he slowly enters me again.

I wrap my arms around his neck. "You make me this way. You make me brave," I say softly, kissing the edge of his mouth.

His gentle thrusts start to become more hurried, more frantic. I know that he feels it too, the surge of chemistry in the air between us.

"Mine." He declares, looking me in the eye.

"Yes, yours." I whimper, rocking my hips up. "Harder baby."

He takes my mouth with his, devouring it as the pace becomes more desperate, the orgasm building from deep within me.

I claw at his back, needing to feel him, having him as close as I can, screaming out from the overwhelming swell of sensations that shove me over the edge as my climax hits hard. I vaguely hear him calling my name out as his release hits. He continues to thrust in and out until his orgasm recedes, then collapses next to me in the bed.

"Oh shit baby." He breathes out. "That was amazing."

"The best," I say, kissing him one last time before he gets up to dispose of the condom.

I close my eyes and roll onto my side, trying to block the tears that are pooling in my eyes. He comes back to bed and slides in behind me, wrapping his arm around my waist and pulling me to him so that my back is firmly secured to his back. He kisses my neck and my cheek.

"Goodnight chief."

"Goodnight baby." *Goodbye* I say in my head, trying to breathe through the very real pain that's taking up permanent residence in my chest. I wait until he falls asleep then carefully disengage from his hold. I walk across the hall to look at a very peacefully sleeping Lily. I sit in her rocking chair, pulling my knees up to my chest and allow myself to silently cry. I let myself cry for the child I used to be, the girl I was forced to leave behind in order to become a mother. I cry for Lily, for having to take her away from this place, from a family who loves her. I cry for what I'm about to do to Logan, leaving him behind to wonder why I did it.

Chapter 17

I pretend to be asleep when Logan leaves for work, there's no way I could handle a conversation with him this morning. I heard him go into Lily's room before he left, I turned to look at the video monitor and caught him just as he leaned over the railing and placed a kiss on her forehead, the same way he did to me moments earlier. My heart is breaking into a million pieces right now but this is my only choice. It's the only way I can make sure I keep Lily and Logan stays safe. I wait for the sound of the car leaving the driveway and get out of bed. I go to the closet, grab my bags and start throwing my belongings into them. In the bathroom, I take my hair products, makeup and toothbrush, everything else can be replaced. Once I'm satisfied that I've taken the necessities, I go into Lily's room and do the same, taking only the necessities.

I bring the bags downstairs, then I quickly feed and change Lily into warm clothes before bringing her downstairs too. I set her down in the playpen and hurry into the kitchen to grab a pen and paper.

I can't just leave without at least leaving a note to let Logan know that I'm leaving. I'm about to start writing when the doorbell rings. The sound startles me causing me to drop the pen. I don't even need to look through the peephole to know who's on the other side of the door. I had hoped to avoid an ugly confrontation with my parents but clearly it wasn't meant to be. My only hope now is to get them out of here as quickly as possible and somehow make sure that they don't follow me when I leave.

I open the door and come face to face with my mother and father; the expressions on their faces are positively glacial. My father's height is intimidating, he's at least 6'2" to my mother's much shorter 5'5" frame. My mother looks stunning, perfectly put together in a dark slacks and a white trench coat. While my dad, ever the business man, is suited up. Behind them is their attorney Felicia; evidently they're wasting no time in trying to get Lily away from me.

"What are you doing here? What do you want?" I ask icily, my tone matching their expressions.

My mother glares at me before she speaks. "Mia. Is that anyway to greet your parents?"

"You're right, how rude of me. Melinda, Michael, what the fuck are you doing here?" I spit out. I'm shocked by how very little their presence affects me. What it does do is make me realize that I'm better off without them.

"That's quite enough young lady." My father scolds. "We've come all this way to see you and the least you could do is invite us in."

I hesitate for a moment, but decide that getting them in and out quickly is my best option for a clean getaway. I open the door wider and step aside allowing them to walk through the doorway. I shut the door behind them and quickly walk past them to pick up Lily. I don't want either of them touching her.

"Is this our granddaughter?" My mom asks with very little emotion.

"No mother, I got rid of her a long time ago. This is a baby I picked up along the way." I say hitting her with sarcasm in response to her very stupid question.

"Mia." My father warns.

"Why did you bring your lawyer on a simple trip to visit your daughter?"

"Because this has gone on long enough young lady. It's high time that you do the right thing. Sign that baby over to the adoptive parents that you promised her to and come home with us."

"I didn't promise her to anyone that was your doing. I made my choice when I left and there's nothing you can say or do to make me give my baby up or go back with you.

"You will do what we say," he says, getting in my face now.

I take a step back to put some distance between us.

"You will sign the papers, hand the baby over to Felicia, and she will make sure that she gets where she needs to go. Then you will get on a plane back home with us this afternoon."

"Over my dead body." Relief washes over me at the sound of his voice. I look over my shoulder to see Logan standing in the doorway, his face hard as stone. I have no idea what he's doing here, but right now I'm grateful that he is. I don't know why I thought that I could handle my parents on my own.

My father turns to face him. "Stay out of this Logan."

Logan? How does my father know his name? Do they... "Do you two know each other?"

My mom comes to stand by my side. "Logan paid us a visit a few weeks ago. Didn't you know?" she asks, rubbing my obliviousness in my face.

My eyes go wide with anger. "You did *what*?"

"We'll talk about it later. ALONE," he says, and I know I need to stand down. The focus needs to be getting rid of my

165

parents. "I spotted a car with dark tinted windows parked down the street and I had a feeling, so I pulled around the corner and waited. When I came back around, I saw the car in the driveway and put two and two together."

He walks over to me and Lily and puts his arm around my shoulder.

"You can't be serious, Mia." My mother states with a scowl. "You would defy your parents because of this man?"

"This *man* has been nothing short of wonderful to Lily and me. I don't know where we'd be right now without him but to answer your question mother, No. I'm not defying you because of Logan. I'm doing it for Lily because she deserves to have her mother with her whether you like it or not. This is not your choice, it's mine. Just go back home, take your crew with you, and leave me the hell alone."

Logan squeezes my arm. "Mia and Lily aren't going anywhere with you. She said her peace, you came, you saw and now you can leave."

"This isn't over young lady!" My father barks.

Logan moves to stand in front of me, tucking me and Lily behind his back. "No. It is. It's over because if you show up here again, I will arrest you for trespassing and we will get a restraining order filed against you."

"You have no idea what you're doing."

"Yes I do, because unlike you I actually love your daughter and your grandchild and I will do whatever the fuck it takes to protect them. If that means I have to take you on then so be it, and I'm pretty sure your little lawyer will tell you that the law is on our side."

They look between each other, casting glances and engaging in silent conversations with their eyes. It seems as if though they're done for now. My mother walks over to us and moves to touch Lily, I quickly retreat taking a step backwards and shake my head at her.

"Mia, for what it's worth we just want what's best for you," she says stoically.

"No, you've never given a damn about what's best for me mother."

She says nothing in her own defense and simply nods. "We're at the hotel on First Street. We'll be there until tomorrow afternoon if you change your mind."

"I won't. Have a safe trip back," I say as they walk through the front door.

Logan follows after them and makes sure they've gone.

I take a deep, calming breath and return Lily to her play yard.

Logan went to see them, he lied to me, I trusted him and he lied. I don't even know what to do with this information. Why would he go see them? Did he want them to come take me away? That makes no sense, he wouldn't have defended me just now if that's what he wanted.

"Were you going somewhere?" he asks, looking at my bags on the floor as he walks back inside.

I stare at him for a minute, not sure of which issue to address first. "That week when you left, you said you were going to training. You really went to see my parents didn't you?"

"I did."

"I can't believe you. How could you do that to me, Logan? I trusted you."

167

"I don't want to argue with you, Mia. It wasn't some devious plot to hurt or lie to you. You'd just told me that you had been thinking about your mother. You said there was no chance of a reconciliation, but I wanted to make sure. I wanted to go out there and see for myself. I thought that maybe you were wrong, maybe there was hope and I could bring you and your family back together."

"Well, you did a great job didn't you? You brought them right to me."

"No. I NEVER told them where you were or how to find you. After meeting with them I knew that you were right that they didn't give a damn about making amends. I left right away and I didn't tell you because I didn't want to make it worse; you were already upset about it. I never meant to hurt you or betray your trust.

I believe him. I know him. I know his heart, and it's clear to me that he's telling the truth. I want to fight with him, to tell him that I'm angry, that I can't forgive him, but after the scene that just unfolded right here in his living room I don't have the heart. He's the only person who's ever really stood up for me. Am I really willing to toss that aside over one bad judgment call?

"I believe you, but that doesn't explain how they found me," I say.

"I don't know, but I'll see if I can find anything out." He looks down at the ground again where my belongings lie. "Why the bags, Mia?"

"Logan... I..."

"Were you planning on leaving me?" He probes. He leans against the wall with his arms crossed over his chest.

I look down at my feet unable to answer him. God, this is hard. This is why I wanted to sneak away, this is why I didn't want to say goodbye.

"You were, weren't you? You were just going to leave me without one word. You were just going to take Lily and run."

I look up at him with tears in my eyes but I still can't find the words.

"Why?" he asks, the hurt evident in his eyes. "Oh wow." He pushes himself off the wall and takes a few steps toward me. "Last night when we made love, you knew you were going to do this didn't you?"

"Yes. I knew." I croak out, the tears now falling down my face.

"How could you do that?"

"I had no choice."

"You always have a choice unless…You knew didn't you?" he asks, catching on to the fact that I had a heads up to the events of this morning.

"Knew *what*?"

"That your parents were coming. You said you weren't in contact with anyone from back home so how could you know?"

"It doesn't matter."

"It matters."

"I can't, Logan. Please, please leave it alone." He takes a step forward as I take one back, needing to keep my distance, fighting the urge to run to him and tell him everything.

"I can't do that."

"You think that I want this? You think that I *want* to leave you? That I want to be away from the man I love, to take Lily away from a good home? It's the only way to keep her protected."

"*I* can protect her!" He yells, throwing out his arms in frustration.

"You can't. They're just going to keep on coming. Logan, this is never going to end. I have to take Lily and go."

He gets in my face now. "You are not leaving. I won't let you go."

"You can't keep me here," I say, pushing up on my tip toes so that I'm in his face as well. "I'm not your prisoner."

"You're right. God, Mia, you're right and I love you. I would hate to see you go, but if that's what you want to do with your life, *fine*. Go. But you are NOT taking Lily with you."

My eyes go wide and I have to control the sudden urge to punch something. "What? You're out of your fucking mind if you think I'm leaving here without my daughter."

"That's exactly what I think. If you go, you go alone."

I take a step forward, using my hands to push him as hard as I can. "She's not your daughter."

"You're wrong! She's as much mine as she is yours. I love that little girl and she loves me. She needs me to protect her even if I have to protect her from you."

"You son of a bitch. I'm leaving with Lily."

He grabs my arms and holds me in place, making me focus my eyes on him. "You're not going anywhere, with or without Lily."

"That's not what you said a minute ago," I say, infuriated by him.

"Yeah, I know what I said. I was bluffing." He lets me go, walks over to my bags and finds the one that holds all of my money and identification. "This is the only way that you can survive on your own," he says, holding it up in the air. "So, I'm going to take it away from you. Problem solved."

"Logan...Please, you can't do that. Don't do this to me."

"Who warned you about your parents coming?"

"Lily's dad."

"Lily's dad?" He looks dumbstruck—*shocked*, and maybe a little hurt.

"You're in touch with her dad?"

"Not normally no. It's the first time I've spoken to him since before she was born."

"How would he know anything that your parents are doing?"

"That's it, Logan. I've said too much. You have to listen to me. It's safer for everyone if I just take Lily and go."

"Are you going back to him?"

"What? No," I say, shaking my head. "No, Logan. I love you, I want you, and that's not the problem."

"Then just talk to me. Tell me what's going on so I can help you babe."

His words hit me hard.

I want to tell him. I want to accept his help, but that would be putting him in danger and I could never live with myself if something happened to him because of me.

"I just can't," I say sadly. I hate hurting him, hate seeing the look of disappointment in his eyes.

171

He nods his head and tosses my backpack full of money over his back. "I have to go to work. Keep the door locked and don't answer it for anyone. Call me immediately if your parents come back here Do you understand?"

"Yes," I reply meekly. I have no choice, he's taken my only option away. I'm stuck here and now Logan and Lily are both in the line of fire.

Chapter 18

I make sure that the doors are locked and then I sit around and stew for the remainder of the day. I'm angry and I don't know where to direct it. I guess in theory I should be directing it at Nick for showing up here and messing with my life, but instead I'm mad at Logan for getting in the way of my leaving. In my heart I know that this is where I want to be, but my head is screaming that it's no longer safe here for Lily and me.

I make an early dinner and put a plate of food in the microwave for Logan. As soon as I'm done eating and the kitchen is clean, I go upstairs with Lily and hide out in what used to be my spare bedroom. If Logan is going to force me to be here against my will then he has another thing coming to him if he thinks I'm going to be in his bed.

He's been home for a couple of hours now but thankfully he's been giving me my space. I heard him as he went into Lily's room to see her while she was napping, she's almost always his first stop when he gets home. He said he thought of her as his daughter and all I could do was yell at him when I should have thrown my arms around his neck and hugged him. He's everything I could have ever wanted for her. I couldn't have handpicked a better father for my daughter and now that she has a chance at that it's being threatened.

I shut off the lights and try to get comfortable in this bed…alone. I have a hard time sleeping when I'm just across the hall from Logan.

How would I make it a lifetime without him?

I feel like I've been awake for hours — tossing and turning and unable to get comfortable enough to sleep, when the door to the bedroom opens. I quickly shut my eyes and pretend to be asleep. Immature I know, but I can't help myself.

I hear his footsteps getting closer and closer, then they suddenly stop and I know he's standing by the bed watching me. I assume that he'll see I'm asleep and leave, but instead he pulls the sheets off of me and scoops me into his arms causing me to gasp in shock.

"What are you doing?" I shriek, wrapping my arms around his neck so that I don't fall.

He walks me across the hall into our bedroom and literally drops me onto the bed.

"*This* is our room. You sleep here."

I stare at him in anger and disbelief, "Well where are *you* going to sleep?"

He smiles seductively and lets out a low chuckle. "I'm going to sleep right here with you baby."

"No, you're not," I declare, pulling the sheets up around me.

He strips down to his boxers and glares my way.

"I'm sorry," he says with a hint of amusement in his voice. He snatches the sheets out of my hands and plops down on the bed next to me. "Did you think you actually had a choice?"

I let out a frustrated huff of air and roll over so that my back is facing him. He lets out an exasperated sigh and shuts the lights off. I feel him settling down next to me and I hate the tension between us. I know that I've caused it, that I'm the reason, but I don't know what else to do. What I do know is that I'm handling this completely wrong.

He throws his hand across my abdomen, gripping me tightly and pulling me back until our bodies are fused together—his front to my back. His face is buried in the nook of my neck and a sense of relief washes over me. I hate that he's angry with me, and though I'm still uncertain of our future together, it makes me happy to know that he still wants this connection between us. I shut my eyes, trying to shut out all of the worry that swims around in my brain. But the more I lie here, the more it festers.

"Logan?" I whisper, not wanting to wake him if he's already fallen asleep.

"Hmm?"

"Everything that I said to you last night, about how much I loved you...It was real." I need him to get that my feelings for him are pure. He and Lily are everything to me and I want him to see that the only reason I'd sacrifice being with him is to keep her safe.

"I believe you."

"I just wanted to show you what you meant to me one last time before I left. I needed to show you so that when I was gone you'd know it wasn't all a lie. That my need to keep Lily safe is the only reason behind me trying to leave."

He tightens his hold on me and kisses the top of my head. "I understand."

I settle down and burrow myself closer to him. I don't care anymore. I don't think I can go through with leaving him now, even if I had the means to do it. I honestly believe that this is where I belong, but that doesn't change the fact that there are very real threats lurking just beyond the walls of this little cocoon we've created.

"Logan?"

"Yes, Mia?"

"I'm scared."

He gives me a gentle squeeze. "I know, but baby no one can hurt you or take Lily away from you. I know you're scared but you can't keep running. It's time for you to stand up and fight."

What Logan doesn't realize is that the real threat is much more real than just my parents coming to town with a lawyer. The threat that he perceives is nothing compared to the actuality and as much as I hate it, as much as I dread it, I'm going to have no choice but to tell him the truth. I need to give it to him completely so that he can decide with eyes wide open if Lily and I are really worth the risk. I make up my mind, I have to tell him the truth... just not tonight. I need to have him hold me one more night before I have to revive all of the demons that I tried to leave behind.

"I'm sorry that I hurt you," I say. "You're the last person I'd ever want to hurt, I just didn't want to bring my mess to your door."

"Your mess is my mess baby. That's what loving you means. Anything that hurts you hurts me. It's my job to make sure you feel safe and protected and I will not let anyone make you feel anything less than that."

I fight for sleep, do my best to fight off the memories of the past and the fears of the future. I hold onto the fact that for tonight at least Logan's love is true.

It's pure and real and I can shelter myself with that.

My eyes flutter open, taking in the bright rays of morning sun that are shining through the window.

I close my eyes again and sprawl across the large bed. I listen for noises but the house is quiet, eerily so. Logan must have left for work already and Lily must still be asleep which is rare. I decide to take advantage of the quiet time and sleep a little longer. It's not like I have a job to get to anymore or anything pressing. I have no money and the sad truth is that I'm not safe leaving the house, not while there's still a possibility of Nick being around. Tonight when Logan comes home from work I'll tell him the truth. I'll tell him all about my history with Nick and hope that he still wants me when I'm done with my story. Assuming he understands and can accept it all, he'll know what to do next, he'll know what steps we should take to ensure all of our safety. I have to believe that everything will work out, that Lily and I will get the life that we deserve.

I toss and turn a bit, unable to get comfortable then finally give up on the notion of sleeping longer than usual. I get up and quickly use the bathroom so that I can go in and check on Lily before making myself some breakfast and starting the laundry. I make my way across the hallway to her bedroom and quietly open the door, careful not to wake her if she's still asleep. I listen for sounds of her cooing or rustling her bed sheet but there are none. I silently tiptoe across the room to her crib, look down, and gasp at the sight of the empty crib before me.

My heart rate doubles and my body goes on instant alert. I try to stay calm and look around the room.

Could Logan have taken her? Left her in her swing or play yard maybe?

My body is in shock, unwilling to move, but I force myself to come unstuck and rush downstairs. I run into the living room, right to the spot where her play yard usually sits. My knees go weak and I have to hold onto the edge of it.

She's not here.

"Lily!" I cry out as panic strikes.

I look around me taking in my surroundings and I know. I know he has her. Nick, he's got Lily. I try to keep control of my emotions. I can't lose it yet, I have to call Logan. He'll know what to do. He'll get her back.

I run into the kitchen and grab the phone, dialing Logan's cell phone number as quickly as I can. It goes to voicemail and I let out a curse before I hang up and try again.

"Please pick up. Please, please, please," I say to myself, biting back the tears that threaten.

"Hey baby, you okay?" he answers. The concern is evident in his voice, I never call him at work.

"Logan, she's gone!" I half shriek, half yell. I'm no longer able to control the tears, the sound of his voice allowing me to let go of the emotions.

"Mia, calm down," he says firmly. "What are you saying?"

"Lily… Lily's gone, he took her Logan. He has her. You have to help me."

"Baby, Lily was in her crib an hour ago." He sounds shaken, scared and confused.

"She's not there. Please, please help me. He's going to do something to her, please." I beg.

"Oh my God, Mia." He breathes out. "I'll be there in ten minutes. Stay by the phone and away from the doors and windows."

"Please hurry," I say before disconnecting the call.

Chapter 19

After hanging up with Logan, I run upstairs and barely make it to the bathroom before I fall to the ground and violently expel the contents of my stomach into the toilet. I sit there for a moment, my body shaking as I try to process what's happening. I pull myself up and throw cold water on my face. I rifle through my drawers for something to wear, anything it doesn't really matter. I just need to be ready to go look for Lily. I toss on a pair of sweats and my sneakers. I pick up my cell phone and check if I have any missed calls or messages. Of course not. Besides Logan and his family, no one knows this number. I search all the rooms again, knowing that it's useless but I do it anyway, saying a silent prayer for Lily to be there as I enter each one. By the time I make it back downstairs, I can barely see through the fountain of tears falling from my eyes.

A few minutes later, I hear a flurry of activity outside.

Logan bursts through the front doors, a swarm of people behind him. I run into his arms and break down in uncontrollable sobs. Logan picks me up and carries me over to the couch, setting me down next to him. I wipe away my tears as I take in the sight before me: Police officers are searching the house, tearing it apart, searching for any evidence of Lily.

"I know that you're freaking out on me but I need you to hold on," Logan says, making me look up and see a pain in his eyes that mirrors my own. "You have to tell me what you know, Mia. I need to know everything if you want me to get Lily back."

I nod my head. "Okay."

He reaches out and strokes my cheek. "Mia, this is John. He's going to listen while I take your statement."

"Why? Why does anyone have to listen?"

"Because baby, you're my girlfriend, and me taking your statement is a conflict of interest. I shouldn't even be the one to do it but I'm going to anyway. John is going to sit in and listen, kind of like a witness."

I look at the officer sitting there, hating that he has to hear what I have to say next but at this point I don't care who hears it. I could care less about who knows what happened as long as I get Lily back.

"Alright," I say softly.

"Who took Lily?" Logan asks, getting right to the point.

"His name is Nick Barnes."

"How do you know him?"

I look past him and gaze out the window, allowing my eyes to focus on anything other than Logan's face. "He's my father's best friend. My godfather."

He gently cups my chin with his hand and turns my face, forcing my eyes back on him. "Why would he take Lily?"

I close my eyes and steel myself for what's about to come because I know my admission is going to shock him. I take a deep breath and open my eyes again letting myself focus on the deep blue of Logan's eyes. "Because he's her father."

"*What?*" His face goes pale and he turns his face away from me, running his hand through his short hair.

"It's not what you think." I blurt out, trying to defend myself before he's too far gone. "It wasn't like that."

His forehead rests on his hand and he angles his head upward to face me. His nostrils flare and I fight the urge to get up and back away, run away from having to explain this to him but this is the only way that I can help Lily now. "What was it like, Mia?"

"We were close while I was growing up. He was always around always there for everything — birthdays, holidays, dance recitals. He was always there cheering me on. I thought I could trust him because he was more of a father to me than my own dad was. He'd spend a lot of time at the house, he and my dad would hang out and drink, and they'd get completely drunk and pass out. Nick would crawl into one of the guest bedrooms and pass out."

"Go on." He urges.

"It started a few weeks before my seventeenth birthday, Nick and dad were on one of their binges. It was a Friday night and I had probably been asleep for hours by the time they were done drinking. Nick came into my bedroom and woke me up. I remember waking up because he scared the shit out of me, you know? But I laughed it off because I just assumed he was so drunk that he didn't know what he was doing, I thought he had just stumbled into the wrong room. Only he wasn't as drunk as I thought he was. No. Actually, I don't think he was drunk at all. He knew exactly what he was doing. He said that I'd grown into a beautiful woman and that I had been taunting him for years, wearing skimpy outfits and bikinis in front of him; giving him hugs and flirting with him while I was practically naked. He said that it was time that he got what I had been flaunting all that time, he said that I owed him that much for acting like a little slut in front of him."

"Mia…" Logan says, reaching his hand out for me, but I move backwards and out of his reach.

"No. It's okay, I'm okay, let me finish."

He nods, but moves closer and grabs hold of my hand. He squeezes it tightly, giving me silent encouragement.

"He climbed into my bed and got on top of me. I was wearing a night gown and he pushed it up as far as he could. I fought him and tried to buck him off of me, tried pushing, but he grabbed my wrists and pinned me down to the bed. He pulled a knife out of his waistband and told me that if I screamed it would wake up my parents and if they came into my room and found us like that he would kill them and then kill me. He told me to stop fighting him, that he wouldn't hurt me if I just calmed down. I was so scared, I didn't know what else to do, so I let him…"

I hesitate, using my free hand to wipe away the tears that have begun to fall down my cheeks.

"It's okay," Logan says, using the pads of his thumbs to wipe away fresh tears.

"I let him do that to me. He held me down the entire time, held my wrists down to the bed and took what he wanted while I cried. After he was done he kissed me on the cheek and told me to rest, told me to gather my strength because he'd be back often. He told me that anytime he was in the house he wanted me ready for him, in a nightgown with no underwear and waiting for him in my bed. And I hate myself, I hate myself because I did it. I did what he said and I let him have me over and over again and I never fought because it was easier that way, because the less I fought the quicker it was over."

"Look at me, Mia. You didn't do anything wrong."

"I was a coward. But I never wanted it, you have to believe me. I hated it and I hated him but I was afraid, I never had the best parents but I didn't want them dead. I didn't want him to kill them, and I didn't want him to kill me and he'd do it. Deep down I knew he would, so I did what he wanted."

"You did what you had to do to survive, Mia. It wasn't your fault. He raped you. You were a minor and he took advantage of you. He used his authority and strength to overpower you."

He's right, I've told myself the same things time and time again, reassured myself that I did the best I could under the circumstances. It's not like I had trustworthy parents to turn to with the truth of my reality. They had done nothing but let me down for most of my life.

"He came to me one last time when he found out I was pregnant. He left me five hundred dollars and told me to get an abortion, told me to never speak a word of what happened between us, that there would be hell to pay if I ever named him as the father of my baby."

Logan straightens his spine and shakes his head at me. "But you didn't get an abortion."

I shrug in response. "I couldn't. I couldn't do it... I didn't care anymore about anything, I just knew I couldn't get rid of my baby. I'm sure he flipped out when he realized I was still pregnant but I started avoiding him altogether and locking my door at night. I know he tried to come to me a few times, but what could he do? Break the door down? Why I didn't think of locking my door from the start I have no idea," I say, realizing how stupid I really was when it came to handling my situation with Nick.

"I think he was the one who eventually planted the adoption bug in my parent's head. He knew that my parents need for a perfect appearance in front of their uptight little world would trump what I wanted."

"Which is when they tried to force you into giving Lily up for adoption," Logan says.

"Yes, you know the rest."

"How do you know it was Nick who took Lily, Mia? What makes you so sure?"

"Because he's here. I saw him two days ago while I was running. He grabbed me and pulled me behind a building. He told me my parents were on their way with their lawyer and he told me that I had better hand Lily over to them. He said that he'd seen you and me together and that if I didn't do what he wanted, he would kill you instead of my parents."

His hands ball into fists and I can almost see the rage rolling off of him. "That's why you were trying to leave yesterday? You were trying to protect me?"

"I didn't know what else to do. I couldn't let him hurt you and I couldn't let them take Lily so I tried to run. And I should have told you when you everything when you caught me. I should have told you what happened because he told me that Lily was a connection between us that couldn't exist, and that if I didn't get rid of her he would."

"You're *lying*." I look up to see my father standing in the doorway like a statue, looking angry and dumbstruck. My mother stands behind him with tears in her eyes, but he continues to talk. "Nick would never do the things you've just accused him of. He would never take advantage of you like that, let alone kidnap a child."

"Michael!" My mother calls to him, grabbing his arm to signal for him to stop.

He turns to his side to face her. "Do not tell me you believe this, Melinda. She's lying."

"She's not. Look at her." She demands. She looks at me somberly, guiltily. I've never seen her look at me with any emotion that wasn't anger. "I said look at her. Look at your daughter."

He turns around to face me and looks at me, I mean really looks at me. His shoulders sag and he stares at me with a tortured kind of pain in his eyes. "Mia. I...I don't know what to say."

"There's nothing you can say," I reply. I turn back to Logan. "I'm sorry, I know this is a lot to take in. I screwed everything up, and I should have told you from the beginning. I understand if you don't want to be with me anymore and I can live with that but please, please help me get Lily back."

"Mia, I love you, that doesn't change just because something bad happened to you. You were a minor, you trusted an adult and he abused that trust. I still want you and I still want Lily. We will get her back, you have to believe that."

"I don't know, Logan. I'm scared."

"I know," he says, pulling me in for a hug. "We'll get our girl back." He turns his face towards John, the officer who had been listening in, the officer I'd forgotten was here. "Do you have enough?"

"I have what I need. I'm going to get to work on this."

Logan moves to stand up, but John shakes his head.

"You can't be involved man. I need you to stay here, but as soon as I know anything I'll let you know."

"This is my family. I need to do something."

"Take care of her," John replies, motioning to me. "She needs you. I'll keep you informed every step of the way, but you have to play it cool. You're too emotionally involved and I can't have you out on the streets like this. You'll just get yourself killed."

He walks away, leaving us both standing there unsure of what to do next. The level of helplessness I feel right now is overwhelming.

"Mia, what can we do? The police came to the hotel to question us. We came as soon as they left," my mother says, coming to stand in front of us.

"*You* sent him here. You sent him right to me when you told him where I was. How did you know where I was anyway? Why couldn't you just leave me alone?"

"Your old boss Sarah called us. She told us that she had just fired you. Said that you were getting into trouble and that she was scared of what might happen to Lily if we didn't come get you both."

"Son of a bitch." I turn just in time to see Logan pick up a glass vase and hurl it across the room. His face is fuming with anger as it shatters into a million tiny little pieces. He walks away and pulls one of the remaining police officers aside, I assume to tell him of Sarah's involvement.

I slump my shoulders in defeat and go grab the broom out of the kitchen. I return and start sweeping up the broken glass. A set of firm hands pulls me back by my shoulders and pulls me into a hesitant embrace.

"I've never been a very good father to you," my dad says, pulling the broom out of my hands. "Let me at least do this for you." He releases me and starts sweeping up the mess. I look at the shards of glass lying on the floor like every single piece is a shattered piece of me, a representation of how my life has fallen apart and without Lily it's not even worth it to try to put it back together again.

I walk over to Lily's play yard and pull one of her blankets out of it. I hold it tightly and raise it up to my nose inhaling her scent, I picture her in my arms sucking on her little pacifier while I rock her back and forth in my arms as she falls asleep. I want to stay strong, to hold it together because I need to be able to think clearly but I can't help how fragile I feel. How on the verge of a complete breakdown I am and clutching this empty blanket is the thing that's about to push me over. I start to cry, unable to fight the tears that overpower me.

"It's okay. Let it go." Logan says, wrapping me up in his arms. I clutch his shirt and hold on tight as if holding on to him is the only way for me to stay upright. I need his strength and light right now, need him to convince me that everything is going to be alright. He scoops me up and carries me up the stairs, with each step he takes I hold onto him tighter, needing him to be my lifeline in this nightmare.

He lays us both down on the bed positioning us so that we're facing one another. My body trembles on its own accord, I get that I need to keep my strength, keep myself together but every moment that I'm here and Lily is not is pushing me closer and closer to a breaking point.

"Shouldn't we be downstairs?" I question softly.

He strokes my cheek and I take in the sight of him. He's trying to be brave, to be solid for me but I can see the fear in his eyes. "It's better if we're out of the way."

"What if John calls?"

"I have my phone with me."

"I was in the house, I was right here." I say, my voice cracking as I try to keep from crying. "How did this even happen?"

"From what we can gather he broke in through an unlocked window downstairs after I left, snuck upstairs, and grabbed Lily while you were still asleep."

"This is all my fault."

"No, it's not." He attempts to reassure me but I'm beyond that point. Kind words can't change the facts and the fact is that I created this situation.

"There's so much that I should have done differently, starting with telling you the entire truth from the beginning, but I was ashamed and scared, and when I started to feel things for you, started to really fall for you I knew I could never tell you because I was afraid that you wouldn't love me anymore when you heard about how things went down. How I stopped fighting and just let him take what he wanted from me."

"You did the best you could, Mia. In a lot of ways you were fighting, you were trying to protect your parents and keep yourself alive, you didn't know what the outcome would be."

I close my eyes and let out a shaky breath. "Sometimes I wonder if she wouldn't have been better off with the adoptive parents, if they could have given her more, a better life."

"Look at me." He demands. His voice is firm and the deep timbre resonates through me. I open my eyes and our gazes lock. "Don't say that. You're her mother, and you've done an amazing job with her baby. She's perfect."

"She's also gone." I wince at my own words, my chest tightens with the type of pain that is indefinable. It's the type of pain that only comes from having your heart ripped out.

"We'll get her back."

"How can you be so sure?"

"I just have faith. I know it."

I wish for sleep to come and claim me, to take me away from this moment in time. I wish to wake up and have it all have been a terrible dream but sleep never comes and pretending that this isn't reality isn't going to help Lily.

"I need to do something, Logan. I can't just lie around and do nothing, this isn't helping."

"I know how you feel, but there's nothing that you can do right now. Everything that can be done is being done," he states calmly, almost too calmly for me.

I'm not sure how long we lie there pretending that falling asleep is actually a possibility, hoping that any minute the phone will ring and it'll be news of Lily. I wonder how Nick is treating her, if he's feeding her, if she's crying, and the thoughts running through my head consume me. After some time I get up and sit on the edge of the bed.

"I can't lay here anymore," I say.

"Let's go downstairs. I'll call John and see if he has any updates for us."

We walk down together hand in hand, I think staying connected is helping us both right now. Him needing to take care of me and me needing to draw from his strength because all I currently feel is weak and scared, and when I don't feel that I'm just numb.

Logan speaks to John, but the only update he has so far is that Nick checked out of his hotel early this morning, most likely before he came for Lily. There's been no sight of him since then.

We know he hasn't gotten on a plane, and the police now have people at the bus depots and nearby train stations. My parents sit on the couch across from me, staring at me, watching me clutch Lily's blanket as if they're terrified of me or what I might do.

They're trying to be supportive, to say all the right things and I know that I should be the bigger person, be the better person and forgive them. Perhaps one day I will, but right now I don't really care what they think or how they feel. They may as well be a pair of strangers sitting in front of me. In fact, they *are* a pair of strangers sitting in front of me and their feelings have no relevance.

"Mia?" My head snaps up at the sound of my name being called, and I see Logan's parents Carol and Steven walking into the living room.

I jump out of my seat and run into Carol's open arms and begin to sob uncontrollably again.

"Oh sweetie, I'm so sorry," she says, holding me tightly while Steven squeezes my shoulder.

She holds me for a few moments, then she cups my face in her hands and gives me a sad smile. "She'll be fine, you'll see. She'll be back with you and Logan before you know it."

I nod my head, wanting so desperately to believe in her words, wishing upon all wishes for it to be true, for any second to have anybody walk through that front door carrying Lily. I glance towards my parents who are looking at my interaction with Logan's parents with mild annoyance and with what I can only describe as envy.

Chapter 20

❦

I jump when I hear Logan's phone ring. I must have dozed off on the couch somehow after spending the majority of the day pacing around the house and crying. Mandy and Chris both stopped by to offer their support. Carol and Steven have gone to buy food which I can guarantee I won't be able to touch. My parents have remained a constant presence in the house but have surprisingly stayed out of my way.

"He's been spotted heading southbound on Park Avenue. I'm going down there to see what I can find out," Logan says.

"I'm coming with you."

"No. I don't want you anywhere near that area. I'm not even supposed to be there. Keep your phone on you and I'll call you." He places a quick kiss on my forehead and before I can argue he's gone, leaving me behind. I look around me at this house that's become my home. I look around wondering what it would be like to live without the two people that make it just that, a home. Logan and Lily are my home and without them I don't want to be in this house. I can't sit here, not even one second longer waiting for news on my daughter, waiting to see if Logan will come back unscathed. Not one more second of playing the victim.

I grab my keys and make a run for the door, ready to plow through anyone who tries to stop me. I can hear my parents calling for me but I keep going, never pausing, never looking back because the truth of the matter is that without Logan and Lily I have nothing. And if there's even a small chance that my presence can make a difference in what's about to go down, I have to be there. I have to try to bring my family back intact; I couldn't live with myself if I sat back and did nothing.

I jump in my car and peel out of the driveway heading toward Park Avenue; it's not a far drive, ten minutes tops. I speed through town praying that I'll make it in time, that Nick hasn't hurt Lily.

I make it onto Park but there's no sign of them and the street is eerily quiet, I pull over to the side of the road and contemplate calling Logan but he'll never tell me where he is, not if he knows I'm out looking for them. Where would they go? What would be the next logical direction to head? Suddenly it hits me. From this point, there's only one way out of town — one way to get away, and that's by crossing the Bay Street Bridge.

I throw the car into gear and drive. I glance in my rearview mirror and see that my parents' car has now caught up to me but I make no moves to slow down or stop. All I care about is getting to my family, my *real* family. Not parents who never gave a damn about me, who never saw or heard me or cared about my feelings. As far as I'm concerned, they can keep driving forever.

It's then when I reach the entrance of the bridge, then when I see the dramatic scene unfolding right before my eyes. I drive as far as I can onto the bridge and come to a screeching halt.

Nick is standing by the ledge of the bridge, pointing a gun at Logan with one hand and holding Lily up to the edge with the other. He's surrounded by countless police officers with guns drawn and pointed at him.

My heart stops and my entire world is a haze, a series of events leading to this moment in time where my entire life is at a crossroads. Where one man has the power to decide which way my fate will go.

I exit the car and run as fast as I can toward where Nick is perched on the side of the bridge. Before I can get too close, a pair of arms go around my waist holding me back. I fight the police officer and try to break free but his hold is too tight, I know it's no use. There's nothing left to be done now, nothing left but to beg.

"Nick!" I yell, desperate to get his attention.

It's as if the sound of my voice is pressing the pause button on a DVD. Nobody makes a move, everyone just freezes, fades away into the background and disappears, and it's only the two of us. Nick and me.

"Mia, I told you. Didn't I tell you? Didn't I warn you to get rid of this kid?"

"You did. You warned me, but she's mine Nick. Only mine. You don't have to do this."

"We had a good thing going and you fucked up everything. You stupid little bitch, why didn't you just get the abortion when I told you to? Then we could have still been together."

I shudder at the thought, of the idea of sustaining more abuse at this man's hands than I already have. "You're not angry at Lily. You're angry at me, Nick Just me. So why don't you give her to Logan. Just hand her over to him and you can take me instead. I won't fight you. I'll go with you and we can be together."

"Mia!" Logan calls out, but I don't look at him, I can't look at him. I'm desperate and determined to get Lily to safety, and I don't care what it takes.

"Nick, listen to me Give Lily to Logan and you and I can go. We'll go anywhere you want. You can do whatever you want to me."

"It's too late baby. They all know now, they'll follow us everywhere, they'll never leave us in peace and it's all this brat's fault," he says, shaking the car seat.

I gasp, finding it increasingly hard to breathe at the sight of him holding my daughter as leverage. I push hard and break free from the officer who was holding me back and slowly make my way into the inner circle, to the point where we're all surrounded by guns. "Let her go."

"I am. Right over this fucking bridge I'm going to let her go." He takes the gun off of Logan and points it at me. "Do not come any closer, Mia. Be a good little girl and listen to me."

I stop dead in my tracks and raise my hands in surrender. "Please. Please put her down on the ground, please. Shoot me. Fucking shoot me already. I don't care, just don't hurt the baby."

He raises Lily's car seat a little higher. "I'll shoot you! I'll fucking kill you, but first I want you to watch me kill her. You love this little brat more than you love me and now I'm going to take away what you love."

My heartbeat pounds in my ears. My body breaks into a sweat and an almost painful panic sets in.

He lifts the car seat out further and dangles it so that it hangs over the bridge.

I watch in horror, my eyes fixated on his hand, his fingers clutching the handle. I can see them twitch, see them move slightly, see him slowly loosening his grip as I lose my grip on the small amount of sanity and control I have. I scream, shriek, and cry out in horror—the sound piercing through the night and carrying over the bridge.

As my knees begin to buckle, the world starts to fade. Pain explodes as I feel my body suddenly hit hard, as it connects to the concrete with a thud, and then there's nothing. Just black.

Chapter 21

I roll onto my side, still tired, exhausted, and unwilling to open my eyes. I want to stretch out but my body is a little sore.

I remember having a dream...a nightmare? I dreamt about a standoff between Nick and the police, the kind that you only see in movies or read about in books. He was mean, crazy and he had...

"Lily!" I shout, panting as I open my eyes and try to sit up. It wasn't a dream, it was real. Nick had Lily, and he was about to throw her over the ledge of a bridge.

"Logan?" I call out looking around the room. I've just come to realize that I'm in a hospital room when I hear the fall of footsteps heading toward me. A hundred pound weight is lifted off my shoulders when I look up and see Logan walking into my room. I burst into tears at the sight of him, relief rolling off of me in waves.

"Oh my God! Oh my God! You're okay." I chant, reaching out for him.

He sits on the edge of the bed and pulls me into a tight embrace. "No, no, no. Don't cry, baby. I'm fine," he says, rocking me back and forth.

"I was so scared for you. I was afraid I'd never see you again."

"I'm sorry. I'm so sorry you had to go through that." He tightens his hold on me. "If I weren't so happy that you're okay I'd be yelling at you. What were you thinking showing up there? You scared the shit out of me."

I rest my head on his shoulder and close my eyes. "I had to get to her. I needed to see her even if it was only for a minute." I pause, bracing myself for the answer to the question I've been too afraid to ask because if the answer isn't what I want it to be my heart will be shattered. "Did he?"

"No," he says, gently pushing me back so that he can look at me. "He didn't. Lily's fine. She's in the waiting room with my mom."

I let out an unsteady breath and blink back the tears that threaten. "He was about to let go. I thought... Can I see her Logan, please?"

"Of course. I'll let the nurse know you're awake and get Lily for you."

"Thank you."

The doctor on duty checks me out and tells me that I have a slight concussion and that I should be okay to go home in the morning. Logan returns a few minutes after the doctor with Lily in his arms. I smile huge at the sight of them, the two people who I've grown to love most in the world. They're here and they're okay and suddenly it's like the world shifts back on its axis and everything that just a few short hours ago was wrong is now right again. He bends over and kisses my forehead and then he hands her to me. I hold her to my chest and lightly rest my chin on the top of her head, breathing in her wonderful baby scent. "Oh Lily, you scared mommy so much. I missed you."

"She missed you too."

"Logan, what happened? One minute Nick was about to throw her over the bridge, the next thing I know I wake up here."

"Oh baby. If there were ever a perfect time for you to faint that was it."

"Huh?"

"When you fainted, it distracted Nick. It gave me enough time to move in and grab the car seat. I backed away from him and he pointed the gun at me, he intended to shoot but he didn't get the chance."

"The police arrested him?"

"They shot him, Mia. He's dead. He will never bother you and Lily again."

"I can't believe it." I'm so happy, elated that he's gone but at the same time I feel guilty for rejoicing in his death. I know that in theory everybody's life has value and without Nick there would be no Lily but he also took something from me. He stripped me of my childhood, my innocence, my choices; all taken away by a selfish, abusive man. "Is it terrible that I'm glad he's gone?"

"No. He was a waste of a human being. He did nothing but hurt you and he wouldn't have hesitated to kill Lily. I think you should be happy that he's gone. I'm fucking ecstatic. Thrilled that he can't get to either of you ever again."

"What about Sarah?"

He lets out a frustrated sigh. "Sarah acted out of anger and jealousy but she didn't really do anything illegal. She was here earlier I think she's pretty shaken up. I think she feels awful Mia, regardless of how she felt about you and me she didn't mean for anything bad to happen to Lily."

"Well she can keep her guilt, she deserves it." I huff.

Movement from the corner of my eye startles me. I look up to see my parents standing there. I'm taken aback by their appearance. They don't look like their normal perfect, put together selves. They look tired, defeated, and just a little disheveled.

I can spot the look of guilt in their eyes immediately, it humanizes them.

My father speaks first. "We're sorry to interrupt but we just wanted to see you and make sure for ourselves that you were alright."

"I'm fine. You can come in." I want to go with my natural inclination to tell them to leave but they did stick around while Lily was missing and they're here now. What kind of person would I be if I turned them away after all that? It would make us too much alike and I've fought for too long to set myself apart from their usual, cruel ways. If I treated them the way they've so frequently treated me, it would make me no better than they are.

They step further into the room, walking around to the other side of the bed where I lie holding Lily.

Mom pulls up a seat and smiles at me. "She's absolutely beautiful, Mia. You've done an amazing job with her."

"Are you here to tell me that I need to give her up again? Because if that's what you want, I have to ask you to leave."

"No. That's not why we're here. Like your father said, we were worried about you. We needed to make sure you were alright, both of you," she says, solemnly.

I nod at her, suddenly aware of how uncomfortable this is, of how little we really know about each other. We have conversations like strangers do, trying to fill in awkward silences with polite phrases and gestures. It's an unfortunate relationship and I promise myself that Lily will never have to feel this way about me.

"We want you to come home with us." This comes from my father who is now seated in the chair next to my mother's. "Both of you, you and Lily."

I look at Logan, whose eyes are wide with disbelief. He looks at me but says nothing. Now that the dust has started to settle, he is leaving the decision to me, letting me make the choice even though I know instinctively he wants to make it for me. He would like nothing more than to kick my parents out of this room and ban them from seeing me or Lily again.

"Why would I do that? Why would I ever go back to that life where I was nothing to you? Where you treated me like I didn't matter?"

"We've made a lot of mistakes where you're concerned, Mia. We know this," my father says, the look of remorse on his face gives me pause. I've never seen him look anything other than confident, decisive. "We won't be winning any parent of the year awards, that's for sure, but what we did to you...The way we neglected you...It's the reason Nick got to you. We left you in the hands of a monster, and even though you could have gone to the police, even though you could have done something, you didn't because you were afraid that he would hurt us. How did we inspire such loyalty from you when we never did anything to deserve it?"

"You're my parents, I loved you. I didn't want anyone to hurt you. It didn't matter how you treated me or what you did. All I ever wanted was for you to love me back."

Tears well in my mom's eyes. It's hard for me to see her show any real emotion, difficult for me to believe it when for so long she's been devoid of anything other than anger towards me.

"We did, we do, we just let our priorities get mixed up. We let our need for status overshadow our responsibility to you. We made it so that you couldn't feel comfortable enough to tell us you were being hurt and when you came to us with your pregnancy we let you down yet again."

"We don't expect you to forgive us right away, but we'd like to try to be a family, all of us — including Lily. We can have a fresh start, make things better, help you give Lily the future that she deserves."

"That's all I want. All I've ever wanted was to give Lily the future that she deserves and I'm sorry, but that's why I've got to stay here with Logan — if he still wants us that is."

"What? Of course I want you. How can you even ask me that? I love you, both of you. We're a family right?"

My heart soars at the sound of his words, hearing him say that he loves us, reaffirming that a life with Lily and me is what he wants is almost too good to believe. I was so afraid that after I told him the truth about my past, about what Nick did to me he wouldn't feel the same way but I couldn't have been more wrong.

"Right," I reply with a smile.

"Well, we'll certainly support your decision. Just know that the door is always open, you'll always have a home with us."

"I appreciate you saying that dad."

He stands up and nods. "We'll get out of your hair now. Please do call us. We'd like to keep in touch, work on our relationship and perhaps get to know our granddaughter if you'll allow us to."

"Why don't you stay for an extra day or two? I'll be out of here tomorrow and maybe you could come by the house for lunch?" I ask and look to Logan for approval which he gives with a smile.

"We would love that, Mia. Give us a call at the hotel when you get settled," he says, leaning over and placing a kiss on my forehead and on the top of Lily's head. Mom follows suit and then just like that they're gone, and gone with them is a ton of anger and resentment that I no longer want to be a part of my life.

⚶

Logan walks me into the house with one arm around my waist and the other carrying Lily's car seat. He carefully leads me over to the couch and gently pushes me down onto the couch.

"Don't move," he commands. Then he puts Lily's car seat on the floor, unbuckles her, and puts her in her play yard.

"I only fainted, Logan. I'm pretty sure I can function as I normally do."

"You hit your head pretty hard there chief. Let's not take any chances."

Who am I to argue? If it makes him feel better to watch over me and force me to take it easy for a day or two, it's the least I can do for all that he has done for me.

"I felt used. Dirty, too dirty to be with someone like you."

"You know that's not true right?"

"I still think you deserve better than this. You deserve to have someone who doesn't have as much emotional baggage as I do."

"Nobody is perfect, you know? Everyone has something, some part of their life they wish they could change and it's not up to you to choose for me. I want you, I'm very sure about that."

"I want you too. I just don't want you to wake up one day and realize you made a huge mistake."

"The only mistake would be waking up one day and not having you there. I'm not going to let that happen, you can't run away from this, Mia. This is your life, here with me and it will be a good life if you allow yourself to have it."

"I can try."

"You've been dealing with all of this stress for a long time. Nick's abuse and having a baby as a result, the issues with your parents and now Lily's kidnapping...I think you need to see someone babe, talk to someone, sort through all of your emotions so that you can move forward and not be haunted by all this shit."

"I don't want to have to relive it. I don't want to have to think about it, let alone talk about it."

"One day Lily is going to want to go have a sleepover at her friend's house. She's going to want to assert her independence, go to the movies or the mall. Are you going to be able to let her do these things without driving yourself crazy with worry?"

"No," I whisper.

"Will you speak to someone?" he asks, stroking my cheek with his hand.

"Yes. I will."

"Good."

"What will I tell her?"

"What will you tell who?" he asks, shaking his head.

"Lily," I reply, looking up at him. "What will I tell her when she asks me about her father?"

He tilts his head and eyes me for a few moments, I don't wonder for long what's going on in his mind when he finally speaks.

"You tell her the truth. You tell her that her father has loved her since the first time he held her in his arms and rocked her to sleep. You tell her that her father has always been there for her and looked out for her. I'm her father and I will be her father in every way that counts, and if it makes you feel any better we can go to your parents high priced lawyer and have her draw up new adoption papers, ones that will legally make me Lily's dad."

"You would do that?" I question, hardly believing that he can possibly be serious about legally making Lily his daughter. That he would take the child of an obviously evil man and raise her as his own.

"Yes I would do that. As a matter of fact, I want to do that. We're a family so we should make it legal."

"When I found out I was pregnant I thought that my life was over, that my entire future had been destroyed. I never would have imagined that things would turn out this way, that I would have a beautiful daughter and amazing man by my side. I never would have believed that this could be possible."

"I want to marry you, Mia, and if you think that it's too soon I'll understand that. I know you're only eighteen and if you'd rather wait a few years then I'll give you that, but this is it for me. You and Lily are it for me and I'm never going to be able to let you go. I don't want to ever let either one of you go."

"Was that a proposal?" I ask, unable to hide the hope in my voice. I know that I'm young, I'm only eighteen but I've been through more in that short time than some people go through in a lifetime. Having a child has forced me to mature earlier than I would have liked but I can't change that. All I can do is go with it and look forward to my future. All I know is that a future with Logan is more than I could have ever hoped for, having him in my life is just proof that good things can happen even in the hardest of times, that there is light beyond the darkness.

He pulls my hand into his. It's a simple touch that sends a rush of warmth throughout my body. "Do you want it to be a proposal?"

"I think so."

"Then it definitely was."

I let out a sigh as I try to wrap my head around this come to terms with all that has transpired over the last few months. I try to understand how I could have gotten so lucky as to end up in this town, running into Logan at that hospital and having him take an interest in me.

What if we hadn't met, if I had truly been left to fend for myself? Would I have been able to make it with a baby on my own or would I have ended up like Logan's sister Amy? He told me once that he joined the police force so that he could do some good, so that he could help someone, and maybe save someone the way he couldn't save her.

"What do we do? What happens now?" I ask.

"Now we live our lives. We make plans together and build a future."

A future with Logan is absolute and utter perfection to me.

"Do you have any ideas about what plans we should make together?"

"As a matter of fact I do. For starters, I'm quitting the police force."

"What?" I nearly shriek out in shock. "Why? I thought you loved your job."

"I loved the idea of it, the thrill of getting criminals off of the streets and helping people who need it, but Tim getting shot was a wakeup call for me. I never want someone to come and knock on our front door to tell you that I've been shot or worse. I never want you to lose sleep at night wondering if I'm coming home, or to have Lily afraid of her dad leaving the house because he might not come back. I never want you to have to mourn for me. I wanted to help and save people. That's all I ever wanted."

"You helped me, you saved me. You saved Lily."

He lowers his head to mine and rests his forehead against mine.

"Then I fulfilled my goal, I did what I set out to do and I can leave the force feeling like I made a difference and I can feel good about that."

"Well, what will you do?"

"I will do what was planned out for me since the day I was born," he says with a chuckle. "I'll make my father a very happy man and go work for him at his company and make way more money than I ever could being a cop."

"But will that make you happy?" I stroke his cheek the way he always does to me.

"Yeah, it will. It's what I wanted to do before we lost Amy. I always felt like that was my place, helping to carry on my dad's company. It's what I always assumed I'd do. I just had to take a slight detour for awhile, but now I'm ready, I'm ready to take my place at the company."

"If you're sure that'll make you happy then I'm happy for you, and I have to admit a little relieved too."

"I'm glad," he says, kissing the tip of my nose.

"I just have to figure out what I'm going to do now."

"I know what you're going to do."

"Yeah? What?"

"You'll see. Just trust me."

Trust me he says, two words that for so long caused me nothing but anxiety, words that I could never really believe in because "trust" to me was always a lie. A thing that people used to manipulate my feelings and emotions so that they could bend me to their will. Trusting people in my life always came with a nice heaping dose of disappointment and consequences. Logan came along and changed that, he showed me that trust is possible, it's real and it's beautiful when it's given to the right person and giving it to him wasn't easy but it was the act that pulled me out of the darkness and brought me to love.

I take in the sight of him, all of him, all mine and I give him the words I know he's been waiting for since we met. "I trust you."

Epilogue

Three Years Later

-Logan-

I hang up the phone on the conference call that I've been stuck on for the last hour and a half. I love my job but phone calls like that are seriously not why I decided to come and work at my dad's company. Days like today are few and far between but I can't wait to get the hell out of this office. I pack up my papers and shove them in my briefcase while I simultaneously off of my computer. It's not even five o' clock yet but I'm pretty much done with this day.

I get on the elevator and press the button for the fourth floor. I look up watching the numbers of each floor light up as the cart descends.

After several stops on numerous floors the doors finally open on fourth one and I slide through the few bodies still lingering on the elevator. I come to the brightly colored double doors and enter the four digit passcode on the wall. The doors unlock and suddenly I'm transported into a whole other world. This is by far the best part of my day.

I'm greeted by a young lady with brown eyes and matching hair. "Hi, Mr. Tate. She's been waiting for you."

I smile and nod at her and swiftly head down the hall, I enter the last room on the left and as if on cue she spots me before I do her.

"Daddy!"

"Lily!" I call, bending down just enough to scoop her up as she runs into my arms. She wraps her little arms around my neck as I place kisses all over her face. "I missed you peanut. How was your day?"

"Miss Lori tried to make me take a nap again, Daddy."

"She did?" I ask exaggerating my tone for her. I snatch her lunchbox and coat from the hooks that line the wall and give a smile to Lily's teacher as I carry her out of the room.

"So what happened? Did you take a nap?" I smile at her and press the call button on the elevator once again.

She sighs. "Can I still watch Yoyo Bears tonight?"

I hold back an urge to chuckle and step onto the elevator. "You can if you took a nap."

"Daddy..." She whines.

"So you didn't take a nap?"

"I don't like sleeping on the floor, Daddy."

"It's not on the floor, Lily. You have a mat and a sleeping bag. It's very comfortable and you should at least try. When you take your nap, you get to stay up later to watch Yoyo Bears."

"Okay," she says, resting her head on my shoulder.

This little girl has the power to turn the shittiest day around with just a flash of a smile. I can't even remember what life was like without her now. I hurry out of the building and hop into the back seat of the awaiting car.

I buckle Lily into her booster seat and settle in. I hate being driven around but living in New York City and driving to work is pretty much impossible. On the days that Lily has day care I opt to use the company car otherwise I use other means of transportation. Getting around this city with a child takes careful planning but it's worth it for the life that we get to live.

Mia, Lily, and I moved to New York shortly after Lily was kidnapped by that psychotic son of a bitch, Nick. I realized when we got her back that my reason for becoming a police officer had been achieved. Yes I wanted to fight crime and make the city safer but I think really I just wanted to help people in trouble the way that I couldn't help my sister Amy, and every time I did it made me feel a little bit like less of a failure. I never really understood how deep the guilt was that I carried where Amy's death was concerned but then I met Mia. Scared but brave Mia with a tiny newborn baby and no one to help her. She came into my life and turned it on its axis; her presence sent me reeling and threw me deep into uncharted territory.

Becoming Mia and Lily's protector became all-consuming for me, it was as important as taking my next breath. Failure was not an option, never an option when it came to making sure that they didn't end up facing the world alone. I knew from the moment I met her that Mia was different for me, she wasn't like any one I had ever met. I could sense her intense determination and will to survive from our very first conversation. I never however imagined that I would end up falling in love with her or having the overwhelming need to claim Lily as my own. Having a family was not on my radar, not even close but Mia and Lily changed that for me and I'm grateful for that every single day.

Fifteen minutes later, I'm unlocking the front door and ushering Lily into our apartment. Well... My parents' apartment that they graciously let us use when we decided to move to the city which allowed us to keep the house in Pennsylvania which we still use often.

"You want to watch a little TV while I start dinner peanut?" I bend down to unbutton her coat.

"Yes."

"Okay." I smile at her and touch the tip of her nose with my finger. I get her settled in the living room and head into the kitchen. A few moments later my phone chimes alerting me to a text message. I check the screen and see Mia's name flash across it.

On my way home! ☺

Mia is in her third year at NYU majoring in social work. After everything that she went through she wanted to be able to make a difference and help others. She realized the importance of having qualified professionals to assist people in need.

It took her seeing a therapist extensively to finally come to terms with the events of her past, to understand the effects of what she went through and be able to live her life free of fear and guilt.

Fifteen minutes later, I hear the front door open and the usual "Mommy!" cry. It makes me smile every single time; it never gets old.

"Hi Lily Bee." I hear in response.

"Mommy, can I watch Yoyo Bears tonight?" My body shakes with silent laughter. If there's one thing I can say for certain about Lily it's that she's relentless.

"Did you take a nap at school?"

"Do you and Daddy always say the same things?" she responds.

I shake my head, the kid is really a piece of work.

"Yes," Mia says, and with that the conversation is over and I can pretty much guarantee that Lily plants herself back in front of the TV set with a pout on her face.

A set of arms slide around my waist from behind.

"Hi baby," she says and rests her head on my back.

"Hi chief," I reply, turning around so that we're face to face. "I bend down and kiss her until her body relaxes in my arms. "How was your day?" I ask when I break the kiss.

"It was good. We had a review for my sociology final, nothing major."

"How many more finals do you have?"

"Just two."

"Have you gotten yourself registered for next semester already?" I ask, lowering the heat on the stove.

"About that..." She pulls back and looks up to the ceiling, and I immediately think that this can't be good.

"What?"

"I've just been thinking a lot lately and..."

"And what?" I say, crossing my arms over my chest and leaning against the kitchen counter.

"Lily's getting older now and as much as I love being in the city, I miss our home. I miss being around the family and I want Lily to go to a school where she can be safe on the playground and..."

"The schools here have safe playgrounds, Mia."

"Well, I know but the city is just so loud and...big. We don't have a backyard here for her to play in during the summertime She can only do that when we spend the weekends at the house and she really loves it there."

I tilt my head and smile at her. For a long time after we got Lily back she'd always hesitate when it came to telling me how she felt. I think that maybe she was scared of my reaction, maybe she was scared that I'd reject her or get angry at her because it's all she'd never known. I found that smiling at her always helped to relieve some of her tension, it made her see that I was a safe place for her to come to, someone who would love her instead of judge her.

"What are you saying?"

"You can transfer to the office in Pennsylvania can't you?"

I nod my head slowly, still smiling at her. She really is adorable when she gets flustered like this. "I can do that, yes, but you have another year left of school. If we're going to move back to the house in Pennsylvania shouldn't we do it once you've graduated?"

"Our wedding is a month away."

I throw my head back and laugh. "Why are you changing the subject?"

"I'm not," she responds defensively. "I just miss our house, Logan."

It's funny how she's never considered this apartment home. It holds special memories for both of us — we made love here for the first time but to her "home" is always the house in Pennsylvania where everything between us started out.

"I've just been thinking that once we're married I'd like to spend more time with you at home, and that I'd like to spend as much time as I can with Lily before she starts kindergarten, which I would like for her to do in Pennsylvania."

"So you want to quit school?"

"Well, when you put it like that," she says rolling her eyes. "I don't want to quit. I want to take a break."

"A break so that we can move back home? What about when the break is up and you want to go back and finish? We'd be in Pennsylvania with a kid in school, and it's not like we could uproot her at that point and I doubt that you'd want to commute into the city every day."

"Trust me baby," she says, running her hands up my arms and circling hers around my neck. "I spoke to my advisor and when I'm ready, I can finish my coursework online, and they'll even help me find a place nearby where I can do my internship."

"Why are you just telling me about this now?"

"I wanted to know my options before I said anything just in case it wasn't possible. Logan, this isn't home. You gave this to me because it was my dream at the time. NYU was my dream and it's been great but sometimes dreams change and now I just want to raise our family in our pretty house in Pennsylvania. Plus, I miss driving my car. I'm sick of the subway and mass transportation."

"Oohhh mass transportation. The horror!" I mock her. "How could I ever have subjected you to that all these years?"

"Don't be a jerk," she says with a giggle.

I get serious for a moment because as amazing as being back home sounds I need to know that this is really what she wants to do.

"I'll give you anything you want, you know that. As long as it's what you really, truly want. I think going home would be great for all of us."

She lets out a squeal and tightens her hold on me, pulling me in for an all-out hug.

215

"o you think the break is really necessary though? If you're going to be finishing up your degree from home anyway why not just get it over with?" I question.

I think a part of me is just scared that if she settles into being a stay at home mom she won't ever finish her social work degree. It's not that I would mind her staying at home to raise Lily if that's what she really wanted to do, but I know that her dreams stretch far beyond that. I know that she has a deep need to help people, especially young women and children.

"Yeah. About that."

"I cringe every time you say that." I sigh.

"Well, there's just something else that I think you should know."

I roll my eyes at her now. "Oh God Mia, I love you babe but just spit it out already."

"I'm pregnant."

I open my mouth, then close it again unsure of what to say. I look around searching for cameras or any other indication that this could be some type of hoax or sick prank. I look back at her and she's still grinning at me.

"You're full of shit."

"I'm not," she says with a gleam in her eyes.

"How?" I question skeptically.

"Well Logan, it all starts when a man and a woman…"

I cover her mouth with my hand and grin at her. "I know how smartass but *how?* I thought you were on the pill." I uncover her mouth and she lets out another giggle.

"How quickly we forget huh? Remember a while back when I told you I ran out of my pills and had to get a new prescription?"

"Vaguely," I respond. It's a lie, I totally remember her telling me that.

"And remember how you said. 'Oh don't worry babe, I'll just use condoms until you get that squared away?'"

"That might sound familiar." I can practically recite the conversation verbatim. I did tell her I'd protect us until she got back on the pill.

"Only you weren't exactly consistent with that."

I can't help but to chuckle, what man in a monogamous relationship ever really wants to use a condom. I was most likely horny and didn't want to wait so I said what I had to say to get some. "Well did you ever go back on the pill?" I ask trying to deflect some of the blame.

"Yes. But evidently the damage had already been done."

"Well, aren't you just a mess?" I grin.

God, I love her. I don't know that I was doing before she came into my life. I thought that I was happy with the way things were, I enjoyed being a cop, I liked being single and having no real ties to anyone but once she stepped foot in my house it was like she absolutely belonged there. It wasn't until she stepped foot in that house that it really became a home.

"What am I supposed to do with you now huh?"

"You're going to marry me?"

"A shotgun wedding?"

She smacks me on the arm. "We've been planning this wedding for a year it's hardly a shotgun wedding."

"You're a real troublemaker you know that?"

"Yeah, but I'm worth it."

And she is... worth it, worth everything I have. I'm just glad that she understands it herself now, that she understands how much she means to me. That my whole world begins and ends with her and Lily and now this baby.

"You know I'm happy, right? I love you and I'm excited to be a dad again. I'm excited to get to experience this pregnancy with you and I'm sure as fuck happy that you're not going to have to go through this one alone..."

"But—"

"But, I just want to make sure you're okay with it. You're only twenty one and you already gave up a lot of your wild and crazy years in order to keep Lily. I just want to make sure that this is what you really want."

She scowls and smacks me across the head,

"Enough with the abuse already," I say with a laugh.

"Of course it's what I want. I've gotten to do a lot of those things over the last few years. You've given me the freedom to make friends and go out and experience college life, and I'm pretty sure I can remember stumbling in here drunk off my ass a couple of times."

"And I took advantage of those times."

She giggles again and places a kiss on my lips. "My point is that I'll be forever grateful for what you've given me but at this point in my life there's nothing more important to me than my family. A new baby will only add to that and you're right, we're going to get to experience it together and it's going to be amazing."

"Alright," I whisper in her ear.

"Alright?"

"Yup, let's go home baby," I say pulling her back into my arms where she belongs. The truth is, we could stay here in this apartment in the city forever. We could go back to Pennsylvania or move somewhere else, I don't care. Home isn't about shelter, home is where Mia is; it's wherever Lily and our new baby are.

Nothing else matters, nothing else even comes close.

Alice
Montalvo-Tribue

About the Author

Alice Montalvo-Tribue lives with her husband and daughter in New Jersey. She has a bachelors degree in communications and is currently working on her masters degree. She spends most of her free time reading, writing, and when the weather permits sitting on the beach sipping a margarita.

For more news about upcoming books, teasers, and happenings, follow her on

Facebook

http://www.facebook.com/pages/Alice-Montalvo-Tribue/216980565108887

Twitter

@AMTribue

Website

http://alicemontalvotribue.wordpress.com/

Acknowledgements

To my readers, thank you for your words of encouragement, amazing reviews, and enthusiasm. You have no idea how much I appreciate each and every one of you.

To all the amazing bloggers who share every sale, every teaser, cover reveal and who help all of us authors tirelessly spread the word about our work. Thank you to the ladies of Love Between The Sheets for hosting my cover reveal and blog tour.

To my beta readers, Monica Martinez, Stephanie Locke, Anji Albis, Kristy Garbutt, Whitney Williams, Danielle Sanchez and Mindy Guerreiros. You all make this process so easy for me, It's hard to find betas who are as honest as they are supportive and I'm so lucky to have you ladies to turn to.

To Monica Martinez, once again I can't thank you enough for all that you do for me, from great advice to amazing covers and teasers and your ability to always make me laugh.

To Whitney Williams, from the first email I sent you I knew that we were going to be great friends. Well I hoped at least… Your friendship has not disappointed me. I'm in awe of your amazing talent and grateful for your support. I'm your biggest STAN EVER!

To Stephanie Locke for the best brainstorming sessions EVER. For our continued KA addiction, I'm sorry that I didn't tell you she comes back as a wolf. For our brand new Reaper's obsession, you're welcome for that by the way. I've had my share of ups and downs in the last year and your friendship has meant the most to me. Thank you for always being there for me, I only hope you get the same from me.

*Alice
Montalvo-Tribue*

Turn the page for a sneak peek of

Three of Diamonds

By W. Ferraro

Followed by excerpts of Books #1 and #2 in the
"Of Love" Series by Alice Montalvo-Tribue:

Translation of Love

and

Desperation of Love

Both Available Now!

Excerpt from Three of Diamonds by W. Ferraro

Lola Nash looked at the enormous warehouse in front of her, thinking Rebecca must have given her the wrong address. The building in question looked deserted, but massive. Lola pulled her old green Wrangler into a spot in front of the only door she could see. She hopped out, adjusting her sunflower yellow dress to fall loosely around her. She wore her brown suede heels, praying that she would not have to remain on her feet too long, because in all honesty, they were the most uncomfortable shoes to wear. Getting an uncomfortable feeling in her stomach, Lola double-checked the paper that had the address and time of her interview. Lola looked at her reflection in the large unlabeled glass door, deeming her appearance suitable for her interview, she reached for the door. However, there was no door handle, only a large red button to the left of the door. Squaring her shoulders and taking a deep breath, Lola pressed the button. She was just about to give up, when the door opened. A small petite woman opened the door and said in a thick German accent, "Ms. Nash, I presume?"

"Please, come in." Backing away and gesturing with one of her stiff arms. "My name is Gitta," she said finishing with a tight smile; an unfriendly aura surrounded her.

Lola slowly walked toward the woman who was holding the door open and led the way into the building. The hallway was dark, limiting Lola's quick and erratic gaze trying to see anything through the darkness.

"Just this way Ms. Nash." Gitta said, as the distinct clicking of Gitta's heels was the only clue to which direction she was being led through the darkness. Suddenly, Lola was in a naturally lit area with huge windows at the top of two story walls. She finally was able to get a good look at Gitta as they continued walking with a purpose. For such a small woman, she looked anything but delicate. Her drab brown hair was pulled back in a severe bun. Her gray tweed suit looked dated and stiff. She wore a thick black scarf around her neck with its ends tucked into the top of her suit coat. Her simple black pumps were just as boring as her outdated suit. The only part of her attire that was surprising was her stockings; a thick black seam ran down the back of her calves. Generally,

Three of Diamonds by W. Ferraro

not something you would see in the woman's fashion department, but rather, only seen in the fetish section of lingerie catalogs.

Finally, they reached a set of doors that looked to be at least fifteen feet high. They looked impenetrable. Lola watched as this small woman turned the handle and eased the huge door open.

"Whoa," escaped Lola as she walked into a club looking area; the size of a football field. Even though the room was stripped bare, it was easy to see the balconies adorning the far left walls and the large central staircase leading up to what looked like a stage. The cold industrial looking décor sent a chill through her system. Off to each side of the central staircase where large tunnels leading to more darkness.

Lola was lost in thought as she took in the enormous room, she didn't see when Gitta came to an abrupt stop and turned around, almost causing Lola to crash right into her. "Ms. Nash, the position I am offering you is to serve refreshments. Does that sound like something you could handle?" Gitta asked in a curt, heavy accented, clipped voice.

Yeah, I think I can handle that. If not, I wouldn't be here, now would I? But Lola thought better of it and decided to hold her tongue. Remembering that Rebecca said this job paid more in one night than she made all month at the restaurant she worked at, the thought had peaked Lola's interest.

"Yes, I'm a bartender." Lola answered.

"Your experiences tending bar is not what you will be using." Without a change to her facial expression, "You will be delivering refreshments to the members. Do you understand?" Gitta asked.

Now Lola's annoyance was creeping up. She was not one to be intimidated by anyone, let alone be spoken to as if she was four years old. She was just about to say as much when Gitta spoke.

"You will be paid $800 cash for a six hour shift. That does not include whatever tips you receive, which of course, are yours to keep as well. You will be supplied a uniform. There will be no employment paperwork. This is strictly cash only employment. You were recommended for this position by Ms. Thatcher, because of your ability to use discretion. Upon your arrival, I see you will be acceptable. This

Three of Diamonds by W. Ferraro

position is not something you can discuss with anyone. Am I making myself clear?"

Discretion? Acceptable? What the hell did Rebecca sign me up for? But, that kind of money is enough for her rent for one month. As long as it isn't anything illegal, it cannot be that bad, right?

"Before we proceed any further, are you accepting of my terms?"

"Is it illegal?" Lola asked.

For the first time, Gitta gave a genuine smile; unfortunately, it did not improve her overall look. "No, nothing illegal. Though, perhaps considered, prohibited."

What the hell did that mean?

Turning quickly on her heels, "Come. Follow me. I will get you your uniform and you will need to sign some forms." With that said, Lola was once again following behind Gitta, watching her walk intently back the way they came. As they stepped out of the room, Gitta closed the large doors and stepped toward a small hallway on the left, which Lola did not notice before. Lola followed Gitta into an office that was just as cold and utilitarian as the room they had just come from. Gitta opened a drawer and withdrew a piece of paper, then placed it in front of Lola, along with a pen.

"This is a Non-Disclosure Agreement. It states that you are restricted in divulging any information regarding our existence, including, but not limited to, your position, our location, or information about our members. It is very straight forward and quite common," Gitta explained.

Lola looked over the form. Her internal warning system began to chime at a blaring volume. She asked if it was illegal, and was told it isn't. Something just didn't feel right about this. "What IS my legal obligation regarding a time period? IF I decide this isn't for me after working my shift, am I held to any length of employment?"

Gitta was surprised. No one ever asked her that. This one might not be as squeamish as she had originally thought. The possibilities! Gitta wanted to lick her lips in anticipation.

"Ms. Nash, please see the last clause of the document. It states and I quote, 'The signing party may choose to cease participation at any time without any legal or monetary ramifications. However,

Three of Diamonds by W. Ferraro

confidentiality regarding the actions and its participants of occurrences held at this address, remain legally binding.' Does that answer your question?"

"So I sign this, I deliver drinks, I get paid. If I choose to tell you to go shove it, I'm free to walk out that door, with money in my hand, as long as I don't say what you potentially sick fuck," holding her fingers up in quotation marks, "so called 'professionals' do behind these walls? Is that correct?" God it felt good to say what she was feeling in blunt terms, Lola thought.

Again, Gitta smiled, fanaticizing about Ms. Nash, and that feisty tongue of hers, at her mercy. Gitta felt her arousal skyrocket and knew that her panties were now wet.

"That is correct, Ms. Nash. Nevertheless, let me assure you, our members are all of legal age, and consensual to the activities that occur at our club. No one is here against his or her will and believe it or not, we do have some limits."

So, it's a sex club. Figures. Reading through the document one more time, Lola signed her name on the designated line and pushed it toward Gitta's awaiting hands.

"Very good," Gitta purred. "Now, if you will excuse me, I will just go grab your uniform. Size 14 correct?" Gitta asked as she lazily perused Lola's figure from head to toe and back again.

Chills ran down her spine, Lola didn't even want to know how she knew her size. The way Gitta was leering at her, made Lola definitely not want to know. "Yeah, 14."

Gitta left the room and returned faster than Lola thought possible. In her hand, she held a red satin hanger that held what Lola assumed to be a joke.

"Exactly what am I supposed to do with that?" She said as she eyed the gauze like material that hung from the satin. The size of the white material could not be larger than a placemat.

"Ms. Nash, you wear it. I promise it has plenty of give to cover your voluptuous physique." Gitta purred once again, roaming her dark gaze over Lola's body.

You have got to be kidding! "Looks more like thick floss." That thing wouldn't cover her boobs let alone her entire body. Lola fingered the material noticing it had a spandex consistency.

Gitta asked for her shoe size, telling her that her uniform and accessories would be awaiting her arrival in eight days. Nodding, Lola was happy to get up and finally get out of the place, needing time to process the past hour. Gitta walked Lola back out to the entrance and gave her a curt goodbye. She watched as Lola climbed into her jeep and pulled out of the parking lot. Gitta walked back to her office and pulled up the security surveillance footage she was looking for and paused the image. Lola looked beautiful and alluring. Her bottom lip was plump as if she had been aggressively kissed. With that image on the screen, Gitta leaned back in her chair, slid her hand down under her skirt and relieved herself of her need to climax, all the while looking at Lola Nash's face on the screen.

***

The night had arrived for Lola to go back to Gitta. As she drove, she thought about Boyd and their argument. She felt horrible as these arguments were becoming more frequent and heated. He really didn't understand why she had to work so much.

"Why do you have to leave?" Bawling up his fists and jetting out his chin.

"I have to go to work, I told you. But I'll be here when you wake up in the morning."

"All you do is work. You promised we would go to the movies. You promised! I hate you!"

"Boyd, you don't mean that. You know how it upsets me when you say such things. I work so you and I can have the things we do."

She watched as he crumbled to the floor and cried. The sight was quite common when Boyd got upset, but did not lessen the angst it made Lola feel. She observed as Boyd fixated on his shoelaces as he always did when he was having a crying fit. He would pull and pull on the loops until either his hands hurt from the exertion or he ripped the laces. Lola lost count of how many pairs of shoelaces he would go through in a year's time. Lola walked over, squatted in front of Boyd and gently

Three of Diamonds by W. Ferraro

gripped his hands to stop them in the act. He yanked his hands away, folded his arms across his chest and let out a loud sigh.

"You know I would rather be here with you than out working, but the bills will not pay themselves, so I have to go to work." Lola said quietly, wanting him to understand.

Boyd wiped under his large brown eyes with his thumbs. No matter how upset he got, Lola never lost her temper with him. He was anxious when she had to leave him, but it especially increased when she left at night.

As Boyd remained quiet, changing positions, Lola sat down next to Boyd. She entwined their hands together like she always did and Boyd squeezed her fingers twice, symbolizing their private sign.

"I'm sorry I got mad at you and said those bad things Lola."

"I know kiddo. I promise we will go to the movies tomorrow. We can even see that movie with the guy that gets sucked into a video game and has to play his way out." Lola said smiling knowing that was the movie he had wanted to see since he first saw the preview, weeks ago.

"Really? And can I get my own popcorn? With extra butter?"

Focusing her attention back on the road, Lola laughed as she thought how Boyd could bounce from emotion and topic so quickly. Lola knew he was more upset about where he wasn't going tonight rather than where Lola went. She was firm in her decision regarding that subject and she refused to second-guess herself now. As she pulled into the parking lot, she gave herself the same pep talk she had been working on all week.

Six hours, piece of cake. You got this Lola. You don't need to agree with or watch whatever these kinky fuckers do. All you have to do is serve drinks. No harm, no foul, six hours and you can take your money and walk away.

***

Lola could not put her finger on it, but the building looked different at night. There were dozens of cars in the lot now. She parked as close to the door as she could, gave herself a final reminder of the money she would have in hand in just a few hours, got out and walked

Three of Diamonds by W. Ferraro

toward the door. She was just about to reach out to press the red button, when the door swung open and a massive man stepped out. His menacing look and overwhelming size seemed out of place in the black suit he wore.

"Name?" He barked in a deep raspy voice.

"Lola. Gitta hired me." Lola said with more clarity than she felt, willing herself to look the man in the eye.

Suddenly, his face changed from menacing to cordial. "May I see your ID?" She fumbled around in her bag, pulled it out and showed him. When he confirmed her identity, he smiled and said, "Sorry about the intimidation, but Gitta pays me for it. I'm Jaxon, but everyone calls me Jax." His chocolate colored skin and matching eyes were finally accentuated with a white toothy genuine smile.

"Nice to meet you, Jax." She responded as his large hand engulfed her smaller one. Not knowing what else to say, she stood looking at him nervously.

"I'm one of five security specialists. Our jobs are to maintain the privacy that occurs within these walls, as well as the safety of the members and staff." When Lola just nodded her head, he continued, "So just think of me as your bodyguard. When you are here, you have nothing to worry about. My team and I miss nothing."

Knowing that his statement was meant to put her at ease, it surprised Lola that it actually did. She felt herself take her first real breath since she left Boyd. You can do this Lola. Six hours and $800 richer. Jax offered to show her the way to the female staff's dressing room.

"Lola, you'll be fine. It really isn't as bad as you've imagined it. I've been with them for seven years and I would never work somewhere that bothered me as a human being. Just do your job you've been hired to do. Remember that whatever you see, people choose to be here and to participate; freely." Jax gave her shoulder a squeeze before he winked and whistled as he made his way back to the entrance.

Lola watched his retreating back, covered in black material pulled tight across his shoulders, walk beneath the overhead lighting. His custom fitted suit covered his wide shoulders and broad back effortlessly. His short dark hair shined from the reflection of the lighting. To her

Three of Diamonds by W. Ferraro

surprise, he stopped just before rounding the corner, looking back toward her. He made a motion with his large hand for her to scurry along into the dressing room. Lola smiled and headed in.

She walked into the somewhat spacious area that housed two white leather couches facing one another with a glass coffee table between them. The large basket that sat on the coffee table contained different body sprays, lotions, and cosmetics. As Lola stood taking in the surroundings, two women entered from another room on the left. Each wore a white slip of satin and white stiletto heels.

"Hi, are you Lola?" Asked a beautiful woman with blonde hair that flowed down around her, practically covering more than her outfit did. Her big blue eyes were enhanced with metallic silver false lashes and her lips were painted a pale pink.

"Yeah, that's me. I'm not really sure what I'm supposed to do." Lola said as she once again looked around for any sort of clue as to what she was to do.

"We can help. Your changing station is right over here." Lola followed the seemingly nice blonde-haired woman and her scowl faced friend, into the room they just exited. She was led to a four foot by four foot cubicle. To the left was a dry erase board which had her name on it. Lola looked at the same red satin hanger with the entirely too small uniform on it and huffed out a breath, which caused her bangs to flutter upward.

Perky Blondie asked if she needed anything else. When Lola responded no, both women left Lola to change.

Ok, here goes nothing.

Lola stripped down and put her uniform on. The lightweight material did in fact stretch to cover more than she thought it would. If Lola had to compare it to anything, she would have to say it was like one of those tube tops her mom used to wear when Lola was young. The strapless design hugged her breasts, clinging to her torso as a second skin and ending indecently high on her thighs. The thin material eliminated her option of wearing a bra; however, Lola refused to remove her panties. Grateful she had chosen one of her skimpy thongs, helped her to feel somewhat covered. She slipped her feet into the white stilettos that were in her cubicle and looked at her reflection in the mirror, inwardly

Three of Diamonds by W. Ferraro

groaning. Knowing what the other two women looked like, Lola dug through her bag, pulling out her own cosmetics. She added her usual heavy black liner to her eyes, giving her a cat eye effect. She opted for a nude lip color. She pulled her long inky black hair to the side, draping it over her shoulder. She put everything back in her bag, tucked it into the wicker basket inside her cubicle and made her way out to the hallway, where she heard multiple female voices.

When she entered the area, she noticed a handful of women, wearing either the same as her, or what Blondie was wearing when she showed Lola in. Ahead of the group was another woman who was quite tall even without her six-inch patent leather thigh high white boots. Her stark white miniscule skirt and bra coordinated so well with her sailor style-matching hat, against her dark skin. The whole ensemble would have been noticeable by itself, but her long bright purple hair added just the right amount of balance.

Patent leather Priestess called for everyone's attention. "Remember ladies, we are here to work and not fraternize. If anyone has a problem remembering, I can introduce you to any one of the security team. I have no remorse for last month with Daphne. Who would have thought it would take Jax, Mac and Pierre to carry her thrashing hoochie-ass out?"

With a hum of female laughter at her remark, Lola watched as each woman walked to the Priestess and took something from a box at her feet. Lola remained behind, not knowing what to do. When the last of her fellow employees had disappeared around the corner, the Priestess looked at Lola, lazily taking in her appearance, before a smile spread across her face. Putting shame to any practiced runway model, she strutted smoothly toward Lola "You must be Lola."

Lola didn't respond, assuming it was said not for confirmation but more for reaction. When no response came, Priestess arched a dark eyebrow at her and could not help but chuckle.

"Gitta was right, you are feisty. I like that. I'm Tawne. Come, let's get you fitted with your mask." Lola watched as Tawne walked back to the box and pulled out a small white satin mask just covered the eyes. When she turned, she was surprised to see Lola hadn't moved from her spot.

Three of Diamonds by W. Ferraro

"It's the last piece to your uniform." Tawne explained.

"Why a mask?" Lola asked as she walked toward Tawne's outstretched hand and took the piece of concealment.

"Christ Gitta, did you explain anything?" Tawne said exasperatedly, as she looked toward the ceiling. She smiled toward her new charge, and explained, "Here at Olympus, everyone, employees and members, wear masks. These masks hide both identities, as well as show whom or what a member is game for. Walk with me and I'll explain as we go." Lola walked next to the statuesque woman and tried to ignore the butterflies in her stomach. As they walked into the club portion, Lola couldn't believe the change that had occurred from when she was here with Gitta. Gone was the cold industrialized steel and starkness. Every wall, seat, and surface was draped with magnificent yardage of white silk. The white surfaces reflected the different hues of light from high above. Greens and blues shimmered over reds, pinks and purples. Lola looked around as women and men in various states of undress were running here and there, making sure everything was where it needed to be prior to opening. She turned to the bar, where two men, who were dressed in white vests with nothing but bare skin underneath, stocked shelves and made sure the glasses, were at the ready. They worked side by side in fluid silence. Never invading each other's space but ensuring the task was done in its entirety.

Tawne watched as Lola took everything in, and gave the other woman a moment to become comfortable in the space. Tawne thought back to her first time here at Olympus, and could remember, vividly, the feelings of doubt and unease. Bringing Lola's attention back around, Tawne began explaining further, "No member is known or addressed by their real names here. The Gods are adamant about privacy and rule abiding. Each member, or potential member, has to go through a severe amount of interviews, questioning, and even a fucking written essay portion. I mean, Christ girl, it's like the SATs for sex addicts." Tawne laughed more out of irony than for any other reason. She continued, "Anyway, members have to comply with a strict code of conduct. Kinda like us working folk, who had to sign the NDA." Tawne took a breath to gauge Lola's reaction. It was Tawne's experience, most newbies got anxious when they learned the degree of secrecy that went on here, and by Lola's expression, she was no different.

Three of Diamonds by W. Ferraro

"You are going to work the lower floor; the area from the bar to the staircase. You'll be working with Mac and Caleb at the bar. As I said before, there is no interacting with members other than to do your job. As a Diakonos, your purpose is to serve beverages only, not indulge in their other appetites. Diakonos' are to keep eye contact to a minimum, as well as make themselves scarce when not serving. Our members know the rules, though occasionally one spoils the flow. For that reason, Jax, our security chief, and his team float around. Any questions?"

Yeah, how about a thousand to start? What is with these people getting their rocks off in such a way? Couldn't they just go and use cheesy pickup lines at a regular bar, like everyone else? Lola couldn't contain her tongue any longer. "Yeah, I got a question. What the fuck is a Diakonos?"

Tawne smiled, Lola was feisty and sassy, but likable. She was not vexed by the bite in Lola's voice, as she should have been. Nor was she surprised. If she had been, she would think nothing of flagging Jax over to escort Lola's ample ass out, but as it was, Lola wasn't like the others. If Tawne had to take a guess, this was the last place the voluptuous Lola wanted to be. And for that reason, Tawne's respect for Lola grew a notch.

She found herself answering the question, and then adding on to give Lola as much information as she could. "Diakonos is Greek for waiter or attendant. The simple white mask you have is a symbol of who a Diakonos is. The Oikatase, or domestic slaves, are members showcasing by their mask what they are into or looking for. For instance, unlike your mask, the member's masks are white but they are ornamented with feathers. Each color feather indicates their personal preference. You know, looking for male attention, looking for female play or if they are already obtained. The only masks that deviate from this are the Gods. They wear masks of gold. If a God shows interest in a member, their selection trumps other member's rights."

"Gods?" Lola said, not caring that she interrupted Tawne.

Feisty indeed. "The Gods, are the founding members of Olympus. They sit up there in the VIP area, known as the Mountain. Just like the ancient Greek Gods, looking down from Mt. Olympus." Tawne explained matter-of-factly.

Three of Diamonds by W. Ferraro

Gods, slaves, feathers, trumping rights; the more Lola learned about this club, the more she wished she didn't know. She was not a prude or anything; one person's love is another person's kink, but to have rules and Gods, just seemed to be a little too neurotic for her.

Adjusting her top coverage, Lola decided to stop with the questions and just focus on getting this shift over.

Tawne went over with Lola where she was to stand and introduced her to Mac and Caleb, the two bartenders she noticed earlier. After strutting off to check on the others, Lola strolled to the end of the bar and braced her hands on the edge. Dropping her head and rolling her neck back and forth, she hoped to alleviate some of the stress she was feeling.

"Ready to rock and roll, Lola?" Mac asked, as he came over to where she was preparing herself for her virgin christening by fire. Leaning on his crossed arms on the bar top, the position brought him eye level to her. From here, he could see just how beautiful her gray eyes were.

"If you have any questions, just come and ask me. Once it is in full swing in here, we tend to uh, not be needed too much." Mac said, winking, hoping to put her at ease.

"Thanks. Just not my scene. But money is money." Lola said trying to rein in her unease.

Just then, the gong sounded. The vibrating echo bounced from surface to surface. Mac was embarrassed that he didn't think to mention to her that it was coming. The way she almost jumped out of her skin made him give her an apologetic grin.

Lola watched as the tall heavy doors swung open. Men and women in all types of skimpy and barely there white cloth paraded in. Even though Tawne had explained about the masks and feathers, nothing could prepare Lola for the sight the members made. Knowing she wasn't supposed to be staring, she just couldn't look away. Most cases, there was more material on the members facemasks than there was on their entire body. Then Lola noticed some wore collars; some bland and white, while others looked as if they were made of diamonds. Some were even attached to leashes. Really!?! Leashes…swearing to herself, if she sees any livestock she was out of here, regardless of the money!

Three of Diamonds by W. Ferraro

One after another entered the vast space; some took seats, while others entered the tunnels and disappeared. Not that there was a lot of chatter going on amongst the hundreds of people that now were in the club, but complete silence fell as another gong sounded. Then, from a door to the left, men and women entered wearing scantily covering drapes of shimmering gold. A few of the women wore no more than gold bra and panties while some others wore satin gowns of different lengths; negligée like. The men wore a variety of bling colored boxers or very tight thongs. However, the last man to enter wore a pair of gold satin drawstring pants. It would not be considered as sexual an outfit as the others, but there was something that spoke to Lola, making her think, he was the most alluring of all. Between the flowing gold over what only could be long lean legs, then just a simple eye covering of gold. His short blonde hair almost matched perfectly to the color of the mask, giving the impression you didn't know where the mask ended and his hair began. Lola watched as each climbed the stairs to their perch on "the mountain". She could easily tell that most of the Gods thought they really were magnificent and magical people. Nevertheless, even though Lola already had distaste for these people, it didn't stop her inability to turn away, as the true God like form in satin pants of gold, ascended the stairs last. The swish of his hips only added to the allure of his muscular back and shoulders. Muscle after muscle rippled with strength speaking loudly of his belief that his body was a temple. He held his head high, confident in his footing. Unlike the others that turned to look down on the members when they reached the top, he continued to move gracefully to the back of the platform without turning or looking down on the other members. Lola regained her feeling of indifference when she could no longer see the captivating God.

"Crazy, right?" Mac whispered to her with a sly smile. Soon, Lola was filling orders, delivering drinks and trying to ignore the leering of some or the distaste of others. Back and forth between the tables and bar, Lola's feet were starting to ache.

Mac spoke with her every time she returned to the bar. Whether it was an inquisition of how she was doing or a mock joke of the audacity of such a place. On her final trip, Lola noticed Tawne leaning toward Mac, whispering something into his ear then looking to Lola. Lola could tell whatever it was she said to him, was a reprimand of some kind. Tawne then walked to Lola, and waited for her to fulfill the last order.

Three of Diamonds by W. Ferraro

"You are needed upstairs. The Gods dismissed their assigned Diakonos. You can handle both here and there well enough, I think." Tawne instructed in a purr.

Oh no fucking way! Between Lola's throbbing feet and her lack of confidence in this ridiculous uniform, the thought of going up there was enough to make her want to forget about the $800 bucks. Surely, there was someone else who could do this?

"Your confidence in me Tawne is over exaggerated. Since this is my first night, shouldn't you entrust someone else?" Lola tried to keep the pleading from her voice.

"No, I think you are just right. Now, I will go up with you and announce you. I'll call you by an assigned name, which is part of the role. I'll come and collect you in five minutes." Tawne said, in a dismissive tone.

Lola wanted to slam her tray down against the smooth bar. Could anything else make this one of the most humiliating experiences of her life? Trying to roll her neck again, she didn't see Mac approach.

"So, did I overhear correctly. She is sending you up?" Mac asked.

"I'd rather walk into a lion's cage strapped to a raw piece of meat." Lola said, hating how she so easily spoke her fear. She looked up into Mac's kind eyes and hated that she saw pity there. Knowing if she showed any sort of weakness or unease now would just make this worse. She took a deep breath and turned to face Tawne, as she approached.

"Okay, let's go." Tawne said, as she led the way to the stairs. "Walk behind me, and I'll introduce you."

Lola followed Tawne and focused on the distinctive clicks of each of their shoes as they climbed the metal stairs. Lola prayed her footing would not give out on her. Like the lower floor, there were multiple white circular sofas but these were adorned with gold satin pillows. People were standing, sitting and some were currently indulging themselves.

"Oh Supreme ones, this is your Diakonos, Banilia," and with a quick bow of her head, the click of her heels announced her exit.

Three of Diamonds by W. Ferraro

Lola suddenly felt like she was indeed in a cage with a lion. Most glared at her like she was intruding on their private domain while others ignored her all together. Including him.

She filled order after order, ascending and descending the stairs, repeatedly. Her arches were on fire and her thighs ached from the workout they were receiving. Lola had just given one of the Gods his Crowne Royal and was returning to her spot in the corner, when she heard a voice call to her. She turned toward the horrid sound.

"So, Diakonos, any thoughts of applying for membership? What I wouldn't give to train you." His dark eyes leered towards her from behind their gold covering. For the minimal amount of coverage her uniform allowed, Lola felt it wasn't enough. His eyes roamed over her leaving a feeling of filth behind in their wake. "Or, do you not need any training? With a body like that, I'm sure you are quite effective in pleasing a master."

"Lycus, leave her alone. Just because you can't find someone to your taste, doesn't mean you can forget the rules," the elegant redhead sitting next to the one called Lycus said. Her extremely short red hair stood up in heavily gelled spikes. Her barely there baby-doll was made of shimmering gold mesh, offering complete exposure of her bling pierced nipples. Her deep ruby painted lips caressed the champagne flute containing her Ménage a Trios, which Lola had delivered minutes earlier.

"I'm just having some fun, Themis. But you know as well as I do, it wouldn't be the first time we've made an exception to the usual application process." Lycus said unabashed, as he tipped his rock glass back draining it.

Lola watched through her lashes toward the compact husky man, who had, not only undressed her completely with his eyes, but who was now, trying to strip away the small amount of control she was maintaining on her indifferent attitude. Come on, one more hour, and we will be $800 richer.

Finally, the hour was up. Thank goodness for Mac who was constantly looking up to her. It gave her something to focus on; a link to someone, aside from the sexual encounters and acts partaking all around her. When he tapped his watch and gave her the thumbs up, she started toward the stairs, leaving the darkened corner, which was her refuge

Three of Diamonds by W. Ferraro

while being on the mountain. As Lola reached for the railing with her left hand and lifted her foot to step down, her wrist was grabbed by a beefy hand, which quickly let go. The unplanned shift of weight, was all her heel needed to roll. The action caused pain to shoot out from her ankle and had her grabbing for an anchor, anything. The anchor reached out to grab her; but it wasn't the beefy hand that started the series of events. Instead, a large firm hand, with long fingers that easily wrapped around her forearm's diameter. Before Lola knew it, another hand was holding onto her waist and her breasts were pressed against a tall, well sculpted, and hard chest above gold drawstring pants.

"Are you alright?" A deep baritone voice asked. It didn't sound like the usual New England accent. It definitely had a different ring to it. Lola was still pressed close to that golden smooth chest, even after catastrophe had been averted. She could feel the vibration of his voice under her cheek.

"Yeah, I'm okay." She answered keeping her face cast downward, knowing the rules. The stupid rules, but rules nevertheless.

The hand that held her waist moved upward to her chin, and applied enough pressure causing her to look into his face. "Are you sure you are okay? How's your ankle?"

She was looking into deep blue oceans behind the rim of gold from his mask. His pupils twitched back and forth as if he looked enough, he would find confirmation of her answer. This close she could see every pore on the lower half of his face. His just shaved smooth skin begged to be touched. Her nose breathed in his scent, and her conscience screamed that such a scent should be illegal.

Not wanting to look away, but knowing she had to, she pulled back from the warmth of his body, and answered more firmly, "Ankle is fine. Thanks for making sure I didn't fall down the stairs."

Accepting her answer and stepping back to give her some more space, the heroic angry God, rounded on the beefy man, who still stood off to the side.

"What the fuck is wrong with you, Lycus? You are lucky she didn't topple down the stairs."

240

Three of Diamonds by W. Ferraro

"Well thanks to you, Adonis, she didn't; no harm, no foul. She, like the rest of us, is so lucky you were here." With the last part said with obvious disdain oozing out his mouth, the one called Lycus, pushed passed his fellow God. His eyes, once again, met Lola's, and she suddenly felt the need to cover her exposed skin. Lola found comfort in the sounds of his heavy treads going down the stairs. She was now alone with the gorgeous God of a man.

"Sorry for his rudeness. Do you need help walking down?" The question asked with a small sexy smile teasing from the side of his, oh so, sensual mouth.

Before Lola could respond, Jax joined them. "Do we have a problem?" he asked, with his intimidation persona firmly in place.

Lola was surprised that the question was not directed toward her, but rather Adonis.

"No, Jax. I just stepped in to stop this Diakonos from falling down the stairs." Without a look back toward her, Lola watched as his golden muscular form gracefully descended the stairs. When they were alone, Jax turned toward Lola and asked if there had been a problem. Just grateful that the night was over, Lola assured him that she had just tripped and Adonis was nice enough to keep her from tumbling down the stairs. Lola didn't want to say what led to the misstep, she just wanted this night to be over.

After gingerly walking down the stairs, Lola followed the other ladies into the changing room. Once she was back in her clothes, and her face and hair cleaned, she left the fitting room and noticed Mac leaning against the hall wall.

"Hey, just wanted to check on you, you know, make sure the ankle really is okay?"

"Yeah, it's good, nothing some Ibuprofen won't cure." Lola answered.

Mac was just about to say something else when Jax's echoing voice sounding from the other end of the hall. "Yo, Mac, you bugging our newbie?" he asked finally joining them. He too had changed from his suit to a football jersey and a pair of nylon pants.

Three of Diamonds by W. Ferraro

"Not me, Jax, I'm just a concerned fellow slave." Mac answered, knowing Jax could not resist a ball busting moment.

Jax smiled knowing his eyes missed nothing. Mac hadn't been able to keep his eyes in any direction that wasn't Lola's. Once the club was closed down, Jax didn't usually stick his nose in any ones business. Since always being the last to leave, he knew all too well, many of the Diakonos' would indulge themselves in physical gratification. How could you not, seeing all that sex and fantasy shit that went on behind these walls, he thought. But, coming around the corner and seeing Mac standing with Lola, just did not sit right with Jax.

"How's the ankle, Diakonos?" Jax asked.

"Good. Fine." Lola answered, just wanting to get out of here. "Thanks guys, I'm going to head out though." She said, effectively walking away from both men.

"Well, part of the service we provide here at Olympus is an escort to your vehicle. We can swing by the office, pick up your cash and we will have you out the door before you know it." Jax said from next to her. With his long legs, it didn't take but a moment for him to fall into stride with her. Doing as promised, he waited as Lola signed for her envelope containing her cash and walked her to her Wrangler.

"So, will we be seeing you again, around here?" Jax asked, as he stood leaning his back against her Wrangler and crossing his ankles as if he had all the time in the world.

Lola climbed in, placing her bag on the passenger seat, and throwing the thick envelope on top of the bag. She turned his words around in her head wondering if she could bring herself to do this again. So, she answered him honestly, "Don't know."

"Well, if you want to come to our union meeting, it's next week." Jax stated plainly, as he moved to stand in the space of her open door.

The audacity of this place never ceased. She found herself shouting at him, "There is a fucking union for this shit?"

Jax was about to continue the jest when they were interrupted from a shout from the door. "Jax, I ain't getting any younger. I want to go before the sun comes up." A female figure wearing a pair of purple plaid pajama pants and a black hoodie pulled up over her head.

Three of Diamonds by W. Ferraro

"Yeah, I'm coming, keep your pants on." Jax yelled back, then turned to Lola, "You are way too easy girl. Lighten up." Stepping back, he closed her door with a wide white grin against his dark skin.

Lola rolled down her window, "You're an ass, you know that?" She said, unable to hide her smile or her laughter.

"I've been told that before, come to think of it. I better go, heaven forbid, Tawne doesn't get home before the sun comes up."

"That's Tawne?" Lola gaped.

"Yeah, my little sister sure can transform, can't she?" With a thump of his large fist on the window frame, Jax walked off toward Tawne.

Lola drove out of the parking lot and headed toward home. The only good thing about driving this time of night, was the roads and highways had very little traffic. She made the forty-five minute trek in just over thirty-five. She entered her apartment quietly, acknowledging Aimee sitting on the sofa before peeking in on Boyd. She returned to wearily ask Aimee how he did tonight.

"Lola, your brother is never a problem. Sweet as rain, he is." Aimee stood stretching her tall body, ridding herself of kinks from sitting too long. With a quiet goodnight, Aimee headed out the door and across the hall to her own apartment.

Excerpt from Translation of Love

Book #1 in the "Of Love" Series by Alice Montalvo-Tribue

Available Now!

Prologue

The sleepless nights are what get to me the most. In the daylight, hours there's no time to think; the hustle and bustle of the day serves as a bandage to cover up the gaping hole in my existence. Always knowing that there's something missing but not being able to figure out why or how to fix it. I toss and turn and, though my body is exhausted and begging for sleep, my brain is on a schedule all its own. Running a mile a minute, thinking about lost love, loneliness and the fear of never feeling adored. Or worse yet, feeling like you are adored only to find out that you're wrong. In the silence of the night, there is nothing left to do but to give in to the pain, the emptiness that comes from knowing that the idea of what you once thought was love was nothing more than an optical illusion. Smoke and mirrors clouding your mind and judgment until it fades and you find that everything you once believed in was a lie. A moment of pure clarity that alters the course of your life forever and shatters your heart. It's a memory that plays again and again in my mind, night after night, keeping me awake until finally my body wins the battle and I fall into a restless slumber.

Chapter 1

Why is it that I can't get it together today? From the moment I opened my eyes this morning, over an hour late

Translation of Love by Alice Montalvo-Tribue

because I forgot to set my alarm clock last night, nothing has gone right. I should have just pulled the covers over my head and called in sick. If waking up late wasn't bad enough, I managed to get a flat tire on my way to work (thank goodness my dad was free to save me from that drama), spilled coffee on my blazer after showing up almost two hours late, and now I'm stuck on a line waiting to get into the only bookstore in town that has the latest vampire series in stock. It's the only thing my niece, Gemma, wants for her birthday this year and if I show up to dinner without it she's going to be so disappointed. I can't imagine why there is such a line to get inside. I pull my cell phone out of my purse to check the time. Six forty-seven, plenty of time to get to dinner by seven thirty if I can maneuver my way through this line. I look over my shoulder to a group of three girls standing behind me. They look around the same age as I am but they're dressed more like they're hitting the hottest club in town tonight searching for single guys.

Girl number one has her long, chocolate hair curled and teased to perfection, her black chandelier earrings look like they weigh a ton and she is wearing a black corset top that pushes up her bust just enough to expose the maximum amount of cleavage possible. Her midriff is barely covered and she's rocking some super skin tight jeans which look almost painfully painted on. Her red spiked heels are so insanely high, I'm surprised she can even walk in them.

Girl number two, with her almost black, curly hair is wearing a strapless, grey sequined top which she has paired with countless bangle bracelets and a black, ultra mini skirt that is so short if she bends down she will surely have a wardrobe malfunction. Her black stiletto heels finish off her look making her legs look a mile long.

Girl number three has mahogany hair cut into a stylish bob. Of the three of them, she's wearing the most makeup,

Translation of Love by Alice Montalvo-Tribue

which looks almost caked on. In fact, I'm almost positive that she is wearing fake eyelashes because no one's eyelashes can be that long. Her nude-colored top blends into her skin perfectly, her jean shorts leave little to the imagination and her nude-colored wedges give her optimum height.

Looking around the crowd of people, I realize that I look out of place. My long, brown hair is up in a ponytail. I have barely any makeup on with the exception of some bronzer, mascara, and a nude lip-gloss. I lost my blazer to a coffee mishap hours ago and my green, button down shirt, black trousers and black ballet flats are about as exciting as a cavity. I consider myself to be pretty tall at 5'7" but these girls tower over me thanks to their heels. *Seriously? What's up with the outfits,* I wonder to myself? I turn around completely to face the girls and address the group in general.

"Excuse me? Can you tell me why there's such a long line to get in to the store?" They look at each other and then stare at me, mouths wide open, as if they can't believe the words that have just come out of my mouth.

Girl number three finally speaks. "Are you kidding? This line is for an autograph signing with Victor Garza!!!" She ended in a high-pitched scream as she bounced up and down in excitement.

I try not to roll my eyes at how ridiculous she looks. "Uh, I'm sorry but who is Victor Garza?"

I hear a collective intake of breath as Girl number one shakes her head at me in shock. "You've been on this line for almost forty minutes and you don't even know who you're waiting to meet? Victor Garza is like the hottest Latin singer in the world!" They all nod in agreement. Girl number two chimes in. "We're all waiting for him to sign a copy of his new book." I scan the crowd and finally notice that just about everyone in line is holding a book.

Translation of Love by Alice Montalvo-Tribue

I turn back to the party girls and thank them for the information. I decide to get off of the line, and go to the front of the store to see if I can just go in and buy my book without having to wait. I spot a security guard as I reach the doors.

"Excuse me, I just need to run in and buy a book. Please tell me I don't have to wait on this line," I say as I give him my best pouty face look.

"You can enter to my left to go into the main store, just make sure to stay away from the line for the autograph signing."

Relief floods over me as I smile at him. "Okay, I will. Thank you!" He gives me a barely noticeable head nod and I make my way into the store. The main floor is practically empty, just a few customers flipping through books and a few employees manning the cash registers. To the far right of the store by the escalators, I can see where the line of mostly girls starts for the autograph signing. Why is a singer signing books anyway? Don't they usually do album signings? As I look over the wall to where the escalator goes down to the lower level, I can see a handful of big, burly men which I can only assume is additional security hired to keep the crowd under control. Beyond the men, I spot an empty table with stacks of books, markers, and a few bottled waters. I guess the man of the hour hasn't arrived yet. What was his name again? Something Garza? It doesn't matter. The quicker I find the book I need, the quicker I can get out of here and to dinner. I decide to make a quick pit stop to the ladies room, since I have just spent the better part of an hour standing outside in the chill of the night. The weather in New Jersey is starting to warm after a brutal winter, and an unusually rainy spring. It's mid May and the summer is drawing nearer but even though the days are getting warmer, the nights tend to still be a little bit on the cooler side, especially this close to the ocean. I live less than 2 miles from the beach

Translation of Love by Alice Montalvo-Tribue

and as much as I love living by the shore, the weather can certainly be unpredictable.

I make my way to the back of the store, down an empty hallway where the restrooms are located and proceed to the ladies room. I finish up and wash and dry my hands quickly, taking a quick look at myself in the mirror before leaving the bathroom. As I open the door, I glance out and see a man walking into the otherwise quiet hallway, causing me to stop short. He is quite possibly one of the most handsome men I've ever seen in my life. He is tall, at least 6'1" with relatively short but thick dark brown hair and milk chocolate-colored eyes that are shaped like almonds. His nose is perfectly sloped, and the sight of his full lips makes me pause for a moment. He has a square jaw that lets you know he's all man and a body that can make anyone's heart flutter. I can tell by the fit of his button down shirt and his jeans that he's built. It's obvious that he works out and keeps in shape but he's not too bulky. Simply put, if there was such a thing as perfect, he'd be it. His eyes meet mine and his lips curl up in a tentative smile. I lose all power to move or breathe. I'm pretty sure I look like an idiot but I have no control over my body at the moment. As he makes his way to the door of the men's room, he greets me politely. "Hi."

My body unsticks and I reply with a "Hello" as I look away and walk out of the bathroom. Unfortunately, I don't get very far as the strap of my purse gets caught on the door handle. I lose my grip on it and it drops to the floor, spilling everywhere. Of course, how could I expect anything less with the disastrous day that I've had. I can feel the heat rising to my cheeks as I'm consumed by sheer embarrassment. I shake my head and bend down to pick up the contents of my purse.

"What else can go wrong today?" I murmur to myself. I see a pair of feet appear in my line of sight.

Translation of Love by Alice Montalvo-Tribue

"Here, let me help you with that," the handsome stranger says as he bends down beside me and starts picking up items.

I look up from the ground and my breath catches at the sight of him. What is it about this guy that makes me flustered? It's not like I've never seen a hot guy before. Hell, I've even dated my share of hot guys but there is something about this one that makes me react like a complete loon. I manage to get control of my power of speech. "Thank you, I don't know what's wrong with me today, I can't seem to function properly."

He chuckles at my comment. "It happens. Everyone has those kinds of days." He reaches for my compact mirror at the same time as I do causing our fingers to graze. His fingers against mine sends a shiver through me. I can't remember the last time I had this kind of reaction to a man. In fact, I'm pretty certain that I never have. I gather up the last of my things, toss them in my bag and start to stand as he hands me the items he's picked up. "Here you go."

I look up at him and manage a small smile. "Thanks for your help," I say softly.

"You're very welcome...."

"Elizabeth."

"Elizabeth, it was my pleasure. I hope the rest of your evening goes better," he says.

I look down at the ground and giggle. "Yeah, it's been pretty bad. I'm almost scared to do anything else for fear of what might happen. I should probably just go home and lock myself in till tomorrow." I look up and catch him smiling. Not a forced smile but a genuine one that makes my knees melt.

"You're probably right, but then you won't get your autograph, right?"

Translation of Love by Alice Montalvo-Tribue

"Oh, I'm not here for that. I've never even heard of the guy. I just came in to get a book."

He looks almost surprised. "Oh, I just assumed that you were a fan of…"

"No, no, I mean, I'm sure he's great and all, there are like a thousand girls on line looking like they are waiting to see the crowned prince but I don't know much about Latin music so I'm kind of at a loss."

"Right, of course." He continues to stare at me for a moment. I almost think that he's about to ask me for my number, actually I'm hoping he does…but he doesn't. I have to get away from him and out of this store before I embarrass myself any further.

"Well, thanks again for your help. I have to grab my book and get out of here. I'm in kind of a rush." I don't wait for a reply. I walk out of the hallway and back into the store as quickly as I can. I look at my phone again. Seven nineteen. "I can still make it if I hurry."

I grab the book for Gemma, pay for it and bolt from the store as quickly as I can. I'm not too far from the restaurant so I opt to walk rather than get my car. With the crowd of people still surrounding the bookstore, I figure it will be quicker by foot. As I make my way to the restaurant, I can't help but to think of him, the stranger at the bookstore. I didn't even get his name. I gave him mine but it never even occurred to me to ask for his. No wonder he didn't ask me for my number, he probably thought I wasn't interested. I seriously need to work on my flirting skills. What am I even thinking? Flirting skills? Me? I wouldn't even know how to flirt if I tried. It's been so long since I've even had a date. My life has been filled with nothing more than work, the occasional outing with my best friend, Jordan, and spending time with my family. Men aren't even on my radar and I'm not sure that I'd ever allow them to be again. Maybe it's a good thing Hot Stranger didn't ask for my number. I don't need anything or anyone messing with my life right now. The life that I've worked so hard to get control of again. No, I cannot let anyone destroy my peaceful existence, not even someone who made my knees weak with a simple smile. I enter the restaurant and the hostess escorts me to the small, private room in the back where my family is surely waiting for me.

"Auntie Elle!"

"Hey, Gemma. Happy Birthday, honey!" I say as I hug my niece. "How's it feel to be 13? You're officially a teenager now." Gemma is tall for her age, almost as tall as I am. She has the signature Brooks family brown hair and brown eyes and already knows more about fashion than I do.

"It feels absolutely no different," she says with a smile. She looks down at the bag in my hand "Whatcha got there?" she asks expectantly.

"What, this?" I ask teasingly. "You want this?"

"Please tell me that's what I think it is!" she begs.

I can't help but giggle. "Oh alright, I'll put you out of your misery. Here you go."

"Ahhh, thank you so much, Auntie Elle!" she shrieks as she throws her arms around me.

"You're welcome, honey."

I walk further into the room greeting some cousins, uncles and aunts until I finally reach my brother, Gavin, and my father. "Hi, Dad. Sorry I'm late," I say as I kiss his cheek. My father, at first glance, is an intimidating man. At 6'2", he towers over me. He has the body of a linebacker, well, maybe a retired linebacker, salt and pepper hair and dark eyes. The eyes are what I found to be most intimidating when I was growing up.

Translation of Love by Alice Montalvo-Tribue

Of course, now I know that my dad is a big softie at heart but he could aim his eyes at you and glare a certain way that would make even the bravest man cower. I think he perfected that look in his years as a police detective. He retired from the force last year, much to my relief, and has spent most of his time since then traveling.

"It's okay, kiddo. You haven't missed anything,"

I turn to my brother and give him a hug. "Hey Gav."

"Hey, I see you found the book?"

"Yeah, I did. I had to fight my way through a massive crowd of girls waiting to meet some Latin singer but I got it."

"Well thanks, sis. I'm glad Gemma can count on you for stuff like that." I smile and give him a nod.

Gavin is as tall as my dad, slender, with brown hair that needed to be cut about two weeks ago but still looks good on him. He is a catch but my brother just doesn't want to be caught. He has dedicated himself to being the best dad he can be and women are secondary. I guess you can say that he is a bit of a serial dater. I, on the other hand, also don't want to be caught but I don't even bother dating.

Gavin is older than me by four years. He was 22 when Gemma was born and completely unprepared to be a father. The girl he had been dating for a little over a year got pregnant and decided that she wasn't ready to be a mother. I can't necessarily say that I blame her, having a child at 20 can't be easy. She tried to convince Gavin that the best option would be to give the baby up for adoption but Gavin would not consent to that. They fought about it for the majority of the pregnancy until near the end when Gavin finally fessed up to Mom and Dad about what was going on. They supported him and together they convinced his girlfriend to sign away her rights to the baby and give Gavin full custody. I've always looked up to my brother but the way he fought for Gemma made me completely idolize him. As a family, we all chipped in and helped him to take care of Gemma until Gavin was able to finish college, get a job in a marketing firm and move into his own home with her.

Three hours later, dinner is finally over and the only people left in the restaurant are Dad, Gavin and myself. Gemma sweet-talked her way into a sleep over at a friend's house. I sit at the table sipping flat cola from a straw. As I stare out the window, my mind goes back to the bookstore, back to those milk chocolate eyes that did something unexplainable to me. It was an unfamiliar feeling. I'm still not sure what to make of it. I can't, however, deny that it was a good feeling. It had the power to scare me and excite me all at once. I've had my share of lovers and relationships but the concept of love is foreign to me. I had thought I'd been in love once but it turned out to be a bad imitation. A relationship which left me so torn and tattered that it took me years to come back from the emotional damage that it caused. Hell, if I'm being honest with myself, I'm still kind of an emotional misfit. Some scars never really heal and because of my newfound need for self-preservation, I've constructed a coat of armor so strong that it will never be penetrated. It's a price I am willing to pay to make sure that I never get hurt again.

"Kiddo, you okay? You look miles away." I snap out of my daze and turn my head to face my father.

"Yeah Dad, I'm fine. Just tired. It's been a long day." He has a look that says he doesn't believe me but he lets it go and gives me a small smile.

"Let's get out of here," he says to Gavin and I. They both move to get up. I join them but decide that I need a moment alone.

"You guys go on ahead. I have to use the bathroom."

Translation of Love by Alice Montalvo-Tribue

Gavin, picking up his jacket and putting it on, says, "Are you sure, Elle. We can wait for you?"

"Yes, Gav, I'm sure. I'll give you both a call tomorrow." I hug and kiss them both and, as they leave, I head to the bathroom. I walk in, go to the sink and splash some cold water on my face. I dry myself off and take a look in the mirror. I barely recognize the reflection. Looking back at me is a woman who is very different from the woman I used to be. Dark hair that used to be blonde, little makeup where there used to be more, conservative clothing where there used to be young trendy fashion. I mean, I don't look like a nun or anything. I actually look good, but it's certainly a far departure from what I looked like two years ago. I take one final glance in the mirror and turn to leave the bathroom. It's definitely about time for this day to come to an end.

Excerpt from Desperation of Love

Book #2 in the "Of Love" Series by Alice Montalvo-Tribue

Available Now!

Desperation of Love by Alice Montalvo-Tribue

Prologue

I don't want to open my eyes this morning. To face the day after the beauty of the night before seems almost cruel. Keeping my eyes firmly closed, I try to shut out the memories of my past. They always seem to surface at times like these, overshadowing the moments of joy. Being the product of divorced parents is never easy, but when you spend the majority of your childhood being used like a pawn in a vicious chess game, it's kind of hard not to be at least a little screwed up. On top of that, add the feelings of abandonment that I've struggled with for years and now I'm nothing but a mess. Here I am, 32 years old, and you'd think that I'd be over it by now. You'd assume that I'd be smart enough to understand that I shouldn't let my issues and my parents' ugly relationship affect me. Well, I'm not that smart, and for as long as I can remember, I have single-handedly sabotaged every relationship I've ever had with a man. It's not that I don't long for something more, for the kind of love that could last a lifetime, I do. But the paralyzing fear of ending up broken and alone is enough of a motivator to keep me rooted in solitude. My need for self-preservation has become greater than my need for love. It's not even that I'm afraid to date, I date all the time. I take what I can for as long as I can get it and then I move on. I dated Mark for seven months. That is a new record for me. But when he started pressuring me for more of a commitment, I began to push him away. He knew what I was doing and thought that the best way to combat my commitment issues was for us to move in together. Dumb suggestion on his part. That was the last nail in the coffin for me. Much like my best friend, Elle, I made a decision to close the door on romantic relationships. She had endured a traumatic experience that resulted in many physical and emotional scars. That's why it was so gratifying to see her walk down the aisle toward Victor last night. Her path to love

Desperation of Love by Alice Montalvo-Tribue

gives me hope that maybe I can get out of my own way long enough that I might be able to experience it one day. I sincerely doubt it, but it certainly doesn't hurt to hope.

When I finally decide to open my eyes and face the day, I'm blinded by the sun shining through my drapes. The bright rays are doing nothing to ease my hangover. I partied with reckless abandon last night and I have the headache to prove it. I turn my back toward the window, trying to block the potent morning rays and what I encounter sobers me up pretty quickly. In all honesty, I'm stunned to find the figure of a man lying next to me. A man that with one look can send me spiraling out of control. I knew from the moment I met Alex Garza that, given the opportunity, he would cause nothing but trouble for my heart. I fought a good fight but ultimately he's gotten his way and somehow has ended up in my bed. *Fuck*!

Chapter 1

Four months later.

I haven't seen him since the morning after Victor and Elle's wedding when I found him in my bed. The sad part is that I can't even remember the events of that night. I know I partied and got drunk, well wasted, really, but the moments that led up to me waking with Alex are all a blur. And I sure as hell don't want to ask *him* what happened. So, I did what any self- respecting woman would have done in my situation. I snuck out...*of my own house*. I did the walk of shame out my front door, slid into my car, and drove to my friend's house, where I hid out for the remainder of the day. He called me several times that day but I let every call go to voicemail. I just couldn't face him, and I made sure to avoid him over the last few months. He eventually gave up trying to contact me, but I knew my luck wouldn't last forever and now he's back.

Victor and Elle finally found a house that they love, right on the beach, and moved in last weekend. This left Elle's little cottage empty, and since Alex is Victor's only brother and they are going into business together, opening up a recording studio, it only makes sense for Alex to move into it. He gave up his apartment in New York and is moving to town this weekend. I'd been hoping to stay far away from him, but Elle insisted that the four of us go out to dinner tonight to welcome him to town. She basically backed me into a corner. If I decline, I'm afraid that she might suspect that there's something going on between me and Alex. I also don't want Alex to think I can't sit through a meal with him especially when he's done nothing wrong.

That leads me to now, sitting in my car, in the parking lot of the restaurant where we're all supposed to meet up. Elle sent a text a few minutes ago, letting me know that the three of them are waiting for me inside, yet I can't move. I'd never admit this to anyone but the thought of seeing Alex again is attacking my system with an overload of emotions. A part of me is actually excited to see him because I'm very attracted to him, but I'm also cautious because I don't want him to know how he affects me. More importantly, I'm just plain embarrassed for getting trashed, bringing him home to do God knows what, and then bailing immediately afterwards. It wasn't one of my better plans. Under normal circumstances, I would have no issue with a one night stand. I might've even embraced it. But this is different. This is my best friend's brother-in-law, and it's all just a little too close for comfort. I'm going to have to see this guy and be around him for years to come, and it's best to just put that night behind us.

Stalling for time, I pull down the car visor and check my makeup in the small mirror. I wore my hair down tonight, in loose waves cascading down my back and framing my face. My

Desperation of Love by Alice Montalvo-Tribue

make-up is minimal, with only a light coating of bronzer, nude lip gloss, a bit of mascara, and a light brown eye shadow, which makes my blue eyes a little more vibrant. Confidence is definitely not something I've ever been lacking. I may not be a supermodel, but I can stare in a mirror and be pleased with the reflection staring back at me. Maybe my assurance comes from the fact that I'm an only child. My parents struggled for years to have a baby, trying everything from holistic medicine to in vitro fertilization. When they finally had me, they were so ecstatic that they spoiled me rotten. Don't get me wrong, I'm not a brat or anything, but my parents never let a day go by without telling me how beautiful I was. They always said how proud they were, and there was little that I wanted that I didn't eventually get. When my luck ran out, it was a hard lesson that I learned. The one thing I really wanted as a child didn't happen. I wanted my parents to stay together, but no matter how much I begged, cried and fought, nothing would save their marriage. When they went down, they did so in a blaze of glory, dragging me down with them and putting me through a horrific custody battle.

The sound of an incoming text message brings me back to the present. I pull my phone from the center console and see that it's from Elle.

Our table is ready. Are you almost here?

I guess it's now or never. I can't keep them waiting all night. I quickly type out a reply.

In the parking lot, be right in.

Exiting the car, I straighten out my black and white shift dress. It hits just above the knee and, paired with my black heels, it makes me look taller than my normal five feet four inches. The sound of my shoes clacking on the pavement matches the increased rhythm of my heart. I don't know why I'm so nervous. I've hung out with Alex on several occasions,

Desperation of Love by Alice Montalvo-Tribue

up until the night of the wedding. We even made out a couple times. In fact, the night we met at Elle's house, we had a hot and heavy make out session on her couch, not that I would ever admit that to her or anyone else. And when I was a complete and total wreck while Elle was hospitalized after being brutally beaten by her low life ex boyfriend, Alex was there to comfort me. And I let him. I've never been one to show weakness. I learned early on that the only way to survive in this world is by exuding nothing but strength. That's why I lift my head up, straighten out my back, and square my shoulders as I enter the restaurant. I look around for Elle but I don't see her in the small waiting area. I open my purse and pull out my phone to call her.

A feather light touch at my waist sends a shiver down my spine. I don't need to turn around to know who it is. I recognize his familiar scent, a mixture of soap and his usual cologne, a combination that always intoxicates me. He inches closer, the feel of his gentle breath on my neck makes my eyes close.

"I'd almost forgotten just how beautiful you are." The deep timbre of his voice makes my breath catch. I open my eyes and turn around so that we're face to face. One look at him and my heart goes into overdrive. Clearly, I've forgotten just how handsome he is. He's tall, at least 6' 2", and I have to tilt my head up to meet his gaze. I do my best to look composed and unaffected, even though my body is betraying me. His light olive skin and honey brown eyes are warm and inviting and his full lips, which I've had the pleasure of tasting a time or two, make my imagination run wild. His brown hair is shorter than I remember, the top is spiked up a bit and the sides are shaved close. It's a different look for him but he carries it very well. His dark green Henley is fitted just tight enough to hint at how ripped his muscles are, while his dark jeans fit like they were

Desperation of Love by Alice Montalvo-Tribue

tailor-made. Simply put, Alex Garza is as mouthwateringly sexy as they come.

"Hi, Alex," I say. He smiles and it radiates through me. It's infectious and immediately calms my nerves. I can't help but smile back.

"Ahh, there she is! You do remember me, huh?" He goads me and pulls me into a sweet embrace. If there's one thing I can say about Alex, it's that he's always been kind to me. He's the type of person that people just naturally gravitate to. I hug him back and say, "Of course. How could I forget you?" There's only a hint of sarcasm in my voice.

He tilts his head and grins at me. "Do you want me to answer that?"

I'm really hoping we can get through this evening without reliving that unfortunate incident. "Not particularly, no," I say, shaking my head. I immediately realize that in order to avoid an uncomfortable conversation, I'm going to need a buffer between us. "Where are Elle and Victor?"

"Elle's in the bathroom. You know, baby on the bladder and all that, and Victor is paying the bar tab."

"Nope, I'm right here. Hey, Shorty," Victor calls, walking up to us. He's taken to calling me Shorty lately since he's so much taller than me. He looks every bit of the superstar that he is. His black shirt and jeans just scream designer. While Alex's hair could be called messy, Victor's is styled to perfection. Alex is ripped, Victor is toned. Victor is just a tad shorter than Alex, and his complexion is just a bit darker, but the fact that they are siblings is undeniable.

"Hi," I say, giving him a hug. "How's our girl?"

"Uncomfortable, but beautiful as ever." He grins at me and I can see the excitement and happiness written all over his face. Elle is in her seventh month of pregnancy and every time I

Desperation of Love by Alice Montalvo-Tribue

see her and Victor together, I know that this baby is going to be so loved. Victor somehow managed to bring Elle out of her shell, showing her the kind of happiness that she never thought was possible. Even though he was able to heal all of her emotional scars, she's given him just as much in return. Love, peace, simplicity, and above all, a normal life and a family.

"It'll be worth it in the end," I say.

Elle is at Victor's side before I can finish my sentence. "Say that when you're eight thousand weeks pregnant and swollen." She's semi joking but more irritated than anything else. "No one is happier about this baby than me, trust me, but good God I'm ready for this to be over."

We all smile, carefully biting back laughter because she's just too cute. Even swollen and uncomfortable, Elle is probably the prettiest pregnant woman I've ever seen. Her adorable baby bump gets a little bigger every time I see her. She can complain all she wants but the truth of the matter is that she's glowing and clearly happy.

Victor pulls her to his side and kisses the top of her head, soothing her in a way that only he can. "It's okay, love, there's not much longer to go now." She wraps her arms around his waist and melts into him.

As sickening as they are, seeing them together always does something to me. A pang in my chest is filled with both joy for them and a hint of envy. The feeling of being in love is something I've purposefully never experienced.

"Alright, enough with the mushiness. Can we have dinner or what?" I say, eager to get this meal over with. The quicker I can escape Alex, the better I'll be.

Dinner isn't as uncomfortable as I thought it would be. Alex sits next to me and, thankfully, he seems normal, totally unphased by our hookup. Once the check is taken care of, I say

Desperation of Love by Alice Montalvo-Tribue

my goodbyes to everyone and promise Elle to have dinner with her later in the week.

"Come on. I'll walk you to your car." Alex is standing right beside me. I'd rather he didn't walk me *anywhere*. Being alone with him always seems to get me in to trouble but denying him would cause suspicion, and I'm not ready to admit to anyone what an idiot I am.

Reluctantly, I agree. "Alright, thanks." He follows me out of the restaurant and as soon as we're out of view, he grabs my hand, linking his fingers with mine. I look down at our joined hands, unsure of what to make of the gesture. It seems bigger than what we are, almost too intimate for us. Once at my car, I let go of his hand and open the door. I turn to face him but keep the door between us, using it as a shield. His eyes are dark, focused, like he's trying hard to read my thoughts. I'm unsure of what comes next and slightly uncomfortable by the intensity of his stare, making me feel vulnerable. Needing to break the moment, I finally speak. "Thanks for walking me. Goodnight, Alex."

His eyes never leave mine as he runs a hand through his hair. "I think you and I need to talk."

"About what?"

He maneuvers around the car door and places his hands on the frame, effectively blocking me in. "About why you left me alone in your house the morning after the wedding and about why you've ignored me ever since."

I bring my hands up to his chest and give a slight push. He doesn't budge. I shake my head. "No. I think some things are better left unsaid, don't you?"

"Jordan." The sound of my name coming from his mouth feels like a warning. With one word, he's letting me know that he's not moving until he gets what he wants.

Desperation of Love by Alice Montalvo-Tribue

The smartass in me gears up for battle. "Alex," I return, mimicking his tone. He leans in closer, our chests practically touching now. I start to feel lightheaded, and I'm not sure if it's because of the line of questioning or the fact that he's so close to me.

"What happened?" He's persistent, not going to let this go and I know that I need to put some distance between us. I don't like how he manages me. He creeps under my skin. It's unwelcome and unfamiliar. I'm good at holding people at bay, keeping my emotions on lockdown. But he gets to me in a way that no one has before. I figure the best line of defense is to give him something.

"Fine! I was embarrassed, alright," I say, rolling my eyes. "I'm not exactly thrilled that you had to see me all sloppy drunk."

He picks up a strand of my hair and gives it a gentle tug. "You weren't sloppy."

"I was trashed," I reply with another roll of my eyes. "You don't have to make it sound better than what it was."

"It doesn't matter." He chuckles.

"I'm sorry that I left you there. It was childish."

He looks away, just for a moment, like he's trying to carefully choose what he wants to say next. He looks back at me with a hint of a smile tugging at his lips. "You can make it up to me."

"How?" I question, dragging out the word and squinting my eyes at him.

"Breakfast."

"Breakfast?" I ask, sounding confused.

"Yes. Tomorrow morning, nine o' clock, Laura's Café."

I can tell by the tone in his voice that it's not a request, but I try to get out of it anyway. "I don't know."

"You don't have a choice." I knew that was coming. Alex doesn't strike me as the type to just walk away when he wants something and, evidently, breakfast with me is what he currently wants. "I'll see you there, princess." He leans in, placing a kiss on my forehead before walking away and leaving me to wonder what the hell just happened.

Made in the USA
Lexington, KY
01 April 2014